Christmas on the
Great Plains

Christmas on the

Great Plains

EDITED BY

DOROTHY DODGE ROBBINS

AND KENNETH ROBBINS

University of Iowa Press | Iowa City
A Bur Oak Book

University of Iowa Press, Iowa City 52242

Copyright © 2004 by the University of Iowa Press

All rights reserved

Printed in the United States of America

Design by April Leidig-Higgins

http://www.uiowa.edu/uiowapress

The University of Iowa Press is a member of Green Press Initiative and is committed to preserving natural resources. This book has been printed on acid-free paper that is 60 percent recycled.

Library of Congress Cataloging-in-Publication Data
Christmas on the Great Plains / edited by Dorothy Dodge Robbins and Kenneth Robbins.
p.   cm. — (A Bur oak book)
ISBN 0-87745-901-0 (cloth)
1. Christmas stories, American.   2. Great Plains—Social life and customs—Fiction.   3. American fiction—Great Plains.   4. Christmas—Great Plains.   I. Robbins, Dorothy Dodge.   II. Robbins, Kenneth.   III. Series.
PS648.C45C4495 2004
813'.0108334—dc22   2004044025

04 05 06 07 08 C 5 4 3 2 1

Scratchboard illustrations by Claudia McGehee

For Mary Lou Dodge,
beloved mother and
mother-in-law and
descendant of Dakota
Territory pioneers

CONTENTS

PREFACE

FOR INHABITANTS of the Great Plains, the month of December is thirty-one days of progressively receding sunlight, days shortening and nights lengthening in recognizable increments. These darkening weeks are accompanied by unremitting temperatures that average below freezing, frequently dip beneath zero, and are exacerbated by potentially lethal windchills. It's the front end of a difficult winter season that can linger into what dwellers in other parts of the country term spring. Christmas is not a singular day in this region but a holiday season extended as far as possible on both sides of the December 25 dateline by many observant residents of South Dakota, North Dakota, Minnesota, Nebraska, Iowa, and Illinois. Men, women, and children anticipate the festive respite from their often too-bleak, too-harsh winter environment. As a softening measure, Nature provides, most years, a canvas of white against which images of gliding sleds and cross-country skiers can be realized, a holiday tableau reminiscent of Currier and Ives if one does not mind the absence of formidable trees, which are scarce on the vast plains. This land harbors few windbreaks, aside from human structures, and can be transformed topographically by shifting snow in a matter of hours or minutes, in the middle of a night or a day. On the Great Plains, December needs Christmas.

Bess Streeter Aldrich proposes in "Journey into Christmas" that, for midwesterners, the holiday both commemorates a special birth in a less cold, more distant clime and allows for seasonal reflections that extend in multiple directions, not just back in time to the Bethlehem manger. Her protagonist journeys from the isolation of a rare holiday endured alone to recollections of previous Christmases shared with family members and toward visions of Christmases to come spent with additional descendants. Aldrich's story is an homage to a Dickensonian insight that human memories in and of the Christmas season have the potential not only to haunt but to revive relationships past, present, and future. Other stories, including Willa Cather's retelling of the prodigal son in "The Burglar's Christmas," Ann Boaden's ghost story "One Christmas in the Darkness of the Plains," and Jane Smiley's examination of culture and gender in "Long Distance," continue this theme of the human desire to traverse great distances at Christmastime, whether the expanse exists between places, people, or ages.

In these and other writings in this volume, characters travel by truck, car, sleigh, horse, and foot, invariably braving inclement conditions in an effort to reunite ranchers with their livestock, children with their parents, the desired with the estranged, even the living with the dead. These authors suggest that despite human conflicts and severe weather, separations created by geographic, generational, or spiritual divides can be bridged this time of year. By dint of sheer will and reliable transportation, an overwhelming need to connect with others is met. In "Winter Break," by Jon Hassler, a mother and son make their annual pilgrimage to Nebraska to share town and country Christmases with paternal and maternal relatives. A recovered phonograph record stirs holiday memories of a previous decade and allows a long-deceased father to be home once more for Christmas. Recorded music features as well in a holiday memoir by Mari Sandoz. "The Christmas of the Phonograph Records" commemorates the year Old Jules recklessly spends his inheritance on the luxury of recorded melodies that draws neighbors near and far to his rustic home. Together they engage in a celebration of sound and dance that shatters the prairie's icy stillness.

Still, some emotional distances cannot be broached, despite the lauded merriment of the season. One person's Christmas joy is countered by another's annual depression, the latter state reinforced by the bleak landscape of the wintry plains. Family members do not necessarily reunite willingly or peaceably, and for many a person the holidays are dreaded rather than treasured. Joseph Ditta recounts a troubled homecoming in "The Shop," in which the myth of Santa Claus and his pristine polar factory reappears darkly in the guise of a downtown merchant and his seedy pawnshop; in this inversion of Christmas traditions, wishes are denied and gifts rejected. O. E. Rølvaag's "The Christmas Offering" chronicles a marriage facing a monetary crisis brought on by the season of giving. The imbalance of power between husband and wife is not corrected in Rølvaag's tale; it is merely exchanged. In Constance Vogel's "Family," spousal tensions increase as the nest empties. When adult offspring decide to forgo the inconvenience of holiday travel, the parents' solution to their children's absence, although comic in execution, provides only temporary comfort. And in Larry Woiwode's "Marie," a young teen, troubled by fading memories of her mother, labors to give her siblings a festive and memorable holiday gathering, an attempt first ignored, then derided by her self-absorbed father.

A number of memoirs in this collection were penned by descendants of immigrants from northern Europe, countries whose climate and contours found their counterparts on the Great Plains of North America. Accompanying the travelers on their journey were traditional Christmas dishes and rituals that would become endemic to their new home and soon intermingle with indigenous delicacies and rites. Paul Engle's "An Iowa Christmas," set in an era when the family farm provided all necessary sustenance, offers lavish descriptions of preparations for, and indulgences in, the holiday feast. "My First Christmas Tree," by Hamlin Garland, recounts the wonder and gratitude of a rough-hewn boy who receives a modest gift at a church party from the hands of a lovely girl. The flickering light of candles in the branches of a scrawny pine and the generosity of her smile entwine in his memory. Ted Kooser's "Making Bows" assays the virtues and labors of fashioning ribbons into gift-box toppers at his father's department store during one busy holiday shopping season.

Several stories in this collection update these inherited rituals and comment upon new ones. "What I Took from Minnesota Christmases" provides an outsider's perspective on the holiday dietary requirements of a typical midwestern family. Though never acquiring a taste for reindeer or lutefisk, Rosanne Nordstrom does adopt other culinary essentials for her table, like Swedish meatballs and potato sausage, ingredients of a feasting tradition that she admits "looked and tasted so much better than the Christmases [she] grew up with." "Julebukking," by Beth Dvergsten Stevens, describes a silent masquerade in which roving neighbors replace porch-to-porch caroling with an elaborate guessing game. And Kenneth Robbins's "Stringing Lights" questions the wisdom of one particular yuletide practice as his car salesman perches delicately on a steep icy roof while bedecking his house with electronic bulbs.

From the dung-encrusted floor of a garden shed to the sterile labor and delivery wing of the aptly christened Holy Family Hospital, crèche scenes and their stories are central to a celebration of Christmas on the Great Plains. Mary Swander's "The Living Crèche" describes her delight in providing friends a nondenominational, gender-neutral, multicultural depiction of the birth of Jesus, replete with a midwestern hot-dish supper. In "The Christmas That Would Not Stop," Ron Robinson confesses a triumvirate tale of holiday, anniversary, and birth, when he anxiously awaits the arrival of his firstborn child on the second day of Christmas. Another living crèche is offered in James Calvin Schaap's "First Profession." While reluctantly preparing for her unglamorous supporting role in a rural Christmas pageant, an adolescent transplant from the city comes to acknowledge in her family's barn both the humble realities surrounding the birth of the Christ child and the wondrous miracles that accompanied it.

Lest we forget that sometimes the land and its demands loom larger than the holiday, Linda Hasselstrom's "December" recalls to us in a series of journal entries that Christmas is no excuse for shirking one's work ethic: there are drifts to be maneuvered and cattle to be fed before enjoying an evening's respite playing cards with friends in front of the fire on the twenty-fourth. Brian Bedard's "Christmas Letter, 1997" answers Hasselstrom's gritty account of furious blizzards, blinding whiteouts, and surprise encounters with ditches with another reminder. In a rare year Nature spreads the gift of a warm Chinook across the length and breadth of the Great Plains at Christmastime, wrapping all—native peoples, descendants of immigrants, recent arrivals, and diverse wildlife—in its unanticipated but gratefully accepted warming embrace.

Christmas on the
Great Plains

Journey into Christmas

BESS STREETER ALDRICH

MARGARET STALEY STOOD at her library window looking out at the familiar elms and the lace-vine arbor. Tonight the trees were snow-crusted, the arbor a thing of crystal filigree under the Christmas stars.

Some years the Midwest stayed mild all through December, donning its snowsuit only after the holidays. But tonight was a Christmas Eve made to order, as though Nature had supervised the designing and decorating of a silvered stage setting.

Margaret Staley visualized all this perfection, but she knew that the very beauty of the scene brought into sharper contrast the fact that for the first time in her life she was alone on Christmas Eve.

For fifty-nine Christmases she had been surrounded by the people she loved. On this sixtieth, there was no one. For not one of her four children was coming home.

She could remember reading a story like that once, about a mother who was disappointed that no one was coming—and then, just at dusk on Christmas Eve, all the children and their families arrived together to surprise her. But that was a sentimental piece of fiction; this was cold reality.

The reasons for none of the four coming were all good. Three of the reasons were, anyway, she admitted reluctantly. Calling the roll she went over—for the hundredth time—why each could not make the trip.

Don. That was understandable. Don and Janet, his wife, and young Ralph in California could not be expected to come half way across the continent every year, and they had been here last Christmas. She herself had visited them the past summer, returning as late as September.

Ruth. Ruth was her career daughter, connected with a children's hospital and vitally important to her post. Long ago she had accepted the fact that Ruth could give her only the fragments from a busy life and never had she begrudged it; indeed, she had felt vicariously a part of her capable daughter's service to humanity.

Jean. Jeanie and her husband, Roy, lived in Chicago. Jeanie was a great family girl and certainly would have come out home, but the two little boys were in quarantine.

Lee. The hurt which she had loyally pushed into the back of her mind jumped out again like an unwanted and willful jack-in-the-box. Lee and his Ann could have come. Living in Oklahoma, not too far away, they could have made the trip if they had wished. Or if it had not been convenient for Lee to leave, she could have gone down there to be with them. *If they had asked her.*

The only time Christmas had been mentioned was in a letter, now several weeks old. Lee had mentioned casually that they were going to have company for Christmas. That would be Ann's folks of course. You mustn't be selfish. You had to remember that there were in-laws to be taken into consideration.

Standing there at the window, looking out at the silver night, she remembered how she once thought the family would always come home. In her younger years she had said complacently, "I know my children. They love their old home and whenever possible they will spend Christmas in it. Of course there will be sickness and other reasons to keep them away at times, but some of the four will always be here." And surprisingly it had been true. Someone had been here every Christmas.

Faintly into her reveries came the far-off sound of bells and she opened the casement window a bit to locate their tinkling. It was the carolers, carrying out the town's traditional singing on Christmas Eve.

She closed the window and drew the drapes, as though unable to bear the night's white beauty and the poignant notes of young voices.

"I'm alone . . . I'm alone . . . it's Christmas Eve and I'm alone." Her mind repeated it like some mournful raven with its "nevermore."

Suddenly she caught herself by a figurative grip. "Now, listen," she said to that self which was grieving. "You are not a weak person and you're not neurotic. You have good sense and understanding and even humor at times. How often have you criticized people for this very thing?"

She walked over to the radio and turned it on, but when *"Silent Night . . . Holy Night"* came softly forth, she snapped it off, afraid she would break down and weep like old Niobe.

"Oh, go on . . . feel sorry for yourself if you want to. Go on. Do it." She smiled again wryly, and knew she was trying to clutch at humor, that straw which more than once had saved her from drowning in troubled waters.

She went over to her desk and got out the four last letters from the children, although she knew their contents thoroughly.

There was the fat one from Don and Janet with young Ralph's hastily scribbled sixth-grade enclosure. They said the poinsettias were up to the back porch roof, that the Christmas parade had been spectacular, and that they would all be thinking of her on Christmas day when they drove to Laguna Beach.

Then the letter from Jeanie. She had been experiencing one of those times which mothers have to expect, but they were over the hump now and although still in quarantine, she thought Bud could be dressed and Larry sit up by Christmas day. They would all miss the annual trip out home but would be thinking of her.

Ruth's letter was a series of disconnected notes written in odd moments at her desk. Almost one could catch a whiff of hospital odors from them. They were filled with plans for the nurses, the carols, the trees for the convalescents, but as always she would think, too, of home and mother on Christmas day.

From Lee and Ann, nothing but that three-, no *four*-weeks-old letter with its single casual reference to Christmas. There was a package from them under the tree, attractively packed and addressed in Ann's handwriting. It, too, had been here for weeks. But no recent letter. No special. No wire. No "We will be thinking of you" as the others had written. She tried to push the hurt back and close the lid on it, but she could not forget it was there.

She put the letters away and went into the living room. It looked as big as Grand Central Station. Last year there had been eleven sitting in these chairs which tonight were as empty as her heart. Half ashamed at her childishness in trying to create an illusion, she began pulling them out to form the semicircle of last year when the big tree had been its pivotal point. She could even recall where each had sat that morning at the opening of the gifts. Jeanie and Bud on the davenport, Ruth curled up on the hassock, Ann and Lee side by side in the big blue chairs—and on around the circle.

She had to smile again to remember the red rocking-chair which she brought from the storeroom for young Larry. It had been her own little rocker and was fifty-eight years old. A brown tidy hung limply on its cane back, an old-fashioned piece worked in cross-stitch, the faded red letters reading: FOR MARGARET. Larry had squeezed into it, but when his name was called and he rose excitedly to get his first present, the chair rose with him and they had to pry him out of it and one of the chair's arms cracked. There had been so much hilarious laughter where tonight was only silence. And silence can be so very much louder than noise.

With the chairs forming their ghost-like semicircle beside her, she turned her own around to the fireplace and sat down to give herself the pleasure and the pain of remembering old Christmases. Swiftly her mind traversed the years, darting from one long gone holiday season to another.

The Christmas before Don was born she and John were in their first new home. They had been very happy that year, just the two of them; so happy in fact that she had felt almost conscience stricken to think she could be contented without her own old family at holiday time. Why, she thought suddenly, that was the way Lee was feeling now, and she could not help a twinge of jealousy at the parting of the ways.

Then Don's first Christmas when he was eleven months old. After these thirty-six years she could still remember how he clutched a big glass marble and would not notice anything else. Strange how such small details stayed in one's mind.

The Christmas before Jeanie was born, when she did not go out to shop, but sent her gifts by mail, so that the opening of them was almost as much a surprise to her as to the recipients.

Then there was the whooping-cough Christmas, with the house full of medicated steam and all four youngsters dancing and whooping spasmodically around the tree like so many little Indians.

There was the time she bought the big doll for Ruth and when it proved to have a large paint blemish on its leg, she wanted to return it for a perfect one. But Ruth would not hear of it and made neat little bandages for the leg as though it were a wound. It was the first she ever noticed Ruth's nursing instincts.

Dozens of memories flocked to her mind. There had not always been happy holidays. Some of them were immeasurably sad. Darkest of all was the one after John's death, with the children trying to carry out cheerfully the old family customs, knowing that it was what Dad would have wanted. But even in the troubled days there had been warm companionship to share the burden —not this icy loneliness.

For a few moments she sat, unmoving, lost in the memory of that time, then roused herself to continue her mental journeying.

Soon after that dark one, Christmas was no longer a childish affair. Gifts suddenly ceased to be skates and hockey-sticks and became sorority party dresses and fraternity rings, and the house was full of young people home for vacation. Then the first marriage and Don's Janet was added to the circle, then Jeanie brought Roy into it. In time the first grandson . . . and another . . . and a third—all the youthful pleasure of the older members of the family renewed through the children's eyes.

Then came that Christmas when the blast of the ships in their harbor had sent its detonations here into this very living room, as into every one in the country. And though all were here and tried to be natural and merry, only the children were free from forebodings of what the next year would bring. And it brought many changes: Don with his Reserves, Roy enlisting in the Navy, Lee in the Army. That was the year they expected Lee home from the nearby camp. His presents were under the tree and the Christmas Eve dinner ready, only to have him phone that his leave had been canceled, so that the disappointment was keener than if they had not expected him at all.

Then those dark holiday times with all three boys overseas and Jean and the babies living here at home. Ruth in uniform, coming for one Christmas, calm and clear-eyed as always, realizing perhaps more than the others that at home or abroad, waking or sleeping, Death holds us always in the hollow of his hand.

Then the clouds beginning to lift and, one by one, all coming back, Lee the last to arrive. And that grand reunion of last year after all the separations and the fears. All safe. All home. The warm touch of the hand and the welcoming embrace. Pretty Ann added to the circle. The decorating of the tree. The lights in the window. The darting in and out for last minute gift wrapping. The favorite recipes. Old songs resung. Old family jokes retold. Old laughter renewed. In joy and humility she had said, "My cup runneth over."

Recalling all this, she again grew stern with herself. How could one ask for anything more after that safe return and perfect reunion? But the contrast between then and tonight was too great. All her hopes had ended in loneli-

ness. All her fears of approaching age had become true. One could not help
the deep depression. The head may tell the heart all sorts of sensible things,
but at Christmastime the heart is stronger.

She sat for a long time in front of the fire which had not warmed her. She
had been on a long emotional journey and it had left her tired and spent.

From the library, loud and brazen, the phone rang. It startled her for she
had never outgrown her fear of a late call. With her usual trepidation she hastened to answer. There was some delay, a far off operator's voice, and then Lee.

"That you, Mother?"

"Yes, Lee, yes. How are you?"

"Fine. Did Jeanie come?"

"No, the boys are still quarantined."

"Ruth?"

"No."

"You there alone?"

"Yes."

"Gosh, that's too bad on the old family night. Well, cheer up. I've got news
for you. Our company came. She weighs seven pounds and fourteen ounces."

"What . . . what did you say, Lee?"

"Our daughter arrived, Mom. Four hours ago. I waited at the hospital to
see that Ann was all right."

"Why, Lee . . . you never told . . . we never knew . . . "

"It was Ann's idea of a good joke. And listen . . . we named her Margaret
. . . for you, Mother. Do you like it?"

"Why, yes . . . *yes,* I *do* like it, Lee."

There was more, sometimes both talking at once and having to repeat.
Then Lee saying, "We were wondering if you could come down in a couple
of weeks. Ann thinks she'd like to have an old hand at the business around.
Can you arrange it?"

"Oh, yes, Lee . . . I'm sure I could."

"Good. Well, I'll hang up now. Spent enough on my call . . . have to save
my money to send Margaret to college. Be seeing you."

"*Lee* . . . " In those last seconds she wanted desperately to put into words
all the things her heart was saying. But you cannot put the thoughts garnered
from a life of love and service into a sentence. So she only said: "Be a good
dad, Lee. Be as good a dad as . . . " She broke off, but he understood.

"I know . . . I'll try. Merry Christmas, Mom."

"Merry Christmas, Lee."

She put down the receiver and walked into the living room, walked briskly as though to tell her news, her heart beating with pleasant excitement. The semicircle of chairs confronted her. With physical sight she saw their emptiness. But, born of love and imagination, they were all occupied as plainly as ever eyes had seen them. She had a warm sense of companionship. The house seemed alive with humans. How could they be so real? She swept the circle with that second sight which had been given her. Don over there . . . Ruth on the hassock . . . Jeanie on the davenport . . . Lee and Ann in the big blue chairs.

Suddenly she turned and walked hurriedly down the hall to the closet and came back with the little red chair. She pushed the two blue chairs apart and set the battered rocker between them. On the back hung the old brown tidy with its red cross-stitching: FOR MARGARET.

She smiled at it happily. All her numbness of spirit had vanished, her loneliness gone. This was a good Christmas. Why, this was one of the best Christmases she had ever had!

She felt a sudden desire to go back to the library, to look out at the silvery garden and up to the stars. That bright one up there—it must be the one that stops over all cradles . . .

Faintly she could hear bells and voices. That would be the young crowd coming back from their caroling, so she opened the window again.

Oh, little town of Bethlehem,
How still we see thee lie . . .

The words came clearly across the starlit snow, singing themselves into her consciousness with a personal message:

Yet in thy dark streets shineth
The everlasting light
The hopes and fears of all the years
Are met in thee tonight.

The hopes and fears of all the years! She felt the old Christmas lift of the heart, that thankfulness and joy she had always experienced when the children were all together . . . all well . . . all home.

"My cup runneth over."

At the door of the living room she paused to turn off the lights. Without looking toward the circle of chairs, so there might come no disillusion, she said over her shoulder:

"Good-night, children. Merry Christmas. See you early in the morning."

Long Distance

JANE SMILEY

KIRBY CHRISTIANSON IS standing under the shower, fiddling with the hot-water spigot and thinking four apparently simultaneous thoughts: that there is never enough hot water in this apartment, that there was always plenty of hot water in Japan, that Mieko will be here in four days, and that he is unable to control Mieko's expectations of him in any way. The thoughts of Mieko are accompanied by a feeling of anxiety as strong as the sensation of the hot water, and he would like the water to flow through him and wash it away. He turns from the shower head and bends backward, so that the stream can pour over his face.

When he shuts off the shower, the phone is ringing. A sense that it has been ringing for a long time—can a mechanical noise have a quality of desperation?—propels him naked and dripping into the living room. He picks up the phone and his caller, as he has suspected, is Mieko. Perhaps he is psychic; perhaps this is only a coincidence, or perhaps no one else has called him in the past week or so.

The connection has a crystalline clarity that tricks him into not allowing for the satellite delay. He is already annoyed after the first hello. Mieko's voice is sharp, high, very Japanese, although she speaks superb English. He says, "Hello, Mieko," and he *sounds* annoyed, as if she called him too much, although she has only called once to give him her airline information and once to change it. Uncannily attuned to the nuances of his voice, she says, "Oh, Kirby," and falls silent.

Now there will be a flurry of tedious apologies, on both sides. He is tempted to hang up on her, call her back, and blame his telephone—faulty American technology. But he can't be certain that she is at home. So he says, "Hello, Mieko? Hello, Mieko? Hello, Mieko?" more and more loudly, as if her voice were fading. His strategy works. She shouts, "Can you hear me, Kirby? I can hear you, Kirby."

He holds the phone away from his ear. He says, "That's better. Yes, I can hear you now."

"Kirby, I cannot come. I cannot go through with my plan. My father has lung cancer, we learned this morning."

He has never met the father, has seen the mother and sister only from a distance, at a department store.

"Can you hear me, Kirby?"

"Yes, Mieko. I don't know what to say."

"You don't have to say anything. I have said to my mother that I am happy to stay with her. She is considerably relieved."

"Can you come later, in the spring?"

"My lie was that this Melville seminar I was supposed to attend would be offered just this one time, which was why I had to go now."

"I'm sorry."

"I know that I am only giving up pleasure. I know that my father might die."

As she says this, Kirby is looking out his front window at the snowy roof of the house across the street, and he understands at once from the hopeless tone of her voice that to give up the pleasure that Mieko has promised herself is harder than to die. He understands that in his whole life he has never given up a pleasure that he cherished as much as Mieko cherished this one. He understands that in a just universe the father would rather die alone than steal such a pleasure from his daughter. All these thoughts occur simultaneously, and are accompanied by a lifting of the anxiety he felt in the shower. She isn't coming. She is never coming. He is off the hook. He says, "But it's hard for you to give up, Mieko. It is for me, too. I'm sorry."

The sympathetic tones in his voice wreck her self-control, and she begins to weep. In the five months that Kirby knew Mieko in Japan, and in the calls between them since, she has never shed a tear, hardly ever let herself be caught in a low moment, but now she weeps with absolute abandon, in long, heaving sobs, saying, "Oh, oh, oh," every so often. Once, the sounds fade, as if she has put down the phone, but he does not dare hang up, does not even dare move the phone from one ear to the other. This attentive listening is what he owes to her grief, isn't it? If she had come, and he had disappointed her, as he would have, this is how she would have wept in solitude after swallowing her disappointment in front of him. But her father has done it, not him. He can give her a little company after all. He presses the phone so hard to his ear that it hurts. The weeping goes on for a long time and he is afraid to speak and interfere with what will certainly be her only opportunity to give way to her feelings. She gives one final wailing "Ohhh" and begins to cough and choke. Finally she quiets, and then sighs. After a moment of silence she says, "Kirby, you should not have listened."

"How could I hang up?"

"A Japanese man would have."

"You sound better, if you are back to comparing me with Japanese men."

"I am going to hang up now, Kirby. I am sorry not to come. Good-bye."

"Don't hang up."

"Good-bye."

"Mieko?"

"Good-bye, Kirby."

"Call me! Call me again!" He is not sure that she hears him. He looks at the phone and then puts it on the cradle.

TWO HOURS LATER he is on the highway. This is, after all, two days before Christmas, and he is on his way to spend the holidays with his two brothers and their wives and children, whom he hasn't seen in years. He has thought little about this visit, beyond buying a few presents. Mieko's coming loomed, imposing and problematic. They had planned to drive out west together— she had paid extra so that she could land in Minneapolis and return from San Francisco—and he had looked forward to seeing the mountains again. They had made reservations on a bus that carries tourists into Yellowstone Park in the winter, to look at the smoky geysers and the wildlife and the snow. The trip would have seemed very American to her—buffalo and men in cowboy boots and hats. But it seemed very Japanese to him—deep snow, dark pines, sharp mountains.

The storm rolls in suddenly, the way it sometimes does on I-35 in Iowa, startling him out of every thought except alertness. Snow swirls everywhere, blotting out the road, the other cars, sometimes even his own front end. The white of his headlights reflects back at him, so that he seems to be driving into a wall. He can hardly force himself to maintain thirty-five miles an hour, although he knows he must. To stop would be to invite a rear-end collision. And the shoulder of the road is invisible. Only the white line, just beside the left front corner of the car, reveals itself intermittently as the wind blows the snow off the pavement. He ejects the tape he is playing and turns on the radio, to the state weather station. He notices that his hand is shaking. He could be killed. The utter blankness of the snowy whirl gives him a way of imagining what it would be like to be dead. He doesn't like the feeling.

He remembers reading two winters ago about an elderly woman whose son dropped her off at her apartment. She discovered that she had forgotten her key, and with the windchill factor at eighty below zero, she froze before she got to the manager's office. The winter before that a kid who broke his legs in a snowmobile accident crawled three miles to the nearest farmhouse, no gloves, only a feed cap on his head.

Twenty below, thirty below—the papers always make a big deal of the temperature. Including windchill, seventy, a hundred below. Kirby carries a flashlight, a down sleeping bag, a sweatshirt that reads UNIVERSITY OF NEBRASKA, gloves and mittens. His car has new tires, front-wheel drive, and plenty of antifreeze. He has a thermos of coffee. But the horror stories roll through his mind anyway. A family without boots or mittens struggles two miles to a McDonald's through high winds, blowing snow, thirty below. *Why would they travel in that weather?* Kirby always thinks when he reads the papers, but of course they do. He does. Always has.

A gust takes the car, just for a second, and Kirby grips the wheel more tightly. The same gust twists the enveloping snow aloft and reveals the Clear Lake rest stop. Kirby is tempted to stop, tempted not to. He has, after all, never died before, and he has driven through worse than this. He passes the rest stop. Lots of cars are huddled there; but then, lots of cars are still on the highway. Maybe the storm is letting up.

As soon as he is past the rest stop, he thinks of Mieko, her weeping. She might never weep like that again, even if she heard of his death. The connection in her mind between the two of them, the connection that she allowed to stretch into the future despite all his admonitions and all her resolutions, is broken now. Her weeping was the sound of its breaking. And if he died here, in the next ten minutes, how would she learn of it? His brothers wouldn't call her, not even if she were still coming, because they didn't know she had planned to come. And if she were ever to call him back, she would get only a disconnect message and would assume that he had moved. He can think of no way that she could hear of his death, even though no one would care more than she would. These thoughts fill him with self-pity, but at least they drive out the catalogue of horror: station wagon skids into bridge abutment, two people are killed, two paralyzed from the neck down, mother survives unharmed, walks to nearby farmhouse. Kirby weighs the boredom and good fellowship he will encounter sitting out the storm at a truck stop against possible tragedy. Fewer cars are on the road; more are scattered on the median strip. Inertia carries him onward. He is almost to Minnesota, after all, where they really know how to take care of the roads. He will stop at the tourist center and ask about conditions.

But he drives past the tourist center by mistake, lost in thought. He decides to stop in Faribault. But by then the snow seems to be tapering off. Considering the distance he has traveled, Minneapolis isn't far now. He checks the odometer. Only fifty miles or so. An hour and a half away, at this speed. His mind eases over the numbers with customary superhighway confidence, but at once he imagines himself reduced to walking, walking in this storm, with only a flashlight, a thermos of coffee, a University of Nebraska sweatshirt —and the distance swells to infinity. Were he reduced to his own body, his own power, it might be too far to walk just to find a telephone.

For comfort he calls up images of Japan and southern China, something he often does. That he produces these images is the one tangible change that his travels have made in him. So many human eyes have looked upon every scene there for so many eons that every sight has an arranged quality: a flowering branch in the foreground, a precipitous mountainside in the background, a small bridge between. A path, with two women in red kimonos, that winds up a hillside. A white room with pearly rice-paper walls and a futon on a mat-covered floor, branches of cherry blossoms in a vase in the corner. They seem like pictures, but they are scenes he has actually looked upon: on a three-day trip out of Hong Kong into southern China, with some other teachers from his school on a trip to Kyoto, and at Akira's house. Akira was a fellow teacher at his school who befriended him. His house had four rooms, two Japanese style and two Western style.

He remembers, of course, other scenes of Japan—acres of buses, faces staring at his Westernness, the polite but bored rows of students in his classroom—when he is trying to decide whether to go back there. But these are not fixed, have no power; they are just memories, like memories of bars in Lincoln or the pig houses on his grandfather's farm.

AND SO, HE SURVIVES the storm. He pulls into the driveway of Harold's new house, one he has not seen, though it is in a neighborhood he remembers from junior high school. The storm is over. Harold has his snowblower out and is making a path from the driveway to his front door. With the noise and because his back is turned, he is unaware of Kirby's arrival. Kirby stops the car, stretches, and looks at his watch. Seven hours for a four-hour trip. Kirby lifts his shoulders and rotates his head but does not beep his horn just yet. The fact is that he has frightened himself with the blinding snow, the miles of slick and featureless landscape, thoughts of Japan, and the thousands and thousands of miles between here and there. His car might be a marble that has rolled, only by luck, into a safe corner. He presses his fingers against his eyes and stills his breathing.

Harold turns around, grins, and shuts off the snowblower. It is a Harold identical to the Harold that Kirby has always known. Same bright snowflake ski hat, same bright ski clothing. Harold has spent his whole life skiing and ski-jumping. His bushy beard grows up to the hollows of his eyes, and when he leans into the car his moustache is, as always, crusted with ice.

"Hey!" he says. He backs away, and Kirby opens the car door.

"Made it!" Kirby says. That is all he will say about the trip. The last thing he wants to do is start a discussion about near misses. Compared with some of Harold's near misses, this is nothing. In fact, near misses on the highway aren't worth mentioning unless a lot of damage has been done to the car. Kirby knows of near misses that Harold has never dared to describe to anyone besides him, because they show a pure stupidity that even Harold has the sense to be ashamed of.

Over dinner, sweet and savory Nordic fare that Kirby is used to but doesn't much like, he begins to react to his day. The people around the table, his relatives, waver in the smoky candlelight, and Kirby imagines that he can feel the heat of the flames on his face. The other people at the table seem unfamiliar. Leanne, Harold's wife, he has seen only once, at their wedding. She is handsome and self-possessed-looking, but she sits at the corner of the table, like a guest in her own house. Eric sits at the head and Mary Beth, his wife, jumps up and down to replenish the food. This assumption of primogeniture is a peculiarity of Eric's that has always annoyed Kirby, but even aside from that they have never gotten along. Eric does his best—earnest handshake and smile each time they meet, two newsy letters every year, pictures of the children (known between Harold and Kirby as "the little victims"). Eric has a Ph.D. from Columbia in American history, but he does not teach. He writes for a conservative think tank—articles that appear on the op-ed pages of newspapers and in the think tank's own publications. He specializes in "the family." Kirby and Harold have made countless jokes at Eric's expense. Kirby knows that more will be made this trip, if only in the form of conspiratorial looks, rolling eyes. Eric's hobby—Mary Beth's, too, for they share everything—is developing each nuance of his Norwegian heritage into a fully realized ostentation. Mary Beth is always busy, usually baking. That's all Kirby knows about her, and all he cares to know.

Across the table Anna, their older daughter, pale, blue-eyed, cool, seems to be staring at him, but Kirby can hardly see her. He is thinking about Mieko. Kirby looks at his watch. It is very early morning in Osaka. She is probably about to wake up. Her disappointment will have receded hardly a particle, will suck her down as soon as she thuds into consciousness. "Oh, oh, oh": he can hear her cries as clearly as if they were vibrating in the air. He is amazed at having heard such a thing, and he looks carefully at the women around the table. Mieko would be too eager to please here, always looking after Mary Beth and Leanne, trying to divine how she might be helpful. Finally, Mary Beth would speak to her with just a hint of sharpness, and Mieko would be crushed. Her eyes would seek Kirby's for reassurance, and he would have none to give. She would be too little, smaller than Anna, and her voice would be too high and quick. These thoughts give him such pain that he stares for relief at Kristin, Eric's youngest, age three, who is humming over her dinner. She is round-faced and paunchy, with dark hair cut straight across her forehead and straight around her collar. From time to time she and Leanne exchange merry glances.

Harold is beside him; that, at least, is familiar and good, and it touches Kirby with a pleasant sense of expectation, as if Harold, at any moment, might pass him a comic book or a stick of gum. In fact, Harold does pass him something—an icy cold beer, which cuts the sweetness of the food and seems to adjust all the figures around the table so that they stop wavering.

OF COURSE, HIS EYES OPEN well before daylight, but he dares not move. He is sharing a room with Harold the younger, Eric's son, whose bed is between his and the door. He worries that if he gets up he will stumble around and crash into walls and wake Harold. The digits on the clock beside Harold's bed read 5:37, but when Kirby is quiet, he can hear movement elsewhere in the house. When he closes his eyes, the footsteps present themselves as a needle and thread, stitching a line through his thoughts. He has just been driving. His arms ache from gripping the wheel. The car slides diagonally across the road, toward the median. It slides and slides, through streams of cars, toward a familiar exit, the Marshalltown exit, off to the left, upward. His eyes open again. The door of the room is open, and Anna is looking in. After a moment she turns and goes away. It is 6:02. Sometime later Leanne passes with Isaac, the baby, in her arms.

Kirby cannot bear to get up and face his brothers and their families. As always, despair presents itself aesthetically. The image of Harold's and Leanne's living room, matching plaid wing chairs and couch, a triple row of wooden pegs by the maple front door, seems to Kirby the image of the interior of a coffin. The idea of spending five years, ten years, a lifetime, with such furniture makes him gasp. But his own apartment, armchair facing the television, which sits on a spindly coffee table, is worse. Mary Beth and Eric's place, where he has been twice, is the worst, because it's pretentious; they have antique wooden trunks and high-backed benches painted blue with stenciled flowers in red and white. Everything, everything, they own is blue and white, or white and blue, and Nordic primatif. Now even the Japanese images he calls up are painful. The pearly white Japanese-style room in Akira's house was bitterly cold in the winter, and he spent one night there only half-sleeping, his thighs drawn to his chest, the perimeters of the bed too cold even to touch. His head throbbing, Kirby lies pinned to the bed by impossibility. He literally can't summon up a room, a stick of furniture, that he can bear to think of. Harold the younger rolls over and groans, turning his twelve-year-old face toward Kirby's. His mouth opens and he breathes noisily. It is 6:27.

Not until breakfast, when Leanne sets a bowl of raisin bran before him on the table, does he recall the appearance of Anna in the door to his room, and then it seems odd, especially when, ten minutes later, she enters the kitchen in her bathrobe, yawning. Fifth grade. Only fifth grade. He can see that now, but the night before, and in the predawn darkness, she had seemed older, more threatening, the way girls get at fourteen and fifteen. "Cereal, sweetie?" Leanne says, and Anna nods, scratching. She sits down without a word and focuses on the back of the Cheerios box. Kirby decides that he was dreaming and puts the incident out of his mind.

Harold, of course, is at his store, managing the Christmas rush, and the house is less festive in his absence. Eric has sequestered himself in Leanne's sewing room, with his computer, and as soon as Anna stands up from breakfast, Mary Beth begins to arrange the day's kitchen schedule. Kirby rinses his cup and goes into the living room. It is nine in the morning, and the day stretches before him, empty. He walks through the plaid living room to the window, where he regards the outdoor thermometer. It reads four degrees below zero. Moments later it is five degrees below zero. Moments after that he is standing beside Harold's bar, pouring himself a glass of bourbon. He has already drunk it when Anna appears in the doorway, dressed now, and staring at him again. She makes him think of Mieko again—though the child is blond and self-contained, she is Mieko's size. Last evening, when he was thinking of Mieko, he was looking at Anna. He says, attempting jovial warmth, "Good morning, Anna. Why do you keep staring at me?"

She is startled. "I don't. I was looking at the bookshelves."

"But you stared at me last night at dinner. And you came to the door of my room early this morning. I know because I was awake."

"No, I didn't." But then she softens, and says with eager curiosity. "Are you a socialist?"

While Kirby is trying not to laugh, he hears Mary Beth sing from the kitchen: "Anna? Your brother is going sledding. You want to go?"

Anna turns away before Kirby can answer, and mounts the stairs. A "No!" floats, glassy and definite, from the second floor.

Kirby sits down in one of the plaid armchairs and gazes at an arrangement of greenery and shiny red balls and candles that sits on a table behind the couch. He gazes and gazes, contemplating the notion of Eric and Mary Beth discussing his politics and his life. He is offended. He knows that if he were to get up and do something he would stop being offended, but he gets up only to pour himself another drink. It is nearly ten. Books are around everywhere, and Kirby picks one up.

People keep opening doors and coming in, having been elsewhere. Harold comes home for lunch; Leanne and Isaac return from the grocery store and the hardware store; Harold the younger stomps in, covered with snow from sledding, eats a sandwich, and stomps out again. Eric opens the sewing-room door, takes a turn through the house, goes back in again. He does this three times, each time failing to speak to Kirby, who is sitting quietly. Perhaps he does not see him. He is an old man, Kirby thinks, and his rear has spread considerably in the past four years; he is thirty-six going on fifty, round-shouldered, wearing slacks rather than jeans. What a jerk.

But then Kirby's bad mood twists into him, and he lets his head drop on the back of his chair. What is a man? Kirby thinks. What is a man, what is a man? It is someone, Eric would say, who votes, owns property, has a wife, worries. It is someone, Harold would say, who can chop wood all day and make love all night, who can lift his twenty-five pound son above his head on the palm of his hand.

After lunch the men all vanish again, even Isaac, who is taking a nap. In various rooms the women do things. They make no noise. Harold's house is the house of a wealthy man, Kirby realizes. It is large enough to be silent and neat most of the time, the sort of house Kirby will never own. It is Harold and Eric who are alike now. Only Kirby's being does not extend past his fingertips and toes to family, real estate, reputation.

SOMETIME IN THE LATE afternoon, while Kirby enjoys sitting quietly and his part of the room is shadowed by the movement of the sun to the other side of the house, Kristin comes in from the kitchen, goes straight to the sofa, pulls off one of the cushions, and begins to jump repeatedly from the cushion to the floor. When he says, "Kristin, what are you doing?" she is not startled. She says, "Jumping."

"Do you like to jump?"

She says, "It's a beautiful thing to do," in her matter-of-fact, deep, three-year-old voice. Kirby can't believe she knows what she is saying. She jumps three or four more times and then runs out again.

At dinner she is tired and tiresome. When Eric tells her to eat a bite of her meat (ham cooked with apricots), she looks him right in the face and says, "No."

"One bite," he says. "I mean it."

"No. I mean it." She looks up at him. He puts his napkin on the table and pushes back his chair. In a moment he has swept her through the doorway and up the stairs. She is screaming. A door slams and the screaming is muffled. When he comes down and seats himself, carefully laying his napkin over his slacks, Anna says, "It's her body."

The table quiets. Eric says, "What?"

"It's her body."

"What does that mean?"

"She should have control over her own body. Food. Other stuff. I don't know." She has started strong but weakens in the face of her father's glare. Eric inhales sharply, and Kirby cannot restrain himself. He says, "How can you disagree with that? It sounds self-evident to me."

"Does it? The child is three years old. How can she have control over her own body when she doesn't know anything about it? Does she go out without a coat if it's twenty below zero? Does she eat only cookies for three days? Does she wear a diaper until she's five? This is one of those phrases they are using these days. They all mean the same thing."

"What do they mean?" As Kirby speaks, Leanne and Mary Beth look up, no doubt wishing that he had a wife or a girlfriend here to restrain him. Harold looks up, too. He is grinning.

Eric shifts in his chair, uncomfortable, Kirby suddenly realizes, at being predictably stuffy once again. Eric says, "It's Christmas. Let's enjoy it."

Harold says, "Principles are principles, any day of the year."

Eric takes the bait and lets himself say, "The family is constituted for a purpose, which is the sometimes difficult socialization of children. For a certain period of their lives others control them. In early childhood others control their bodies. They are taught to control themselves. Even Freud says that the young barbarian has to be taught to relinquish his feces, sometimes by force."

"Good Lord, Eric," Leanne says.

Eric is red in the face. "Authority is a principle I believe in." He looks around the table and then at Anna, openly angry that she has gotten him into this. Across Anna's face flits a look that Kirby has seen before, has seen on Mieko's face, a combination of self-doubt and resentment molded into composure.

"Patriarchy is what you mean," Kirby says, realizing from the tone of his own voice that rage has replaced sympathy and, moreover, is about to get the better of him.

"Why not? It works."

"For some people, at a great cost. Why should daughters be sacrificed to the whims of the father?" He should stop now. He doesn't. "Just because he put his dick somewhere once or twice." The result of too many bourbons too early in the day.

"In my opinion—" Eric seems not to notice the vulgarity, but Harold, beside Kirby, snorts with pleasure.

"I don't want to talk about this," Leanne says. Kirby blushes and falls silent, knowing that he has offended her. It is one of those long holiday meals, and by the time they get up from the table, Kirby feels as if he has been sitting in a dim, candlelit corner most of his life.

There is another ritual—the Christmas Eve unwrapping of presents—and by that time Kirby realizes that he is actively intoxicated and had better watch his tone of voice and his movements. Anna hands out the gifts with a kind of rude bashfulness, and Kirby is surprised at the richness of the array: from Harold he has gotten a cotton turtleneck and a wool sweater, in bright, stylish colors; from Leanne a pair of very fancy gloves; from Isaac, three pairs of rag wool socks; from Eric's family, as a group, a blue terry-cloth robe and sheepskin slippers. When they open his gifts, he is curious to see what the wrappings reveal: he has bought it all so long before. Almost everything is some gadget available in Japan but not yet in the States. Everyone peers and oohs and aahs. It gives Kirby a headache and a sense of his eyeballs expanding and contracting. Tomorrow night he will be on his way home again, and though he cannot bear to stay here after all, he cannot bear to go, either.

He drifts toward the stairs, intending to go to bed, but Harold looms before him, grinning and commanding. "Your brain needs some oxygen, brother," he says. Then they are putting on their parkas, and then they are outside, in a cold so sharp that Kirby's nose, the only exposed part of him, stings. Harold strides down the driveway, slightly ahead of him, and Kirby expects him to speak, either for or against Eric, but he doesn't. He only walks. The deep snow is so solidly frozen that it squeaks beneath their boots. The only thing Harold says the whole time they are walking is, "Twenty-two below, not counting the wind chill. Feels good, doesn't it?"

"Feels dangerous," Kirby says.

"It is," Harold says.

The neighborhood is brightly decorated, and the colored lights have their effect on Kirby. For the first time in three Christmases he feels a touch of the mystery that he thinks of as the Christmas spirit. Or maybe it is love for Harold.

Back at the house, everyone has gone to bed except Leanne and Mary Beth, who are drying dishes and putting them away. They are also, Kirby realizes —after Harold strides through the kitchen and up the stairs—arguing, although with smiles and in polite tones. Kirby goes to a cabinet and lingers over getting himself a glass for milk. Mary Beth says, "Kristin will make the connection. She's old enough."

"I can't believe that."

"She saw all the presents being handed out and unwrapped. And Anna will certainly make the connection."

"Anna surely doesn't believe in Santa Claus anymore."

"Unofficially, probably not."

"It's Isaac's first Christmas," Leanne says. "He'll like all the wrappings."

"I wish you'd thought of that before you wrapped the family presents and his Santa presents in the same paper."

"That's a point, too. They're his presents. I don't think Kristin will notice them."

"If they're the only wrapped presents, she will. She notices everything."

Now Leanne turns and gazes at Mary Beth, her hands on her hips. A long silence follows. Leanne flicks a glance at Kirby, who pretends not to notice. Finally, she says, "All right, Mary Beth. I'll unwrap them."

"Thank you," Mary Beth says. "I'll finish this, if you want." Kirby goes out of the kitchen and up to his bedroom. The light is already off, and Harold the younger is on his back, snoring.

WHEN HE GETS UP an hour later, too drunk to sleep, Kirby sees Leanne arranging the last of Santa's gifts under the tree. She turns the flash of her glance upon him as he passes through the living room to the kitchen. "Mmm," he says, uncomfortable, "can't sleep."

"Want some cocoa? I always make some before I go to bed."

He stops. "Yeah. Why not? Am I mistaken, or have you been up since about six A.M.?"

"About that. But I'm always wired at midnight, no matter what."

He follows her into the kitchen, remembering now that they have never conversed, and wishing that he had stayed in bed. He has drunk himself stupid. Whatever words he has in him have to be summoned from very far down. He sits at the table. After a minute he puts his chin in his hand. After a long, blank, rather pleasant time, the cocoa is before him, marshmallow and all. He looks at it. When Leanne speaks, Kirby is startled, as if he had forgotten that she was there.

"Tired?" she says.

"Too much to drink."

"I noticed."

"I don't have anything more to say about it."

"I'm not asking."

He takes a sip of his cocoa. He says, "Do you see much of Eric and family?"

"They came last Christmas. He came by himself in the summer. To a conference on the future of the family."

"And so you have to put up with him, right?"

"Harold has a three-day limit. I don't care."

"I noticed you unwrapped all Isaac's presents."

She shrugs, picks at the sole of her boot. She yawns without covering her mouth, and then says, "Oh, I'm sorry." She smiles warmly, looking right at him. "I am crazy about Kristin. Crazy enough to not chance messing up Christmas for her."

"Today she told me that jumping off a cushion was a beautiful thing to do."

Leanne smiles. "Yesterday she said that it was wonderful of me to give her a napkin. You know, I don't agree with Eric about that body stuff. I think they naturally do what is healthy for them. Somebody did an experiment with one-year-olds, gave them a range of foods to choose from, and they always chose a balanced diet. They also want to be toilet trained sooner or later. I think it's weird the way Eric thinks that every little thing is learned rather than realized."

"That's a nice phrase." He turns his cup handle so that it points away and then back in his direction. Finally he says, "Can I tell you about something?"

"Sure."

"Yesterday a friend of mine called me from Japan, a woman, to say that she couldn't come visit me. Her father has cancer. She had planned to arrive here the day after tomorrow, and we were going to take a trip out west. It isn't important, exactly. I don't know."

Leanne is silent but attentive, picking at the sole of her boot. Now that he has mentioned it, the memory of Mieko's anguish returns to him like a glaring light or a thundering noise, so enormous that he is nearly robbed of the power to speak. He pushes it out. "She can't come now, ever. She probably won't ever call or write me again. And really, this has saved her. She had all sorts of expectations that I couldn't have . . . well, wouldn't have fulfilled, and if she had come she would have been permanently compromised."

"Did you have some kind of affair when you were there?"

"For a few months. She's very pretty. I think she's the prettiest woman I've ever seen. She teaches mathematics at the school where I was teaching. After I had been with Mieko for a few weeks, I realized that no one, maybe in her whole adult life, had asked her how she was, or had put his arm around her shoulders, or had taken care of her in any way. The slightest affection was like a drug she couldn't get enough of."

"What did you feel?"

"I liked her. I really did. I was happy to see her when she came by. But she longed for me more than I have ever longed for anything."

"You were glad to leave."

"I was glad to leave."

"So what's the problem?"

"When she called yesterday, she broke down completely. I listened. I thought it was the least I could do, but now I think that she is compromised. Japanese people are very private. It scares me how much I must have embarrassed her. I look back on the spring and the summer and yesterday's call, and I see that, one by one, I broke down every single one of her strengths, everything she equipped herself with to live in a Japanese way. I was so careful for a year and a half. I didn't date Japanese women, and I was very distant—but then I was so lonely, and she was so pretty, and I thought, well, she's twenty-seven, and she lives in this sophisticated city, Osaka. But mostly I was lonely."

Leanne gazes across the table in that way of hers, calm and considering. Finally she says, "Eric comes in for a lot of criticism around here. His style's all wrong, for one thing. And he drives Harold the younger and Anna crazy. But I've noticed something about him. He never tries to get something for nothing. I admire that."

Now Kirby looks around the room, at the plants on the windowsill, the hoarfrost on the windowpanes, the fluorescent light harsh on the stainless-steel sink, and it seems to him that all at once, now that he realizes it, his life and Mieko's have taken their final form. She is nearly too old to marry, and by the end of her father's cancer and his life she will be much too old. And himself. Himself. Leanne's cool remark has revealed his permanent smallness. He looks at his hands, first his knuckles, then his palms. He says, "It seems so dramatic to say that I will never get over this."

"Does it? To me it seems like saying that what people do is important." And though he looks at her intently, seeking some sort of pardon, she says nothing more, only picks at her boot for a moment or two, and then gets up and puts their cups in the sink. He follows her out of the kitchen, through the living room. She turns out all the lights, so that the house is utterly dark. At the bottom of the stairs, unable to see anything, he stumbles against her and excuses himself. There, soft and fleeting, he feels a disembodied kiss on his cheek, and her voice, nearly a whisper, says, "Merry Christmas, Kirby. I'm glad you're here."

The Christmas That
Would Not Stop

RON ROBINSON

IF EVER THERE WAS A PLACE suited for wallowing in self-doubt, it was the waiting room of the maternity ward at Holy Family Hospital in Estherville, Iowa, on the second day of Christmas, 1966. The walls, institutional off-white, were sparsely dressed. A color lithograph of Jesus at Gethsemane adorned one wall. A print of Mary, full of compassion, faced her Son at the other end of the narrow chamber. Noticeably missing, despite the name of the hospital, was a representation of Joseph. I assumed that I was to take his part, that of the hapless, clueless onlooker, unsure of what his role actually was.

Battered wood and vinyl furniture, designed by a Danish-modern sadist, offered scant comfort. Scattered about were ragged issues of *Reader's Digest*, filled with articles both curt and smug; ancient condensed books by the same publisher, wrung juiceless by severe editing; and religious brochures warning me that while bad things happen to good people, worse things happen to bad people. Opposite the rack-like sofa was a rectangular window which gave upon a brick wall. A sliver of iron-gray sky was visible above, and a few flakes of snow sifted insidiously downward.

There was no television in the room, so that I was deprived of even that mild anesthetic. I was left alone with my thoughts, mostly along the lines of self-condemnation. I had just read a solemn declaration posted in the hall of the maternity wing warning that, in case complications arose and given a choice between saving the life of the newborn and the life of the mother, hospital policy was to save the child. The warning had filled me with dread, because given my genetic history, there was an off-chance that complications might arise, and because I loved my wife more than anything else, certainly more than I loved that alien being that had invaded her body some nine months earlier. What had I gotten us into?

Margaret had for the past several weeks been stuck in the limbo of the last trimester, weary of being pregnant and afraid of childbirth. Not only was she sure it would be painful, but in those years there was little effort at DNA, amniotic, or ultrasound gender- or fortune-telling, hardly a way of knowing whether the baby would be normal. Her doctor wasn't even sure of the due date. "About mid January," he'd guessed.

When the morning-sickness stage had waned and the Moby Dick stage waxed, Margaret couldn't bear to have me even looking at her. She said, "If you tell me one more time how creamy my complexion is or what a warm glow I have about me, I swear I will clobber you with the kitchen sink."

"You blame me," I said.

She hissed back, "Yessss!"

Margaret worried she would turn out to be a bad mother, and evidence suggested she might be right. Children got on her nerves. Our scant experience in sitting a friend's baby girl had ended with Margaret retching repeatedly while attempting to change a messy diaper. She could endure her sister's two daughters as long as they played quietly with paper dolls, but when they started playing tug-o'-war with Barbie and screaming accusations, as they had during our recent Christmas Eve gathering at her parent's farmstead, Margaret's eyes filled with panic and disgust. During the two-hundred-mile Christmas Day trek between her parent's place in South Dakota and mine in Iowa, she had confided yet again that children tried her patience and that she found them selfish, noisy, and grubby. What would she do, she asked, when our baby wouldn't stop bawling? I had no answer.

Just that day, during a visit to my aunt's place outside Estherville, we had been confronted once again with the realities of parenthood. My dad's sister Mabel (one of five sisters) was a capacious soul who had birthed ten or twelve children of her own. Everyone else in the family had lost count, and Mabel herself seemed a bit uncertain of the number. Now her house swarmed with grandchildren whose names she could not keep straight. It was not encouraging for Margaret to discover that large broods ran in my family.

That was the year when Gumbies were the gift of choice for children, and Mabel's living room was littered with carcasses of the green rubber monstrosities. Unlike plastic toys, most of which were already in pieces, the Gumbies were virtually indestructible. When my little second cousins discovered that Gumby did not really walk and talk like his television counterpart, they invented other uses for him. They found that Gumbies made excellent clubs, for example.

In the midst of howling and shouting children and parents urgently commanding their offspring to let go, get down from there, stop doing that, and share with their younger siblings under threat of corporeal punishment, my Aunt Mabel sat serene, as though at the eye of a human hurricane.

Following our third Christmas Dinner in as many days, at a table the approximate size of a basketball court, Margaret begged me to join her in a walk outside.

"How can she stand it?" Margaret asked me as we ambled down the lane, the hubbub of children's voices receding behind us.

Once again I had no answer. I was getting good at that.

"I think I'm sick," Margaret said.

"Come on," I said, "the kids aren't that bad."

"No," she said, "I mean unwell. I think it's a gas pain."

NOW, OUTSIDE the window of the waiting room, the sky transmuted from iron into a heavier metal. The snowfall seemed to be picking up. The oncoming night would be among the longest of the year, and tomorrow would be our second anniversary.

THE DATE FOR our wedding had been chosen casually, as a convenience, because the Christmas holidays would afford some time for a honeymoon before we both had to go back to our teaching jobs. We had no idea how the choice would complicate our lives, irk our relatives and friends, and haunt us for untold years to come.

The wedding was held at the bride's stately white-steepled Norwegian-Lutheran church on a hill dominating the windswept prairie of southeast South Dakota, about ten miles from the town of Howard. The service proceeded during a ground blizzard, with those in attendance shifting their attention back and forth between the ceremony and the wind screeching past the stained-glass windows. The guests were disappointed that the groom, who at one point seemed on the verge of providing some real entertainment by fainting, had managed to mumble his way through. At the reception they began to worry lest they all be trapped in the place, living on dried remnants of wedding cake and stale punch until dug out sometime the following spring. The wedding photographer was missing in action, and a substitute photographer had to be brought in from Howard to make the obligatory shots. The delay further postponed escape. It was dusk before the wedding party fled to cozier shelter, just as the originally engaged photographer arrived to set up for what he had mistakenly marked down as an evening wedding. While the bride and groom headed through the snowy night toward New Orleans, friends and relatives were wondering whether they henceforward had to give two cards to mark the events of the season or whether they could get by with one.

And now it seemed likely that yet another life passage would mark the season.

THE SUDDEN LIGHT startled me. I realized that I had been meditating in almost complete darkness. I swiveled around to see a nurse in green scrubs poised in the doorway, her hand on the light switch.

"The contractions have stopped," the nurse said. "Looks like it will be a while."

"Can I see her?"

The nurse knitted her brows while retaining her smile, giving her a look of benign resignation much like that on the face of the Madonna. "She's resting," the nurse said.

I took that to mean that I could see my wife, if I wanted to be a horse's rump.

This was a decade before it became fashionable for the husband to be present at the delivery, to act as cheerleader for his wife, to remind her to breathe, to fight down his nausea, and to share in the joy and mystery of birth. In the dark ages during which this scene is set, doctors and nurses treated husbands like the clumsy, irrelevant oafs they really were.

"Why don't you go home and get some sleep?" the nurse suggested. "We can call you when the contractions get closer together."

I considered this option, glancing briefly at the window. With the overhead light on, all I could see was my own reflection in the glass, a shady, unshaven character you'd pick out of any lineup as the prime suspect. "I'll stay."

The nurse shrugged. "Light on or off?"

"Off."

"I can get a pillow."

"No, thank you." Hey, I told myself, I deserved to suffer.

The nurse shrugged again, absolving herself of responsibility, clicked off the light, and was gone. With the light gone, the window glowed ghostly gray, like a charcoal sketch on tinted paper. Ice granules pinged on the glass.

I HAD WHAT I thought was good reason to stay. The Holy Family in Estherville was some one hundred miles east of our little house in Sioux Falls, twelve miles from my parents' home in Graettinger, to the south. Twelve miles doesn't seem like much, but thirty years before that winter I had been born at the old hospital in Estherville during a massive February blizzard. My father had gone home to Graettinger to attend to some chores and did not get back to Estherville until a week later by following a snowplow through house-high drifts. He arrived finally to find my mother distraught, nearly inconsolable. I had been born clubfooted.

The defect had been corrected by a series of innovative procedures undertaken at the University Hospital in Iowa City during the summer of 1936, a summer as hot and dry as the previous winter had been cold and snowy. Records at the extreme of cold and hot were set during that year that have not yet been broken. The braces that I was to wear for a year following the final operation caused me great distress at first. My parents could not get me to stop howling. During the cool fall I started to grow used to encumbrance, and one day, using the steel braces as ballast, I amazed my mother by sitting bolt upright in bed. Soon I was staggering around in my wooden playpen at home or in the cardboard Wonder Bread packing boxes in the kitchen of my grandparents' café, swinging the braces clumsily but without complaint. By my first Christmas I was getting around well enough to clamber onto my new wooden rocking horse and to ride obsessively, going nowhere fast, for hours on end.

One problem had arisen during that first Christmas, my parents informed me. At bedtime on the first day of Christmas, I insisted on hanging my stocking again. My parents, happy that I was on the mend, could not deny me. The next morning I found that Santa had come once more. That night I hung my stocking a third time. My parents thought I was cute and indulged me. By New Year's Eve it was clear that I did not want Christmas to stop.

The year 1936 was the low point of the Great Depression. My mother waited tables in her parents' restaurant and would have been astonished ever to have received a tip. My father operated a portable grain grinder, often bartering his skilled labor for potatoes, eggs, chickens, or other commodities. My parents were deeply in debt for my medical treatment. They weren't exactly poor by the standards of the day, but they could hardly afford a child who expected every day to be Christmas. They drew the line on further gifts after a week. I kept hanging my stocking a few nights more, but eventually I gave up. Still, I think there lingered in my unconscious the possibility of a time when my stocking would be endlessly refilled.

I AWOKE TO THE gray light of dawn on the third day of Christmas, groggy, bleary-eyed, and sore. The Danish-sadist sofa had done its work. When I turned to look out the window, I found my neck locked at an oblique angle to the line of my shoulders. I had to shuffle my whole body around and swivel my eyes to see the steady, abundant snow falling past. When I heard my name called, I repeated the series of moves, head, body, eyes, in the opposite direction.

"Mr. Robinson?" She was a different nurse, but she had the same pinched-eyebrow, beneficent smile as the previous one. They must teach that in nursing school, I guessed.

"Yes?"

"It's a baby girl."

Some time passed while the words fought their way through my foggy brain. What was the reference for the pronoun *it*? my benumbed, English-teacher mind wished to know. Why the unnecessary adjective *baby*? Had someone been expecting a fully grown girl?

"Mr. Robinson?"

"Yes?"

"Do you want to see her?"

"Who?"

"Your daughter!" The nurse's benevolent smile had faded. She probably thought I had become somehow mentally deficient.

I tried to feign alertness. "Oh, yes, of course." I attempted to snap to attention, but I was grabbed by a muscle spasm when half erect and remained bent in the shape of an inverted capital letter *L*. Slowly, fighting pain, I managed to attain a less acute angle.

"This way," the nurse snapped. And I stumbled through the door after her.

Now, I always imagined that a father viewed his newborn child through multiple layers of glass, the little bundle wrapped tidily in a blanket with its little face squinting about and its tiny little hands reaching out as though to grasp the world by the horns. Instead I was led to a full-sized gurney upon which lay this impossibly small, writhing red thing, reminiscent of a plucked chicken or a mistinted Gumby. I carefully checked the feet, which looked all right, but the rest of the thing left me aghast. It was executing karate chops and kicks while emitting guttural grunts and cries in a tongue resembling Japanese. Its complexion was the color of raw meat, and it didn't seem at all happy to be there. I nodded and tried to fake pleasure, but it was as I had long suspected—my wife had given birth to an alien.

As they wheeled the gurney on down the corridor, a sudden horrible thought popped into my head. "My wife," I blurted. "Is she—?"

"She's fine," the nurse said. "Go on in and see her."

Margaret looked tired and deflated but surprisingly happy to see me. I was given to know, however, that the first words out of her mouth following the ordeal of birth were, "When can I start taking the Pill again?" Obviously, whatever I had suffered in the waiting room was like a gnat bite compared to what she had gone through.

"Happy anniversary," I told her. "Some gas pain."

She nodded solemnly, not really getting into the swing of the joke. "Did you see her?"

"She's beautiful," I lied, and offered a kiss.

"We'll have to think of a girl's name," Margaret said. All we had managed to come up with in advance had been fashionable male names like Sean and Zachary. "We can't keep calling her 'Gas Pain,'" my wife said.

After a while the nurse brought in our daughter, now properly cleaned, pink, and swathed, and lay her in my wife's arms. Incredibly, Margaret did not seem to notice that she was pressing an alien to her breast. "Isn't she a sweet little thing?" Margaret asked. I gave what I hoped was a convincing nod. The baby started to cry, and Margaret gently cuddled the bundle until the wail subsided. It was as though the two had suddenly recognized each other. For the second time that morning I was astounded. Apparently Margaret's nurturing gene had at last kicked in.

Twenty-five years later, Tania Noel, grown into a recognizable, normal human being, hit the trifecta by choosing December 27 as her own wedding date. Subsequently she bore three boys of her own, Noel, Josiah, and Sam, now nine, six, and three. When we visit during the holidays to exchange Christmas, birthday, and anniversary gifts, among heaps of torn and gaudy wrapping paper, with the boys running, screaming, literally climbing the walls, clubbing each other with improvised light sabers, and our daughter urging them to cease and desist at the risk of a severe revocation of privileges, Margaret sits smiling and serene, as though at the hub of a hurricane.

As for me, well, my cup runneth over. Although I was but a minor player in this story, I felt like its chief beneficiary. The cornucopia I had wished for that first Christmas is achieved, and without my ever deserving it.

Winter Break

JON HASSLER

NEBRASKA, THOUGH SNOWLESS, wears its wizened, wintry look—the un-varying miles of frosty russet fields and hillocks broken here and there by the sudden neon of fast-food shops along the freeway. Mother wakes from a short doze as we pass a treeless housing development, a sprawling strip mall, an exit sign into Omaha.

"It still seems strange not stopping here, doesn't it, Leland?"

"It does."

"Next year we really should. After all, he *is* your first cousin."

"You said that last year."

She laughs. "But next year we'll do it. Aren't you a tiny bit curious to see him?"

"Not in the least."

"And have a look at that skinny little wife of his? And see what's become of those fat little babies?"

"We know what's become of them. They're fat little husbands and fathers."

This, too, amuses her. "Now, Leland, don't be contrary."

"Sorry, I have a headache."

"Your glasses."

"Glasses! I don't wear glasses"

"You're overdue for a checkup."

"No, it's driving into the sun all day."

We've been making this annual trip since I was a boy. Until eight or ten years ago, we always spent Christmas Eve in Omaha with my father's family, and then early on Christmas morning set out for the O'Kelly farm near Grimsby, where Mother grew up. However, now that Aunt Cora and Uncle Herbert are dead, there's nobody left in Omaha but my cousin Wesley and his wife and twin sons. Cousin Wesley doesn't—nor did he ever—have any interest in seeing us.

Mother examines her face in her sun-visor mirror. "Wrath of God," she sighs, disapproving of it, "but I'm too tired to fix it." She lowers her seat to a reclining position. In a minute she's sleeping again.

Christmas Eve with my father's people in Omaha, during my boyhood, was invariably stiff and unfestive, whereas we always spent a jolly Christmas Day at the O'Kelly farm. Not that the Edwardses were unkind or inhospitable. It's only that the O'Kellys, by nature, were more spontaneous and high-spirited. The minute we entered the farmhouse, we heard stories so uproarious they must have been invented, though they usually began or ended with the phrase "Swear to God." The laughter and tall tales continued through dinner and into the evening as more aunts and uncles and cousins came pouring through the house to greet us. Any given Christmas, we probably saw thirty-five O'Kellys.

A Christmas Eve conversation, on the other hand, followed a serious, predictable line, beginning with the unreliability of the weather and leading on through the deteriorating condition of their ailing friends and neighbors and automobiles. As a boy, I considered this talk painfully dull, but over the years I learned to take a certain pleasure in the constancy of it—the way you will sometimes come to appreciate the cheerless old hymn in church simply because it's so familiar. I suppose, as we age, any sign of permanence consoles us, no matter if it bores us besides.

Isn't it curious, therefore, that despite the high colors of the O'Kelly Christmases, the Edwards family is more clearly etched in my boyhood memories? Grandfather Edwards, a small fragile man with a mustache and a mottled face, was made to seem even smaller by the engulfing overstuffed chair he always sat in. "Come Leland, we'll read," he used to declare before dinner, and I would climb onto his lap and be read to from a book of moralizing tales about a virtuous boy named Henry. Grandmother Edwards, humbly deflecting all credit or praise, would serve the dinner for eight and then take her place at the foot of the table, where she silently nibbled and smiled at me whenever our eyes met.

Aunt Cora was my father's younger sister. She lived on the other side of Omaha with her husband, Herbert, and their son, Wesley. Aunt Cora operated a beauty salon in her living room and smelled of permanent goo. Uncle Herbert was a butcher, a silent man with nine fingers and a full head of red hair. Cousin Wesley, two years older than I, was never any fun. Throughout his teens, he fancied himself a superb baseball pitcher and found me useful as a receiver of his fastball, which numbed my hand up to the elbow. His father called him "Hotshot." Wesley is retired now, after forty years of driving a delivery truck for a lumberyard.

I remember how Grandmother Edwards's smile, never quite joyous, turned very sad on the Christmas when my father was stationed in California and waiting to be shipped out to the war in the South Pacific. I recall the phonograph record he sent home to his parents that winter. *Don't open without Lolly and Leland present,* he'd printed on the envelope, but Cousin Wesley was discovered opening it before we got there. He was reprimanded by his parents and prevented from putting it on the Victrola, and when Mother and I arrived, he was still pleading his innocence—which I found easier to accept than his parents did, for neither Uncle Herbert nor Aunt Cora would admit even to themselves what I knew: their eleven-year-old hotshot hadn't yet learned to read.

It was unlike any phonograph record I'd ever seen—small, thin, bendable, nearly transparent, with grooves on only one side. It had a white and blue label on which

U.S.O.
SAN FRANCISCO

was smudgily printed. Grandfather set it on the spindle, lowered the needle, and we were astonished to hear my father's voice. He was singing, a cappella, "I'll be home for Christmas."

Mother laughed and wept. Grandmother only wept. I felt supremely gratified and far superior to Wesley, for not only did his father have no singing voice, he'd also been rejected as physically unfit for the armed forces, having lost his trigger finger in a meat slicer. We played the record over and over, far into the night.

The next year a glimmer of joy appeared in Grandmother Edwards's smile; the war was over and my father was safely home. But four years after that the smile turned severely sad again, and it remained that way for the rest of her life, for by that time my father had been struck dead by lightning.

My own sorrow, though secret, was devastating. Had I allowed my feelings to be touched by the open air, perhaps they would have evaporated, but Mother made it clear from the start that while a widow might indulge herself in an ongoing sort of lament, her fourteen-year-old son must quickly cast his grief aside and console her with a happy face. Thus my sadness, mostly un-expressed, lingered like a low-grade fever. Fortunately, my father had left me a legacy of absorbing hobbies—fishing, coin collecting, reading history, play-ing the piano—and these I pursued with a kind of mad intensity; yet I could never quite throw off the gloom I felt whenever it struck me that I must go on living in a world bereft of this dear man.

It's too bad that a tragedy of that magnitude was required to bring me into closer union with my paternal grandparents, but that's what happened. I ac-quired an affinity for—indeed I found myself imitating—the Edwards reti-cence, their measured, mournful ways. True, I still enjoyed Christmas Day on the O'Kelly ranch, but every December I found myself looking forward with the same degree, if not the same type, of eagerness to Christmas Eve in Omaha, where my father's memory was held in sacred trust.

When, with time, my memories of him began to fade, my melancholy did not. It was compounded, in fact, by guilt. Why hadn't I written down exam-ples of my father's wisdom? Why, without the help of photos, could I not bring his face clearly to mind? I wanted to be able to dwell on his life the way they did in Omaha. No Edwards ever seemed to tire of my inquiries. Were there snapshots of my father I hadn't seen? How big were the fish he'd caught in the Missouri River when he was my age? What were his favorite piano pieces? Told and repeated every Christmas, the facts of my father's days on earth became as familiar to me as the Gospels, and as holy.

And as intimidating. So intensely reverent was the Edwards form of devo-tion that I began to feel extremely unworthy. In retrospect, of course, I see that my common sense was telling me to quit probing my wound and get on with my life, but to do so then would have seemed a kind of betrayal.

It took the upheaval of a moving day to shake me out of this state of un-healthy nostalgia. I was nineteen or twenty when my grandparents decided to leave their house in Omaha and take a new suburban apartment. In planning to be packed and moved by Christmas Eve, they'd overestimated their endurance, with no idea of how much time it takes to dig the accumulation of a lifetime out of the corners of the attic and closets and little storerooms under the stairs. When Mother and I arrived around noon, we found Grandfather exhausted and deeply asleep in his overstuffed chair and Grandmother full of tearful apologies. The house was in disarray—curtains down, cupboards half empty, dozens of half-packed boxes scattered through the rooms. Aunt Cora was upstairs emptying the linen closet. Soon, Wesley and Uncle Herbert returned for another pickup load and we all pitched in.

Working into the night, we moved about half their belongings, including beds, to the apartment before we all wore out. Christmas Eve dinner was take-out Chinese, eaten around midnight in a new dining nook that smelled of fresh drywall. We were sipping tea, dunking Aunt Cora's holiday cookies, and feeling dislocated when I brought out the celluloid record of my father's voice. Earlier, while helping Grandmother clear out the attic, I'd come across it in a hatbox of mementos. I put it on the turntable. The sound was amazingly clear. So fresh and melodious was my father's voice that he seemed to be present in the room. "I'll be home for Christmas," he sang, and we sat there enchanted. I played it a second time, and we exchanged a few reverent remarks. I played it a third time, and each of us gazed off in a private direction, calling up private memories. Even Cousin Wesley seemed moved.

I switched it off then, and a curious conversation ensued. It began with Grandfather, who declared, "Typical of that boy not to say right out that he was coming home."

"Yes, that was his sweet way," Aunt Cora said of her brother. "Tell us in a song like that. And the next thing there he was."

"Typical," Grandfather repeated with a growl, as though the memory irked him. "Surprise you like that. Never say it straight out."

Uncle Herbert quietly agreed. "Just give us that one clue."

"But he didn't—" began Grandmother, her memory evidently clearer than theirs, but she wasn't given a chance to finish. Aunt Cora was recalling the gifts he'd brought home from Hawaii:

"To this day I keep the Pearl Harbor pillow on the daybed. And, Wesley, don't you still carry that jackknife?"

Cousin Wesley said he did.

Aunt Cora turned to Mother. "Lolly, you must've been the most surprised of all when he showed up. You and Leland."

Mother and I exchanged a look, and before either of us could point out that they had their Christmas memories mixed up, Aunt Cora was going on:

"Or did you and Leland know ahead of time and not tell us?"

"Seems like yesterday," mused Uncle Herbert.

"I thought he'd be in uniform," said Wesley accusingly, "but he wasn't."

Grandmother timidly made another attempt. "I don't think he came home that Christmas . . ."

And Mother came to her aid. "It was the following year he brought the things from Hawaii."

Grandfather declared both of them mistaken. First the record appeared, then my father himself, the next day. Wesley and his parents all nodded their support.

"Oh, so that's how it was," said Grandmother, and I watched a little smile spread across her face as she allowed herself to believe this erroneous version. It made such a pleasing story after all.

I spoke up then, pointing out that the song wasn't about actually coming home for Christmas, only dreaming about it. Mother, too, persisted, repeating the facts—the recording one Christmas, his homecoming the next.

None of this made the least impression. With Grandmother forsaking the truth and going over to the other side, we were outnumbered five to two. There were a few moments of strain, a kind of silent standoff, before Mother laughed and said, "Well, what's the difference? At least we have his voice. Would you play it again, Leland?"

And so we listened once more, all of us sitting there in a kind of stupor of satisfaction: Grandfather, Uncle Herbert, Aunt Cora, and Wesley happily picturing the day they'd invented; Grandmother putting their invention together, piece by piece, in her imagination; Mother not caring what they thought, only relishing the sound of the voice preserved so fortuitously by the U.S.O., San Francisco.

And I, of course, was relieved beyond measure to watch a pleasing myth replace the truth, for I saw how trivial were the memories I'd been trying so hard to preserve. Memories, fading and flawed, were all they had in Omaha, while I had my father's fishing tackle, his coin collection, his library, his sheet music. I lived in his house. I had his knack for catching fish. I didn't have his singing voice, but I had his talent at the piano. I had his smile, I was told by those who knew him. I had his way of walking, said Mother, with my left foot turned out a little. I knew from photographs that I had his hairline and eyes. And I had this family of his, who, I sensed, would go on worshiping his memory over the years, preserving it, in their way, from oblivion, while I went ahead and lived the life he lost.

The Living Crèche

MARY SWANDER

"BY THE POWER INVESTED in me as your emperor, I do decree that everyone in the Roman world must find his way back to his home town to register." Caesar Augustus stood in the middle of Fairview School, fifty shepherds, sheep, kings, and angels gathered around him. He read from a long scroll, enunciating perfectly and booming the words out with clear authority.

"A census will be taken of my entire kingdom."

A few days before Christmas, I assembled friends from all over the area and we reenacted the Nativity scene. The living crèche. A traditional place for Christmas pageants, Fairview School provided the perfect setting, with the ground frozen but not yet impossible, the Iowa flag flying from the pole in a steady breeze but not yet a howling wind, and a few snowflakes just beginning to fall but not yet turning into a blizzard. There was no script, and parts were not assigned, although cross-gender roles were encouraged. And first, we had a good old-fashioned midwestern potluck dinner.

Beginning in the late afternoon, just before the sun set, the guests arrived, toting casserole dishes and bread boards, halos and staffs.

"Peace be with you." A local realtor was the first to appear, with barbecued chicken wings under his arm and a scraggly beard pasted to his face. He stood before me in a long flowing robe studded with rhinestones, a pair of pointed slippers on his feet and a crown on his head. "I come bearing gifts," he said and turned my oven on low to keep the chicken warm.

Next, Donna showed up at the door dressed as another king, and a friend's twelve-year-old daughter as the third. Yet a fourth, a Jewish journalist, came with his press tag dangling from his shirt: Mr. Weissman III. An artist, originally from Alabama, stuffed a pillow under her dress and became the pregnant Saint Elizabeth, cousin of Mary.

"Who are we?" she said, standing next to her husband. "Baptists. Southern Baptists."

Another friend bobby-pinned furry children's mittens in her hair and transformed herself into one of the sheep. Several women musicians, the heavenly hostesses, arrived with tiaras in their hair and numbers designating tables 38, 39, and 40. Caesar Augustus's commanding nature was authentic. He was played by a real English lord, who spends half of his time in Iowa with his law professor spouse and the other half in Parliament. The lord brought along his Lebanese brother-in-law, a Broadway composer home for the holidays, who took up the role of Saint Joseph. I, of course, wrapped in a blue bedsheet, played the Virgin Mary.

The schoolhouse lit up the countryside. In each of the eight tall windows, a candle glowed brightly, reminiscent of the older, traditional Yuletide ceremonies celebrated in this space. In the more modern, "English" fashion, blinking Christmas tree lights, secured by big red bows, looped across the loft and up and over the bookshelves. A tiny papier-mâché Nativity scene, a gift from some vacationing friends in Mexico, took up a quiet but important place on the bureau, its presence seemingly becoming more muted while the pile of coats next to it grew higher and higher.

Invitations to thirty people somehow produced sixty guests. In they poured, grandmothers in hair nets and grandchildren playing kazoos, couples and singles, friends of friends, visitors from California and Hong Kong who just happened to be passing through on their way to Michigan or North Carolina. The table filled with goodies, the offerings as diverse as the crowd. Plates of plump Christmas sausages and hot German potato salad were wedged up against sushi and braised duck in Creole sauce. Children stuffed their mouths with angel food cake and chocolate pie before their parents could encourage them to try some baked beans or a few bites of turkey.

So Joseph went up to Judaea from the town of Nazareth in Galilee, to register in the city of David, called Bethlehem, because he was of the house of

David by descent; and with him went Mary, who was betrothed to him. She was expecting a child, and while they were there, the time came for her baby to be born.

We listened to the Bible reading, then another from a book of myths, tracing all our customs—the wreaths on the door, the trees decorated with ornaments in the corner, and even the Yule log—back to the celebration of the winter solstice. Pagans, Catholics, Protestants, and Jews, we tucked our heavy winter coats under our bedsheets and stepped out into the dark.

"It came upon a midnight clear," we sang at last, assembling on the front stoop. Saint Elizabeth threw me the pillow and I crammed it up under my costume.

Eeeee, aaaaaa, Katie brayed, her mouth open wide, ears pointing straight up into the crisp air. I hopped up on her back, and Joseph, lantern in hand, took the lead. Then we were off, Katie trotting at a faster rate than we'd ever seen her go before. I was Mary, the Virgin Mary, Goddess, queen of the Wild West. A French horn carrying the melody, our voices rising up in harmony, a life-size cardboard star guiding our way, we rounded the garage, heading for Donna and Stu's mudroom door—the Inn.

"That glorious time of old." We ambled along and sang, buggies rolling by on the road, those inside, I'm sure, wondering about the event. For a moment, I felt a tinge of fear that my neighbors would think my party was sacrilegious. Throughout the Midwest, living crèches are a common occurrence around Christmas time, church groups gathering each year for these reenactments. Usually, they have to search for a donkey, though. Of course, I approached this occasion with a sense of irony, but not with the intention of making fun of the significance of the day. On the other side of my world, some of my friends asked how I could celebrate such a patriarchal occasion.

"First of all," I told them, "I'm playing the Virgin Mary, who had a leading role in this chapter of the story."

Second, this is the myth I grew up with. It's as simple as that. I've examined it now from every angle. I've found its cracks. I've figured out its evolutionary roots, and acknowledged my anger over its faults. Yet I've also discovered that I like the celebratory nature of the holiday, as well as the sense of sacredness that it forces me to contemplate. And there is something very dangerous in completely rejecting your heritage. It's good to step back, even move away for a while from one's childhood assumptions and indoctrinations. Even the Amish allow their youth a period of experimentation when they are free to rebel against the mores and strictures of their religion. Fuzzy dice hanging down in front of the windshield of a buggy tell me that the teenage driver is moving through his dissidence period. But if not a return or reconciliation, then at least a reconnoitering of one's original mythical structure seems a key to the health of the human—for both body and soul.

Saint Joseph knocked at the mudroom door, and Stu appeared.

"See if they'll take Mastercard, will you, honey?" I called.

"Could we stay here for the night? My wife's about to have a baby."

"Do you have a reservation?"

"We didn't think to call ahead."

"I'm sorry."

"Ohh-ohhhhhh," I moaned from the donkey.

"My wife's going into labor."

"There's the barn . . ."

We made our way across the yard, up into the pasture toward the barn, the new red building with its sturdy manger where two sheep, Emily, and Scalawag—her own belly beginning to bulge—waited in the freshly strewn straw that Donna and I had laid down that morning. Joseph and I arrived first. I pulled out my stuffing, and from the manger picked up and held in my arms a rag doll that Donna keeps on hand for her grandchildren. We'd planted the prop in the hay that morning when, donned in rubber boots and work gloves, the two of us shoveled and raked the manure out of the barn, then ceremoniously spread it on our gardens.

"Joy to the world!" we sang, flinging the brown crusted clumps with our pitchforks. "Let earth receive her King . . ."

The earth itself seemed to be both king and queen that night in the stable. The star led the shepherds into the stall, and angels suddenly appeared in the barn's "miscellaneous" area. All sixty of us crowded in, Katie looking down on the scene with the nonchalance that only a donkey can provide, the children looking up with awe and amazement. Real sheep and costumed sheep pressed in to create a warmth of body and spirit that suddenly became more hallowed than anyone expected. We stood there in silence for a moment, the laughter, singing, and merriment stopped.

All the Christmases of my past flashed before me, from those of great joy and festivity of my youth, to those rather barren ones of the past few years.

Trees and stockings, wrapping paper and bows, even the great beauty of the choirs during Midnight Mass, all fell away at this moment. Another beauty took over. One of simplicity and starkness. Of living your life on the animal level, of going through the miracle of birth on the basest plane, finding your god, finding your place, your connection to all life in a wooden shelter with the smell of droppings around you. In that instant, the Christmas myth became wilder, more feral, more full of energy and raw female power, closer to the primitive spirit world, closer to me.

Silent night! Holy night! All is calm, all is bright.

"Thank you all for coming to my home and sharing this celebration with me," I said to my friends after we'd finished the last carol and were about to wind back along the path to the school, the stars in the sky shining brightly down upon us. Inside, I had a box of oranges that Moses had sent me from Florida. I planned to give one to every guest. "Have a wonderful Christmas and New Year." I couldn't find the words to say more.

The Christmas of the Phonograph Records

MARI SANDOZ

IT SEEMS TO ME THAT I remember it all quite clearly. The night was very cold, footsteps squeaking in the frozen snow that had lain on for over two weeks, the roads in our region practically unbroken. But now the holidays were coming and wagons had pushed out on the long miles to the railroad, with men enough to scoop a trail for each other through the deeper drifts.

My small brother and I had been asleep in our attic bed long enough to frost the cover of the feather tick at our faces when there was a shouting in the road before the house, running steps, and then the sound of the broom handle thumping against the ceiling below us, and Father booming out, "Get up! The phonograph is here!"

The phonograph! I stepped out on the coyote skin at our bed, jerked on my woolen stockings and my shoes, buttoning my dress as I slipped down the outside stairs in the fading moon. Lamplight was pouring from the open door in a cloud of freezing mist over the back end of a loaded wagon, with three neighbors easing great boxes off, Father limping back and forth shouting, "Don't break me my records!" his breath white around his dark beard.

Inside the house Mother was poking sticks of wood into the firebox of the cookstove, her eyes meeting mine for a moment, shining, her concern about the extravagance of a talking machine when we needed overshoes for our chilblains apparently forgotten. The three largest boxes were edged through the doorway and filled much of the kitchen–living room floor. The neighbors stomped their felt boots at the stove and held their hands over the hot lids while Father ripped at the boxes with his crowbar, the frozen nails squealing as they let go. First there was the machine, varnished oak, with a shining cylinder for the records, and then the horn, a great black, gilt-ribbed morning glory, and the crazy angled rod arm and chain to hold it in place.

By now a wagon full of young people from the Dutch community on Mirage Flats turned into our yard. At a school program they had heard about the Edison phonograph going out to Old Jules Sandoz. They trooped in at our door, piled their wraps in the leanto and settled along the benches to wait.

Young Jule and James, the brothers next to me in age, were up too, and watching Father throw excelsior aside, exposing a tight packing of round paper containers a little smaller than a middle-sized baking powder can, with more layers under these, and still more below. Father opened one and while I read out the instructions in my German-accented fifth-grade country school English, he slipped the brown wax cylinder on the machine, cranked the handle carefully, and set the needle down. Everybody waited, leaning forward. There was a rhythmic frying in the silence, and then a whispering of sound, soft and very, very far away.

It brought a murmur of disappointment and an escaping laugh, but gradually the whispers loudened into the sextet from *Lucia*, into what still seems to me the most beautiful singing in the world. We all clustered around, the visitors, fourteen, fifteen by now, and Mother, too, caught while pouring hot chocolate into cups, her long-handled pan still tilted in the air. Looking back I realize something of the meaning of the light in her face: the hunger for music she must have felt, coming from Switzerland, the country of music, to a western Nebraska government claim. True, we sang old country songs in the evenings, she leading, teaching us all she knew, but plainly it had not been enough, really nothing.

By now almost everybody pushed up to the boxes to see what there was to play, or called out some title hopefully. My place in this was established from the start. I was to run the machine, play the two-minute records set before me. There were violin pieces for Father, among them *Alpine Violets* and *Mocking Bird* from the first box opened; *Any Rags*, *Red Wing*, and *I'm Trying so Hard to Forget You* for the young people; *Rabbit Hash* for my brothers, their own selection from the catalog; and Schubert's *Serenade* and *Die Kapelle* for Mother, with almost everyone laughing over *Casey at the Telephone*, all except Father. He claimed he could not understand such broken English, he who gave even the rankest westernism a French pronunciation.

With the trail broken to the main bridge of the region, just below our house, and this Christmas Eve, there was considerable travel on the road, people passing most of the night. The lighted windows, the music, the gathering of teams and saddlehorses in the yard, and the sub-zero weather tolled them in to the weathered little frame house with its lean-to.

"You better set more yeast. We will have to bake again tomorrow," Mother told me as she cut into a *zopf*, one of the braids of coffee cake baked in tins as large as the circle of both her arms. This was the last of five planned to carry us into the middle of the holiday week.

By now the phonograph had been moved to the top of the washstand in our parents' kalsomined bedroom, people sitting on the two double beds, on the round-topped trunk and on benches carried in, some squatting on their heels along the wall. The little round boxes stood everywhere, on the dresser and on the board laid from there to the washstand and on the window sills, with more brought in to be played and Father still shouting over the music, "Don't break me my records!" Some were broken, the boxes slipping out of unaccustomed or cold-stiffened hands, the brown wax perhaps already cracked by the railroad.

When the Edison Military band started a gay, blaring galop, Mother looked in at the bedroom door, pleased. Then she noticed all the records spread out there, and in the kitchen–living room behind her, and began to realize their number. "Three hundred!" she exclaimed in German, speaking angrily in Father's direction, "Looks to me like more than three thousand!"

Father scratched under his bearded chin, laughing slyly. "I added to the order," he admitted. He didn't say how many, nor that there were other brands besides the Edison here, including several hundred foreign recordings obtained through a Swiss friend in New York, at a stiff price.

Mother looked at him, her blue eyes tragic, as she could make them. "You paid nothing on the mortgage! All the twenty-one-hundred-dollar inheritance wasted on a talking machine!"

No, Father denied, puffing at his corncob pipe. Not all. But Mother knew him well. "You did not buy the overshoes for the children. You forgot everything except your stamp collection, your guns, and the phonograph!"

"The overshoes are coming. I got them cheaper on time, with the guns."

"More debts!" she accused bitterly, but before she could add to this one of the young Swiss, Maier perhaps, or Paul Freye, grabbed her and, against the stubbornness of her feet, whirled her back into the kitchen in the galop from the Edison band. He raced Mother from door to stove and back again and around and around, so her blue calico skirts flew out and the anger died from her face. Her eyes began to shine in an excitement I had never seen in them, and I realize now, looking back, all the fun our mother missed in her working life, even in her childhood in the old country, and during the much harder years later.

That galop started the dancing. Hastily the table was pushed against the wall, boxes piled on top of it, the big ones dragged into the leanto. Waltzes, two-steps, quadrilles, and schottisches were sorted out and set in a row ready for me to play while one of the men shaved a candle over the kitchen floor. There was room for only one set of square dancers but our bachelor neighbor, Charley Sears, called the turns with enthusiasm. The Peters girls, two school teachers, and several other young women whom I've forgotten were well outnumbered by the men, as is common in new communities. They waltzed, two-stepped, formed a double line for a Bohemian polka, or schottisched around the room, one couple close behind the other to, perhaps, *It Blew, Blew, Blew*. Once Charley Sears grabbed my hand and drew me out to try a quadrille, towering over me as he swung me on the corner and guided me through the allemande left. My heart pounded in shyness and my homemade shoes compounded my awkwardness. Later someone else dragged me out into a two-step, saying, "Like this: 'one, two; one, two.' Just let yourself go."

Ah, so that was how it was done. Here started a sort of craze that was to hold me for over twenty years, through the bear dance, the turkey trot, the Charleston, and into the Lindy hop. But that first night with the records even Old Jules had to try a round polka, even with his foot crippled in a long-ago well accident. When he took his pipe out of his mouth, dropped it lighted into his pocket, and whirled Mother around several times we knew that this was a special occasion. Before this we had never seen him even put an arm around her.

After the boys had heard their selection again and *The Preacher and the Bear*, they fell asleep on the floor and were carried to their bed in the leanto. Suddenly I remembered little Fritzlie alone in the attic, perhaps half-frozen. I hurried up the slippery, frosted steps. He was crying, huddled together under the feather tick, cold and afraid, deserted by the cat too, sleeping against the warm chimney. I brought the boy down, heavy hulk that he was, and laid him in with his brothers. By then the last people started to talk of leaving, but the moon had clouded over, the night-dark roads winding and treacherous through the drifts. Still, those who had been to town must get home with the Christmas supplies and such presents as they could manage for their children when they awoke in the morning.

Toward dawn Father dug out *Sempach*, a song of a heroic Swiss battle, in which one of Mother's ancestors fell, and *Andreas Hofer*, of another national hero. Hiding her pleasure at these records, Mother hurried away to the cellar under the house for two big hams, one to boil while the Canada goose roasted for the Christmas dinner. From the second ham she sliced great red rounds for the frying pan and I mixed up a triple batch of baking powder biscuits and set on the two-gallon coffee pot. When the sun glistened on the frosted snow, the last of the horses huddled together in our yard were on the road. By then some freighters forced to camp out by an upset wagon came whipping their teams up the icy pitch from the Niobrara River and stopped in. Father was slumped in his chair, letting his pipe fall into his beard, but he looked up and recognized the men as from a ranch accused of driving out bona fide settlers. Instead of rising to order them off the place he merely said "How!" in the Plains greeting, and dropped back into his doze. Whenever the music stopped noticeably, he lifted his shaggy head, complaining, "Cain't you keep the machine going?" even if I had my hands in the biscuits. "Play the *Mocking Bird* again," he might order, or a couple of the expensive French records of pieces he had learned to play indifferently in the violin lessons of his boyhood in Neuchatel. He liked *Spring Song* too, and *La Paloma*, an excellent mandolin rendition of *Come Ye Disconsolate*, and several German love songs he had learned from his sweetheart, in Zurich, who had not followed him to America.

Soon my three brothers were up again and calling for their favorites as they settled to plates of ham with red gravy and biscuits, Fritzlie from the top of two catalogs piled on a chair shouting too, just to be heard. None of them missed the presents that we never expected on Christmas; besides, what could be finer than the phonograph?

While Mother fed our few cattle and the hogs I worked at the big stack of dishes with one of the freighters to wipe them. Afterward I got away to the attic and slept a little, the music from below faint through my floating of dreams. Suddenly I awoke, remembering what day this was and that young Jule and I had hoped Father might go cottontail hunting in the canyons up the river and help us drag home a little pine tree. Christmas had become a time for a tree, even without presents, a tree and singing, with at least one new song learned.

I dressed and hurried down. Father was asleep and there were new people in the bedroom and in the kitchen too, talking about the wonder of the music rolling steadily from the big horn. In our Swiss way we had prepared for the usual visitors during the holidays, with family friends on Christmas and surely some of the European homeseekers Father had settled on free land, as well as passersby just dropping in to get warm and perhaps be offered a cup of coffee or chocolate or a glass of Father's homemade wine if particularly privileged. Early in the forenoon the Syrian peddler we called Solomon drew up in the yard with his high four-horse wagon. I remember him every time I see a picture of Krishna Menon—the tufted hair, the same lean yellowish face and long white teeth. Solomon liked to strike our place for Christmas because there might be customers around and besides there was no display of religion to make him uncomfortable in his Mohammedanism, Father said, although one might run into a stamp-collecting priest or a hungry preacher at our house almost any other time.

So far as I know, Solomon was the first to express what others must have thought. "Excuse it please, Mrs. Sandoz," he said, in the polite way of peddlers, "but it seem to uneducated man like me the new music is for fine palace—"

Father heard him. "Nothing's too good for my family and my neighbors," he roared out.

"The children have frozen feet—" the man said quietly.

"Frozen feet heal! What you put in the mind lasts!"

The peddler looked down into his coffee cup, half full of sugar, and said no more.

It was true that we had always been money poor and plainly would go on so, but there was plenty of meat and game, plenty of everything that the garden, the young orchard, the field, and the open country could provide, and for all of which there was no available market. Our bread, dark and heavy, was from our hard macaroni wheat ground at a local water mill. The hams, sausage, and bacon were from our own smokehouse, the cellar full of our own potatoes, barrels of pickles and sauerkraut, and hundreds of jars of canned fruit and vegetables, crocks of jams and jellies, wild and tame, including buffalo berry, that wonderful, tart, golden-red jelly from the silvery bush that seems to retreat before close settlement much like the buffalo and the whooping crane. Most of the root crops were in a long pit outside, and the attic was strung with little sacks of herbs and poppy seed, bigger ones of dried green beans, sweetcorn, chokecherries, sandcherries, and wild plums. Piled along the low sides of the attic were bushel bags of popcorn, peas, beans, and lentils, the flour stacked in rows with room between for the mousing cat.

Sugar, coffee, and chocolate were practically all we bought for the table, with perhaps a barrel of blackstrap molasses for cookies and brown cake, all laid in while the fall roads were still open.

WHEN THE NEW BATCH of coffee cake was done and the fresh bread and buns, the goose in the oven, we took turns getting scrubbed at the heater in the leanto, and put on our best clothes, mostly made-over from some adult's but well-sewn. Finally we spread Mother's two old country linen cloths over the table lengthened out by boards laid on salt barrels for twenty-two places. While Mother passed the platters, I fed the phonograph with records that Mrs. Surber and her three musical daughters had selected, soothing music: Bach, Mozart, Brahms, and the *Moonlight Sonata* on two foreign records that Father had hidden away so they would not be broken, along with an a capella *Stille Nacht* and some other foreign ones Mother wanted saved. For lightness, Mrs. Surber had added *The Last Rose of Summer,* to please Elsa, the young soprano soon to be a professional singer in Cleveland, and a little Strauss and Puccini, while the young people wanted Ada Jones and *Monkey Land* by Collins and Harlan.

There was stuffed Canada goose with the buffalo berry jelly; ham boiled in a big kettle in the leanto; watercress salad; chow-chow and pickles, sweet and sour; dried green beans cooked with bacon and a hint of garlic; carrots, turnips, mashed potatoes and gravy, with coffee from the start to the pie, pumpkin and gooseberry. At the dishpan set on the high water bench, where I had to stand on a little box for comfort, the dishes were washed as fast as they came off the table, with a relay of wipers. There were also waiting young men and boys to draw water from the bucket well, to chop stove wood and carry it in.

As I recall now, there were people at the table for hours. A letter of Mother's says that the later uninvited guests got sausage and sauerkraut, squash, potatoes, and fresh bread, with canned plums and cookies for dessert. Still later there was a big roaster full of beans and sidemeat brought in by a lady home-steader, and some mince pies made with wild plums to lend tartness instead of apples, which cost money.

All this time there was the steady stream of music and talk from the bed-room. I managed to slip in the *Lucia* a couple of times until a tart-tongued woman from over east said she believed I was getting addled from all that hol-lering. We were not allowed to talk back to adults, so I put on the next record set before me, this one *Don't Get Married Any More, Ma,* selected for a vis-iting Chicago widow looking for her fourth husband, or perhaps her fifth. Mother rolled her eyes up at this bad taste, but Father and the other old tim-ers laughed over their pipes.

We finally got Mother off to bed in the attic for her first nap since the rec-ords came. Downstairs the floor was cleared and the Surber girls showed their dancing-school elegance in the waltzes. There was a stream of young people later in the afternoon, many from the skating party at the bridge. Father, red-eyed like the rest of us, limped among them, soaking up their praise, their new respect. By this time my brothers and I had given up having a tree. Then a big boy from up the river rode into the yard dragging a pine behind his horse. It was a shapely tree, and small enough to fit on a box in the window, out of the way. The youth was the son of Father's worst enemy, the man who had sworn in court that Jules Sandoz shot at him, and got our father thirty days in jail, although everybody, including the judge, knew that Jules Sandoz was a crack shot and what he fired at made no further appearances.

As the son came in with the tree, someone announced loudly who he was. I saw Father look toward his Winchester on the wall, but he was not the man to quarrel with an enemy's children. Then he was told that the boy's father himself was in the yard. Now Jules Sandoz paled above his bearding, paled so the dancers stopped, the room silent under the suddenly foolish noise of the big-horned machine. Helpless, I watched Father jump toward the rifle. Then he turned, looked to the man's gaunt-faced young son.

"Tell your old man to come in. We got some good Austrian music."

So the man came in, and sat hunched over near the door. Father had left the room, gone to the leanto, but after a while he came out, said his "How!" to the man, and paid no attention when Mrs. Surber pushed me forward to make the proper thanks for the tree that we were starting to trim as usual. We played *The Blue Danube* and some other pieces long forgotten now for the man, and passed him coffee and *küchli* with the others. He tasted the thin flaky frycakes. "Your mother is a good cook," he told me. "A fine woman."

When he left with the skaters all of Father's friends began to talk at once, fast, relieved. "You could have shot him down, on your own place, and not got a day in the pen for it," one said.

Old Jules nodded. "I got no use for his whole outfit, but the music is for everybody."

As I recall now, perhaps half a dozen of us, all children, worked at the tree, looping my strings of red rose hips and popcorn around it, hanging the people and animal cookies with chokecherry eyes, distributing the few Christmas tree balls and the tinsel and candleholders that the Surbers had given us several years before. I brought out the boxes of candles I had made by dipping string in melted tallow, and then we lit the candles and with my schoolmates I ran out into the cold of the road to look. The tree showed fine through the glass.

Now I had to go to bed, although the room below me was alive with dancing and I remembered that Jule and I had not sung our new song, *Amerika ist ein schönes Land* at the tree.

HOLIDAY WEEK WAS much like Christmas, the house full of visitors as the news of the fine music and the funny records spread. People appeared from fifty, sixty miles away and farther so long as the new snow held off, for there was no other such collection of records in all of western Nebraska, and none with such an open door. There was something for everybody, Irishmen, Scots, Swedes, Danes, Poles, Czechs as well as the Germans and the rest, something pleasant and nostalgic. The greatest variety in tastes was among the Americans, from *Everybody Works but Father, Arkansas Traveler,* and *Finkelstein at the Seashore* to love songs and the sentimental *Always in the Way;* from home and native region pieces to the patriotic and religious. They had strong dislikes too, even in war songs. One settler, a GAR veteran, burst into tears and fled from the house at the first notes of *Tenting Tonight.* Perhaps it was the memories it awakened. Many Americans were as interested in classical music as any European, and it wasn't always a matter of cultivated taste. One illiterate little woman from down the river cried with joy at Rubinstein's *Melody in F.*

"I has heard me talkin' and singin' before," she said apologetically as she wiped her eyes, "but I wasn't knowin' there could be something sweet as that come from a horn."

Afternoons and evenings, however, were still the time for the dancers. Finally it was New Year, the day when the Sandoz relatives, siblings, uncles and cousins, gathered, perhaps twenty of them immigrants brought in by the land locator, Jules. This year they were only a sort of eddy in the regular stream of outsiders. Instead of nostalgic jokes and talk of the family and the old country, there were the records to hear, particularly the foreign ones, and the melodies of the old violin lessons that the brothers had taken, and the guitar and mandolin of their one sister. Jules had to endure a certain amount of joking over the way he spent most of his inheritance. One brother was building a cement block home in place of his soddy with his, and a greenhouse. The sister was to have a fine large barn instead of a new home because her husband believed that next year Halley's comet would bring the end of the world. Ferdinand, the youngest of the brothers, had put his money into wild-cat oil stock and planned to become very wealthy.

Although most of their talk was in French, which Mother did not speak, they tried to make up for this by complimenting her on the excellence of her chocolate and her golden fruit cake. Then they were gone, hot bricks at their feet, and calling back their adieus from the freezing night. It was a good thing they left early, Mother told me. She had used up the last of the chocolate, the last cake of the twenty-five pound caddies. We had baked up two sacks of flour, forty-nine pounds each, in addition to all that went into the Christmas preparations before the phonograph came. Three-quarters of a hundred pound bag of coffee had been roasted, ground, and used during the week, and all the winter's sausage and ham. The floor of the kitchen–living room, old and worn anyway, was much thinner for the week of dancing. New Year's night a man who had been there every day, all week, tilted back on one of the kitchen chairs and went clear through the floor.

"Oh, the fools!" Father shouted at us all. "Had to wear out my floor dancing!"

But plainly he was pleased. It was a fine story to tell for years, all the story of the phonograph records. He was particularly gratified by the praise of those who knew something about music, people like the Surbers and a visitor from a Czech community, a relative of Dvorak, the great composer. The man wrote an item for the papers, saying, "This Jules Sandoz has not only settled a good community of homeseekers, but is enriching their cultural life with the greatest music of the world."

"Probably wants to borrow money from you," Mother said. "He has come to the wrong door."

GRADUALLY THE RECORDS for special occasions and people were stored in the leanto. For those used regularly, Father and a neighbor made a lot of flat boxes to fit under the beds, always handy, and a cabinet for the corner at the bedroom door. The best, the finest from both the Edison and the foreign recordings, were put into this cabinet, with a door that didn't stay closed. One warmish day when I was left alone with the smaller children, the water pail needed refilling. I ran out to draw a bucket from the well. It was a hard and heavy pull for a growing girl and I hated it, always afraid that I wouldn't last, and would have to let the rope slip and break the windlass.

Somehow, in my uneasy hurry, I left the door ajar. The wind blew it back and when I had the bucket started up the sixty-five foot well, our big old sow, loose in the yard, pushed her way into the house. Horrified, I shouted to Fritzlie to get out of her way, but I had to keep pulling and puffing until the bucket was at the top. Then I ran in. Fritzlie was up on a chair, safe, but the sow had knocked down the record cabinet and scattered the cylinders over the floor. Standing among them as in corn, she was chomping down the wax records that had rolled out of the boxes, eating some, box and all. Furiously I thrashed her out with the broom, amidst squealings and shouts. Then I tried to save what I could. The sow had broken at least thirty or thirty-five of the best records and eaten all or part of twenty more. *La Paloma* was gone, and *Traumerei* and *Spring Song; Evening Star* too, and half of the *Moonlight Sonata* and many others, foreign and domestic, including all of Brahms.

I got the worst whipping of my life for my carelessness, but the loss of the records hurt more, and much, much longer.

Marie

LARRY WOIWODE

NOW ALL OF THE FAMILY was home for Christmas. When Marie returned from an afternoon of last-minute shopping with an aunt in Peoria, Jerome and Charles had arrived and were sitting at the kitchen table, playing a game of pinochle with Tim and her father. They were away at college and hadn't been home since Thanksgiving, and she was so happy to see them that she almost sang out "Joy to the World!" in a loud, clear voice, as she'd been singing it all the way home in the car.

"Mrs. Claus returneth," Tim said, and Marie wondered, since her hands were full of packages, how Tim pictured the name: Claws?

Charles looked up from his cards and said, "Hey, hey, Marie," and Jerome said, "How have you been?"

"Fine," she said, smiling and studying her older brothers with affection. They were wearing the sweaters she'd sent them for their birthdays—it was like them to be so thoughtful—and Jerome had on a new pair of horn-rimmed glasses that gave his hollow-cheeked face a fuller, more direct look.

She was relieved that they didn't get up from the table to greet her. She felt awkward enough already. They were much older than their ages, it seemed, and both so intelligent she was sure they'd learned things she couldn't possibly learn in her lifetime. She blushed, embarrassed and at the same time comforted by the emotions they aroused in her, and put her packages on the kitchen counter.

"Oh!" she said. She'd tracked in snow and it was melting around her shoes. She went to the sink, took a sponge from its drainboard, and blotted at the water. The house had to be perfect for Christmas, correctly arranged and immaculate, so the spirit of the season could move unhindered through the rooms. It had taken her two weeks to clean and decorate the house, and now, as usual, she was the first to track it up.

"Have you joined the Thespian Club yet?" Charles asked. He'd been the president when he was a senior in high school, and he acted at the university now; his hair was long, halfway down his neck, and she remembered hearing that he was in another play, one by Shakespeare, with "night" in the title. She'd often wanted to go to the university with her father to watch Charles perform, but she was afraid she wouldn't understand the play and then wouldn't know what to say to Charles afterward. He was that sensitive.

"Oh, no," she said. "I'm just a freshman."

"So? I joined when I was a freshman."

"But you're so good. I can't act."

"Sure you can."

"I'd feel too dumb standing in front of all those people."

"Get into makeup or props."

"Maybe next year."

Her father, who'd been staring at Charles, said, "Will it be necessary for her to grow her hair as long as yours in order to act?"

"Oh, for God's sake," Charles said.

"I used to act in school, too, you know," her father said, "but that doesn't mean I ran around looking like a bum. I'll give you five dollars right now if you'll run uptown the first thing tomorrow and have that cut off."

"It's supposed to be long."

"Wear a wig!"

Charles's face flushed and he turned to his cards.

Marie put the sponge in the sink and noticed that Tim and her father, who were paired off against Jerome and Charles, were secretly passing the signals that Tim had devised over the fall. Did Jerome and Charles have their own signals? She hoped so.

Tim crossed his eyes and said through clenched teeth, "Rack 'em up! Wrap 'em up! Whip 'em out!"—he plucked a card from the neat fan in his hand and lifted it high in the air—"Ah, ha! Ah, ya-ha-ha! *Winny*-beat! *Winny*-beat! Whoo, whoo*ooooo!*" His eyes uncrossed. "Feast on this, fond bluver

Jerbloom," he said and flipped the card, an ace, down on the table. "Shazam! Screwdini takes another sizzling trick!"

Jerome, whose play was next, kept staring at his cards and said, in his dispassionate, gravelly drawl, "You're a hebephrenic schizophrenic."

"Oooo!" Tim said. "Large words stream from one so mightily educated."

"Come on, come *on*," her father said. "Either play cards or act the fool, one of the two, or let's just quit right now."

"I choose the former of those, kind sire," Tim said, and tossed down another ace.

"Hmm," her father said, glancing at his cards. "That helps."

"You betchum, Big M," Tim said.

"Play!"

At her father's elbow was a beanbag ashtray filled with cigarette butts, orange peels, peanut shells, and the butts and chewed bits of her father's cigars. She'd have to remember to empty the ashtray before it gave off that awful odor of old cigars she'd grown up with most of her life; and she'd have to remember, too, to set out more ashtrays. Jerome and Charles smoked in the house now, instead of going for a walk.

Jerome closed one eye, pushed out his lips, drew back from his cards like a farmer, and said in a farmer's voice, "Looks like you two are gonna git trounced agin!" And then threw down a trump.

Marie laughed. Jerome, the oldest, was solemn and reserved, and never acted in such an absurd manner unless he was embarrassed. He must be happy to see her. She smiled and the light around the edges of her eyes turned rainbow-colored from tears. She picked up her packages and went into the living room, dimly lit and aromatic of pine pitch from the ceiling-high tree. The television was playing, staining the front wall and half of the ceiling gray-violet, and above the back of the easy chair she could see a half-moon of big hair curlers. Without taking her eyes from the television, without moving the curlers, Susan said, in her rapid, matter-of-fact voice, "What'd you get me, Mare?"

Her younger sister was as intelligent as the boys—a straight-A student who seldom had to study. Although Susan had never taken an algebra course, she was able to solve Marie's algebra problems (how could anybody add x's, letters of the alphabet?), and Marie sometimes felt that she'd been born into this family to remind the others to be grateful.

"You'll have to wait till Christmas to find out," Marie said.

"You never wait."

"I know."

"You see everything everybody's got a week before they get it."

"I know," Marie said.

She couldn't bear the uncertainty. She rewrapped the packages as carefully as she could, sometimes adding touches of her own—a larger bow, an arrangement of bright tape, or a design cut from colored foil or an old Christmas card. Unless they were gifts for her father. She had to rewrap his exactly as she'd found them or he'd realize they'd been opened, and he couldn't stand it if anybody knew what he was getting before he did. She arranged the gifts she'd brought in (she'd redo them later), along with the others already under the tree, to balance colors and display to the best advantage the most artistically wrapped. Then she reached to the stand at the center of the tree and put her finger into it; she'd filled it with water this morning and added a spoonful of molasses for food, and the level was still high.

She realized that she was singing "O Little Town of Bethlehem" under her breath and stopped. It irritated Tim and Charles that she was always singing and humming songs—Tim, especially—and when they were younger Tim had named her Hum-Hound. Lately, whenever a song unconsciously rose from her, she'd be jolted by a punch to her shoulder. "Hum-Hound! Hum-Hound!" Tim would say with eyes so angry his pupils appeared red. "Dirty damn-ass Hum-Hound!"

She arranged a few of the foil icicles hanging from the branches. She'd used eleven packages on the tree. Instead of draping handfuls of icicles here and there, or tossing them at the tree, as the boys usually did, and letting them fall where they would, she had suspended each icicle separately, as she'd seen somebody else (a friend's mother?) do, and now the tree looked like a waterfall of silver. The colored lights were reflected everywhere off the icicles, along with the ornaments (she moved a blue globe with a gold sunburst in its center to another branch), if they were hung in the right places.

Something was missing. She stepped back and looked up. The star at the tip of the tree was lit, casting a red streak across the ceiling. She'd arranged cotton snow around the stand before putting down the packages, the manger scene was set up, and this year she'd repaired a shepherd that hadn't been used as long as she could remember, and had included him in the group of night visitors at the stable. Every room in the house but the one she shared with Susan was clean, the floors were waxed, and the Christmas-tree lights were reflected in the sheen of this one like colored stars at her feet.

A miniature sleigh filled with candy and nuts sat in a circle of pine branches on the coffee table, and she could see the wreath on the front door, through the Venetian blinds. An angel in an attitude of prayer kneeled among greenery on the television set. There was a candelabra behind the angel, and candles of red and green and white stood singly and in pairs on the coffee table, the end tables, the gateleg table, the smoking stand. Candles were much better for the mood of celebration than electric lights. With candles burning, there was room for darkness, for the emotions that arose only in subdued light, and the flames swayed as though to music she could almost imagine. On Christmas Eve, with all of these lit, the family would be surrounded by shadows that would add to the sense that the past had joined them.

Marie went into the kitchen and four pairs of eyes fixed on her.

"Oh," she said. "Do you want coffee?"

They turned back to their cards and in different tones of voice "Sure, sure, sure, sure" went around the table, as though they were bidding. She filled the percolator with water from the faucet and took down the coffee. In this house, the smell of brewing coffee was more common than perfume; any of the four could empty a coffeepot in a few hours, and there were times when Jerome and Charles took their mugs upstairs and had coffee and cigarettes before bed. What did they talk about?

Marie realized that her father's voice was pitched as it became pitched only when he spoke to her—higher, imperative, and for some reason always impatient. She looked over her shoulder at him. "Yes?"

"I said, 'Don't you think it's about time you took off your coat?' Can't you hear?"

"Oh," Marie said. "I forgot."

She folded it and placed it over the back of a chair and went to the refrigerator. She'd also forgotten the platter of cold cuts she'd prepared. The men in this house were always hungry. They ate hearty meals and ate whenever they had the inclination in between, but none of them put on weight. Why? Though she mostly picked at her food, she was always heavier than she wanted to be; not overweight, really, but not as slim as she'd like.

She removed the waxed paper from the platter and exposed wedges of cheese and slices of ham, corned beef, and liverwurst, rayed around a central arrangement of olives. Charles and Tim loved olives. She popped one in her mouth. She carried the platter across to them and placed it on the table, and her father glanced at her in an abrupt, annoyed way. Was he losing at cards? He couldn't stand to lose. He'd say, "Oh, well, it's just a game," and go into the living room and slump in his chair, brooding about it, pulling and punishing the hair at the back of his head, and then he'd be at the kitchen table again, riffling the edge of the card deck and saying, "Well, is there anybody in this house brave enough to take a chance?"

Her father didn't seem as restless and displeased with himself since he'd gone back to teaching, five years ago, and in that time he'd worked his way up from coach and P.E. instructor in the junior high to the principalship of the high school. And since the beginning of the summer he'd been seeing Laura, a spirited and youthful widow in Chicago, and had become more demonstrative than Marie had ever seen him. Though he couldn't carry a tune, he'd walk into the kitchen where she was working, throw his arms out wide, and sing in the nasal voice of that old movie star Eddie Nelson, or whoever, "Oh, Marie! Ah, Marie . . ."

Through the fall, he'd been driving to Chicago nearly every weekend, and he planned to spend part of the holidays there. He slammed down a trump to take a trick, spread out his cards on the table, and said, "I've got the rest," and tossed the cards to Jerome. Then he turned his annoyed look on Marie. "I suppose you spent too much again today."

"I think the checking account might be overdrawn."

"Over*drawn*?"

"Maybe."

"Maybe? Can't you subtract?"

"Well, you know . . ." Her figures never came out right.

"That money was supposed to last till the middle of January!"

"I know."

"What do you expect to buy groceries with?"

She looked down at the shred of ham she was tearing with her fingers. "I saw some things I had to get."

"Some 'things.' *What* 'things'?"

"You'll see."

"Ach!"

He turned back to the game, shaking his head as he gathered up his dealt cards, and heaved a sigh of exasperation. Laura, who was a private secretary and a bookkeeper, planned everything months in advance, and always carried out her plans to the letter, and from observing how she managed, Marie's father had become more intolerant than ever of the way Marie handled money. Marie realized that it wasn't right to spend so much on everybody at Christmas, when they didn't have that much, but she couldn't help it; and anyway, she knew that her father would forgive her when he saw the gift.

She'd bought him a bedroom valet of solid maple. There was a seat where he could sit as he dressed, with a drawer beneath filled with shoe-care equipment (she'd also bought a shoehorn with a handle of deer antler), and a shelf beneath that for shoes; maple shoe presses came with it, and its back was a hanger for suits. Her father had become more particular about his dress and appearance. He was always going into the bathroom to brush his teeth; he combed his hair in a new way, to conceal his bald spot, his shoes weren't dull and scuffed, as they used to be, his suits were always pressed, and Marie no longer had to tell him when a tie and a suit jacket clashed.

"The coffee will be done in a minute," she said. "Is there anything else I can get?"

"You can get me back the money you just spent," her father said.

Jerome looked up at Marie and smiled a faint smile, so relaxed and easygoing Marie envied him. She smiled back, and then Jerome twisted up his lips as though he'd tasted lemon, shrugged his shoulders, and turned back to his cards.

Marie picked up her coat and went into the bedroom she shared with Susan.

IT WAS ABSOLUTELY quiet on this side of the house. Every time Marie walked through the door of the room, she felt she'd stepped into a sanctum of her own creation. She couldn't hear the television or the sound of voices, and all the clothes seemed to hold silence. They were everywhere. The doors of the closet were thrown back, and it was filled with clothes, and clean clothes and dirty clothes were piled on the dressers, on the chairs and the beds, which were unmade, and all over the floor; undergarments hung from dresser knobs.

Her father complained about the condition of the room, especially in the past months, and last week he had walked in on her when she was half naked and shouted, "Gol*dammit,* get this crap cleaned up or I'm going to throw it out the door!" Which frightened her worse than if he'd actually starting throwing things; it was one of the few times she'd heard him swear. His face was crimson.

She had tried to clean it up then, and she'd made an effort almost every day since, but it seemed impossible. She felt comfortable here. Besides the quiet, it was well heated, always warm, not like some parts of the house, and now the room was filled with a shuddering glow from a candle burning on her mother's vanity.

The candle was supposed to last for the twelve days of Christmas, but she doubted that it would, since it was already half a day ahead. Everything she got for herself was imperfect in some way, it seemed, or destined to break down, like the clock beside the candle. The vanity, though, was still in good shape, and over the summer Jerome and Charles had stained and refinished it for her, and now it was the same shade of maple as the valet she'd got for her father. She sat on the vanity bench and put the tip of her index finger into the pool of wax at the top of the candle, and its flame jumped higher. She held up her finger, turning it to allow the wax to harden, and then held it apart from the others as she pushed back her hair.

Her face bothered her; it always had. Aunts and older women said that she was "adorable" or "pretty," but she thought she looked awful. "Scary-Mare," Tim used to call her, and that seemed a perfect description. Her hairline was uneven, her upper lip looked swollen, her nose was too small, though not as small as Susan's, and her eyes too big. It was mostly the eyes, moon eyes, as she thought of them—large and circular, like half dollars, larger even than her father's, which were enormous behind his glasses.

She looked at the photograph she'd placed, several years ago, under the molding at the bottom of the vanity mirror: her mother, standing in front of a snow-covered lilac bush, dressed in a dark suit, her hands hidden in a muff, was smiling directly into the camera. When was the picture taken? And where? It was Marie's favorite photograph of her mother, and she'd removed it from a family album and put it here to have it close, so she could remember how her mother looked. She had died when Marie was three years old—"passed away," they said, gone. When Marie first put the picture on the mirror, she used to stare at it and whisper, as if she were praying, "Oh, Mom, come back, come back," until she began to cry. But after a few months she couldn't cry anymore, it was too difficult to keep doing, and she felt unworthy of being her mother's daughter.

Her aunts would say, "Your mother was a wonderful woman—it's a shame you couldn't have known her better," and that made her feel worse. She couldn't really remember her mother, or say what she was actually like. Tim, though he was two years older, had trouble remembering her, too (with him, however, it sometimes seemed on purpose), and when they were children they tried to re-create the moods they could recall when she had been there. Tim would pretend he was sick with rheumatic fever, and Marie would minister to him as she felt their mother might. Or Tim would cover Marie with a blanket and pat her back and sing a lullaby their mother used to sing, about waking from sleep and riding a silvery pony. He couldn't remember all of the verses and invented some of his own. Or else he told stories about what he and his mother had done the day before.

One afternoon when Tim and Marie were home alone, they shut themselves in the closet off the living room, and Tim began to talk about their mother as he really remembered her. All Marie could make out in the darkness was the shining wand of the vacuum cleaner, while Tim went on about a picnic, a blanket with pink stripes, pebbles around it, putting the pebbles into their mouths, and then their mother walking up and locking the two of them inside a hot, stuffy car in punishment, and suddenly it seemed the wand brightened and the closet filled with cotton. Tim knocked open the door and ran outside, and never mentioned their mother again.

Marie looked at the photograph. Was that you, she thought. Did you actually do that? Could you have? Her mother's smile appeared wider, and it seemed she'd shifted her position slightly, as though to remove her hand from the muff and reach out to Marie and say, "Oh, Marie, of *course* not." But how could Marie know? She couldn't even recapture the tone of her mother's voice.

It was as if all of her childhood had passed in darkness; there were no details. Every week she looked through the family albums, all three of them, hoping to find in their pages some clue to the makeup of that time. The photographs were like scraps of sewing material for a large and elaborate project, but the pattern to it had been lost. The photographs were fascinating in themselves—she could look into a pair of eyes and wonder, What are you thinking? Are you happy? Are you sad? How is the day around you, and what happened next? And perhaps sometime in the future, if she kept at it, she could assemble all of the pieces into—into whatever it was they were intended to be.

She picked the wax off her fingertip, putting it back at the top of the candle, around the wick, and then went into the kitchen. Her father and the boys had taken down mugs and poured their own coffee. At her father's elbow was a loaf of white bread, the ketchup, and a jar of mustard with a table knife sticking into it—everything Marie had forgotten to put on the table.

"Would you like some rye bread?" she asked. "I bought some in town this morning."

"No, this is fine," he said.

"Do you want anything else?"

"Not right now."

"Who's winning?" she asked.

"Whom do you presume, Miss Aberdeen-Anguish?" Tim said, and Marie saw the corners of her father's lips compress and the beginning of a smile. Tim and her father were winning.

"I'll make some popcorn later," Marie said.

"Great," Jerome said.

She went into the living room and found Susan on her knees beneath the Christmas tree, shaking a package close to her ear while she kept her eyes on the television. She turned and said, "Oh, God, you would have to come in just now." She tossed the package under the tree and went back to her chair and slumped down in it, and Marie sat on the couch, behind Susan, and stared at the television screen. She'd developed a habit of watching it out of the corners of her eyes ("Sidewatcher," Tim called her), because she'd sat in front of a television so much when she was a child she'd become skeptical of it. None of the programs were very plausible and she couldn't look at them for long without wondering how people in California or New York could appear inside their living room, engaged in performances she could observe at the second they were taking place, and this caused her to lose the thread of what they were doing.

She glanced around, checking for any detail she might have overlooked. The gateleg table was exactly right with the rest of the furniture. A few months ago, her father had described it, and asked her if she'd seen it anywhere; he said it had been built by a neighbor, a carpenter eighty years old, as a gift for him and Marie's mother when they were married. Marie found it in the upstairs storeroom, underneath an old mattress covered with a tarp. She cleaned it and rubbed it with oil until her reflection appeared over its surface, as though beneath the grain, and then brought it down last week, along with the Christmas decorations, and set it up in the living room as a surprise for her father.

"Ach!" Susan said to the television screen. "Baloney on you!"

She got up and stomped through the living room, through the kitchen, and Marie heard the door to their bedroom slam. The program must have been a love story; Susan was in tears. It seemed that one of the two always was, and their tears had become so commonplace that Tim and her father hardly noticed them anymore. And she and Susan didn't pay that much attention to one another's. Susan would say, "Oh, for God's sake, Mare, are you *crying* again?" and then in a while Susan would be in tears.

Marie stared at the table, at the design cut with a coping saw from its side supports, like a pair of hourglasses set end to end, and the gold grain that lifted from the darker wood into another dimension, and then she remembered looking at it like this another time. It was a Christmas from her past. One of the leaves of the table was raised, and a tiny Christmas tree, sprayed with silver paint, was sitting on it. There were strings of cranberries and popcorn on the tree. Had she helped string them? She couldn't remember any lights, and the tree was too small for icicles. Were they poor then? Was that in this house?

She turned to the kitchen, and through its doorway she could see Tim and Charles and Jerome, but not her father. The three of them were talking with expressions on their faces that meant their voices had risen, and were slamming down cards, but her mind was so crowded she couldn't hear a sound. The kitchen was brightly lit, and from the dark of the living room they seemed to be inside a yellow cube, closed off from the rest of the house and her, as if she were seeing them for the first time, as an outsider: they were brothers, it was Christmas, their mother was missing, and would always be.

Then Marie had an image of her mother whipping batter in a bowl held against her side, bending to the oven to check on her baking, carrying a cookie sheet to the kitchen table, where rows of holiday pastries were spread out on cooling racks, slapping her father's behind with a spatula when he tried to snitch one, and then her laughter at his startled expression. The house was filled with the sweetness of baking for days, and while her mother worked she sang Christmas carols and hymns.

There was a cry of triumph from Tim, and then Jerome tossed down his cards, shoved away from the table, and came into the living room and sat at the end of the couch. He'd brought along an ashtray from the kitchen (she'd *have* to remember to put out ashtrays before tomorrow), and he placed it on the couch between them, and then lifted his chin to blow out smoke, and she saw that the cords of his neck were stiff with tension.

"Are you done playing cards already?" she asked.

"They're playing three-handed."

"Oh."

"It's harder to cheat that way."

Marie smiled. Jerome had known about Tim and her father all along. The light from the television gave the side of his face a gray, statuelike cast, and she felt sorry for his lips; they were thick, not very mobile or expressive, and sometimes it seemed he talked so little because of a self-consciousness about them.

"The house really looks nice," he said.

"Oh, thank you."

"I remember how it used to look two or three years ago."

"I know. I'm sorry."

"It wasn't your fault. Nobody picked up after themselves."

"I was the worst."

"Mmmmm." His mind had jumped beyond the conversation and he was considering something else.

"How long has Dad been this way?" he asked.

"How?"

"Angry at you."

"All the time!"

"More, lately?"

"I guess."

"Mmmmm." Jerome put the cigarette to his lips, and his exhaled smoke rolled in overlapping clouds toward the Christmas tree.

"Are you excited about Christmas?" Marie asked.

"Sort of," he said.

"I am."

"You don't seem in a celebrating mood tonight."

"Oh—" Marie stared down and evened her skirt against a knee with her thumbs. "Oh, I've just been thinking."

"What about?"

"Oh, I don't know. A lot of things." She was embarrassed to mention her mother in front of Jerome.

"About Mom?"

Marie looked up. The Christmas-tree lights were reflected in colored dots on Jerome's glasses and she couldn't see his eyes.

"Yes," Marie said.

"What about?"

"Just her. She made times like this so perfect. Even if I knew exactly how you boys and Dad wanted Christmas, I'd probably ruin it."

"That's how you feel?"

"I can't do anything right."

"Everything you've done here looks great to me."

"You're just being nice."

"Nnnn." There were more clouds of smoke, and then he said, "She made mistakes all the time." And after a moment added, "Mom."

"That's not so."

"Sure it is."

"It's not!"

"She made more mistakes than you."

"You're just saying that."

"She had more opportunity to make them."

"What do you mean?"

"Five kids."

No matter how much Marie kept brushing her cheeks with her fingers she couldn't keep them free of tears.

"When do you think it'll happen?" Jerome asked.

"What?"

"Dad get married."

"This summer," Marie said.

"That soon?"

"He's practically said so to Susan and me. A couple of times."

"That's what I was thinking."

"Why?"

"Nobody seems too happy around here."

"*He* does."

"I'm sure he's worried about a lot of things—especially how we'll all take it."

"No, he isn't."

"Sure, Marie. Also, it's his second wife. He's probably wondering if things will work out the same."

"Why does he have to get married at all? After so many years? Why can't we stay the way we are? We get along just fine."

"I doubt if he wants to spend the rest of his life alone."

"But what about us?"

"I'm sure he's considered our feelings."

"Not Susan's and mine."

"Especially yours."

"But he never really talks to us."

"He will."

Marie wanted to rest her forehead against Jerome. "I was just starting to find out where I belong in this family!"

"You'll keep on finding out."

"I won't have a chance. There'll be too many others!"

"Just Laura. She's nice."

"She has three kids."

"Both her sons are married."

"But her daughter will be here. Her daughter's younger than Susan."

"Mmmm," Jerome said. "Maybe you just don't want to give up the house."

"I don't! I'd never feel right about it! I'd feel like I let somebody else take it from Mom!"

"She's been gone a long time, Marie."

"I know she has, I know that! But I'm still here, aren't I? Can't you see that I am?"

One Christmas in the Darkness of the Plains

ANN BOADEN

I THINK OF HER AS I WALK in the small prairie planting near my home. The grasses stand above my head and rustle with the life in them. In winter they're the color of pale straw. Sunset gleams on their feathered tips so they look like candles in the dusk. Snow bends and blurs but does not cover them.

And I remember that this was how the land looked a hundred and more years ago, when she came to the plains.

We can't know the nuances of the past, one writer has said. Only the crude, blurred contours of its stories, like prairie grass in snow.

And yet.

And yet once the past came to me. It was at Christmas. But as I try to remember, I see that even this story is blurred. I did not know; I was the one known. Like Christmas itself, the story is a mystery. Like Christmas, it shines in the darkness.

I wasn't going to go to the service that year. Loss had swooped down on my life like a crow's wing, and I couldn't take the Currier-and-Ives perfection of the annual village Christmas. When you are vulnerable, what hurts most is the sudden press of old joy.

Every year our college attends a Christmas service at a nearby historic village on the prairies, always on the Wednesday evening before classes are dismissed for break. Typically snow begins as the buses pull out of the campus parking lot and lumber onto the highway, their big wiper blades jerking arcs

across the front windows. In the occasional lights—we take a two-lane country road and lighting is casual—flakes hover like moths.

The village is twenty miles east of us, a half-hour drive on good roads,
longer when pavements are slick. The surrounding fields are dark, the landscape a race of snow. The buses are packed with students. They are wild as
kids because Christmas is coming, and they chatter and laugh and occasionally shriek, and we few faculty and staff smile tolerantly amid the noise that
fills the bus as the snow fills the darkness. On the way back the students sing.
They have been moved, in various ways and for reasons they can't always define, by the service they've attended. Or by the cookies and cocoa served afterward by grandmotherly village women.

We go each year because our college shares history with this prairie village.
Our school's founder came to America leading a band of settlers who'd left
Europe for the usual reasons: religious freedom and freedom from worn earth
that—like the church—gave them stones rather than bread. They came here
with their families and their painted trunks seasoned with herbs and hope.
They saw the prairie grass waving above their heads. They plowed and planted
the dark loam of the plains. Their leader started a school that eventually became our college. They gathered material to build a church.

And one winter—was it in Advent, that most hopeful of seasons?—the
cholera came, and they watched their loved ones sicken and die. Especially
the children. The chapel where we commune in candlelight was half-built when
the illness reached epidemic proportions. The people turned the chapel
basement into an infirmary. And from the good wood that was to have made
walls they built coffins. Not until several years had passed did they finish it—
this monument to grief and to dogged faith.

That was the other reason I wasn't going to go that year. Old pain hurts almost as much as old joy.

So I'm not sure why I did go. The students, maybe. "You're coming to
hear our choir sing, aren't you?" Or maybe it was the speaker, one of those
revered sages every school cherishes, a former professor full of years and wisdom. He knew all the stories of our shared past, and could tell them almost
as vividly as if he'd been there. Perhaps he *was* there sometimes, in his mind.
He was, at any rate, acquainted with their particular joys and griefs. He had
spent a lifetime looking into people's hearts.

So, drawn between young and old, I went.

The day had been iron, sullen-cold, unforgiving. It was a dark coming over the road through the invisible fields. No snow fell as the bus droned into the prairies. The random lights appeared, white as ice, and fell away. The students talked and laughed. I sat alone; colleagues were wary of me, as if loss were a contagion. Sometimes I could see my face, reflected dark and fleshless, in the bus window. Sometimes I couldn't.

As the students say, if the pattern of this event ever varied, the plains would rise up and pour into the Mississippi River. There's the service— readings, liturgy, set music, homily—in the big "new" church (circa 1875) at the center of the village. Then we process across the road, usually snowy and faintly luminous, our boots squeaking, wind knifing our faces, singing carols. We sing until we get to the "old" church—the small chapel, candlelit in the night, that the settlers stopped building when the cholera came.

It doesn't hold all of us, so we line up outside until there's room to squeeze in.

Inside people move in light and shadow, and their boots clump on the hard wooden floor. An atmospherically sensitive pump organ wheezes out the carols. We kneel to commune at the small wooden altar. Our breath smokes in the air. The altar rail and wooden floor are cold as stone.

Then we go back to the big church for cookies and cocoa with those beaming Ur-grandmas.

I knew what to expect, that year I wasn't going to go. Except for one thing.

The revered scholar—emeritus for longer than he'd taught—was marginally frailer this year. He must've been pushing ninety by then, but that only made stronger and more tender the stories he told of dauntless faith against brutal reality, of endurance in the face of pain and sorrow so deep we could hardly imagine it, of light in darkness, like the candles in the window of the chapel. He spoke of those who healed where they could not cure, in the moment of their own piercing grief. Many, he said, were women. His white hair shone in the overhead lights; his voice rose and fell in an almost chantlike pattern, and when he came to the children's deaths it broke, whether from emotion or weakness I don't know.

I sat with the green hymnal held rigidly on my lap. I traced the gold cross incised on its cover, traced it over, up and down and sidewise, till my finger burned.

The wind was relentless as grief when we walked over to the chapel. The shiver in me went so deep it didn't touch muscle or skin. I thought, and tried not to think, of the people walking this way long ago. Walking toward the chapel hospital to tend loved ones.

Did they walk in the dark, or take lanterns that jostled the night? Did they welcome the bitter wind in their faces because it hurt them outside and permitted tears?

Maybe it was those thoughts, new to me. Or the wheezy organ, itself an antique, whose voice broke like that of the revered scholar. Maybe it was the young voices singing, suddenly etherealized in the living shadows of that small chapel. Or the faces, stilled, simplified, made holy by candlelight. Or the hands cupping the bread and wine that were the hands of all love and grace and promise.

Whatever it was, my own hands shook on the communion chalice, I could not swallow the bitter new pain in my throat, and I knew that it had been a terrible mistake to come. I did not see how I could go back on that bus. I knew I couldn't return to the new church for the cookies, couldn't face the merriment and jollity, the shining and boisterous and uncorrupted excitement. So after the last of them trailed out on the last threads of "Silent Night," and the door thudded behind the "heavenly peace," I sat there, in the stone-cold pew in the candlelit chapel. Someone would be coming back to put out the candles and I wanted to freeze before she (it would probably be a she) did. I sat with my face in my hands.

I didn't hear the door, but I knew when she came. It was odd; one moment, my face buried, I saw only the darkness inside my hands. The next moment, in a way I can't define, the darkness eased.

There was no sound of footsteps, no weight of her sitting down next to me, only the sense of complete presence.

She didn't speak till, finally, I raised my head. I can't even say what she looked like; when in memory I try to look at her directly, to focus her, she both blurs and intensifies, like a flame seen through ice. And yet she was there. Nothing, not even sorrow, has ever been realer to me than the fact of her being present.

"I'm so scared."

I must have said it. But I can't remember the sound of the words, only the way they felt in my heart.

"Yes." I wish I could describe her voice. The nearest I can come is that it said she knew. It was matter-of-fact. And it went to the very center of all that hurt me. "It does feel like fear. And fear feels like grief."

"She had such dreams"—I had not said this to anyone, could barely speak her name to kind people who offered sympathy—"she wanted to help them, to help them make a new world, those people—half a world away, new for them, for us all. And I—I loved her, but I didn't really . . . understand, except intellectually; it seemed . . . fanatical somehow, crazy to go out there with all the violence and . . . and . . . what did she know? How could she? She was so young. All she ever said was, 'I have to speak for those who can't. There are children dying.' And then—I was impatient—oh Christ, she was my daughter but I was impatient—and then—so far away—such a terrible death. They had no antibiotics—they couldn't even keep the hospitals clean—"

"Yes." Silence. "When you would have held her against all harm." Silence in the chapel. Silence, deep as the plains and the sky, gathering us. And then, "A sword piercing your heart."

"I'm so afraid," I said. "I'm afraid I'll fall off the edge into the dark." And then—again the moment of it blurs, but blurs to essentials; circumstances fall away. Did I reach out my hand or did she? Did she speak, say "No"? All I know is, there was a touch and there was peace.

I don't know how long I sat there. A minute—an hour.

I heard the thud of the closing door and the slow creak of the wood on the chapel floor.

I looked up into the wise old face of the revered professor. It was crumpled and seamed in candlelight, but also simplified. He said, "She came to you, did she?"

"Yes. How did you—"

He nodded. Smiled a little. "She does, to those on a dark way. The others . . . forget, when the tears are wiped from their eyes. But hers was an extraordinarily strong spirit. She comes, as she came then, to the places of pain." His own eyes shone. His voice rose and fell like the candlelight.

"Who?"

"One of the many who lost. Lost and . . . remember. You have received a most unusual Christmas gift."

"Yes," I said. "Yes."

When we came out of the chapel, the sky had softened. It was snowing on the plains.

December

LINDA M. HASSELSTROM

December 1   Low -20, high zero. Sunrise: bank of blue-gray clouds lying on the horizon, a single clear pink jewel set in the center. Then the gray closed in: the sun rose higher, glowing red, suddenly ripping the curtain and flaring across the plains.

Margaret is still in the hospital, but I called her this morning. She sounds drugged and tired but as cheerful as ever. I was complaining about getting another batch of poems back, rejected by yet another magazine, and she quoted Robert Frost to me:

> *. . . Do you know,*
> *Considering the market, there are more*
> *Poems produced than any other thing?*
> *No wonder poets sometimes have to seem*
> *So much more businesslike than businessmen.*
> *Their wares are so much harder to get rid of.*

As usual, the poet learns from the beekeeper: I'd read "New Hampshire" years ago but forgotten it. Margaret keeps a copy of the complete Frost on her coffee table and reads him often.

I went over east with George. The ice is getting harder to chop every day —it's more than two feet thick now. The cows bawl and follow the truck as we pour out cake behind it. They gobble it down, then huddle with their backs against the north wind, waiting for us to chop enough holes so they can drink. We started around eight o'clock but the drifts are deep and the going slow, so it was after one o'clock when we got back.

In the afternoon George drove through the drifts and went to Buffalo Gap for more cake; we've fed more than normal because the deep snow keeps the cattle from grazing. I worked on poems.

December 2   Low -28, high -20; windchill -51. Over east in a.m. to feed in freezing wind.

Every day we get up in the gray light of dawn, wearily climb into the red long underwear and wool pants, fuel our bodies with hot oatmeal, toast, and jelly that looks and tastes like the ripe berries of fall, and go out to battle Nature again. Only it's not really a battle; it's a war of nerves, of tactics. If we considered it a fight we could only lose; instead, we try to outmaneuver her, to survive, to keep the cattle alive.

We visited Margaret and Bonnie in the afternoon. Plants and bouquets and stuffed animals hang from the traction frame around Bonnie's legs. They're both in pain but calm and making jokes. Margaret's eyes looked tragic and dark in her white face, and an awful cut slashes across Bonnie's fragile forehead. I managed to make wisecracks until we got out of the room, then cried all the way down in the elevator, soaking George's shoulder.

December 5   Low -10, high 15; wind blowing, and lots of drifting.

We went over east together and had to pioneer an entirely new route to get to the dugout. The gullies where our trails run were drifted full, so we drove along ridges swept almost bare of snow. When we got to the end of the last ridge, the drift ahead looked fairly shallow. I was driving, and at the last second, worried about the depth of the drift, I gunned the pickup. As we dropped into the drift, snow exploded over the windshield, completely burying the truck for a few moments.

The slope above the dugout had only a few inches of snow on it. We chopped the ice and let the cattle in a few at a time to drink, so they didn't crowd out onto the ice and break through. After we'd fed, they'd churned up the slope so much the pickup just sat and spun. We tried a dozen times and were just beginning to face the prospect of walking home—ten miles in snow to our knees, with a cold wind and a chill factor the pickup radio said was close to thirty below zero—when we finally got enough traction to get out. On the way home, slowly thawing out, we decided that if it's a passable day tomorrow we have to bring the cattle home.

The Christmas party for the Thunder Mountain Long Rifles, our blackpowder gun club, was tonight in Sturgis, but the weather was so bad we decided not to go. We're always afraid of being stuck up there in a blizzard.

December 6   Low -10, high 15; sunny and felt warm.

Called the county shop and asked them to send the snowplow so the propane truck could deliver.

We led Oliver over east behind the truck and moved 168 cows, heifers, and bulls home. George was able to drive the truck in the lead much of the way, except where he had to detour around gullies drifted full of snow. It was a real test of his knowledge of the landscape, since all the familiar landmarks are drifted under, but between the two of us we managed to keep the truck out of the worst drifts. The cattle moved along well, but the trip was longer because of the detours, and the deep snow wore them out.

At one point, in the Triple Seven pasture, two of the bulls were fighting. The Angus caught the Hereford with his back to a down slope, gave him a boost, and tipped him over. The Hereford rolled over a half-dozen times and landed on his back, completely buried in a drift. There was a long pause, with the cows looking on, while I wondered how in the world I'd get him out of there, if he hadn't broken a leg. Then the snow heaved, and his head popped out. He shook his horns, looked the situation over, picked an easy way out of the gully, and stayed right in front of the cows—a long way from the Angus bull—all the way home.

I've been having diarrhea for several days, which added to my general misery during the six hours it took to drive the cattle home. To hell with laser technology—I'd cheer wildly for the man who invented winter coveralls that would allow a woman to relieve herself in a blizzard without stripping.

December 7   Low -10, high 20; sunny, a little wind.

George and I went to the Lindsay pasture where we'd left the horse, and I had to ride all over to collect everything, the cows we brought yesterday as well as those that were already in the pasture. We brought them all home, as we intend to keep them on feed until we can sell most of the calves. We have less hay than usual, and prices are high so we'd rather not buy any.

I ache everywhere this evening; it's been too long since I spent two solid days in the saddle, and the cold makes tense muscles even sorer. My feet and fingers itch from frostbite.

December 8   Low -10, high 15; nice at first light, then the wind started about 8:30 a.m. and the snow began to drift badly.

We are so glad we have the cows home—it was a struggle just to feed them here.

Harold is back in the emergency room with continuing heart problems. The hospital said he had several small heart attacks. I find it impossible to think of the world without Harold's gruff dawn phone calls.

Father talked to our neighbor Al tonight to ask if he'd feed the main herd of cattle in the creek pasture this winter. They started this arrangement while I was away at college, and it has gone on ever since. Asking Al to do it each winter has become a ritual they both enjoy. Father drives up to Al's house, drinks coffee and eats cake for several hours, and then just before he leaves, pops the question. Al always accepts. In the spring Al visits my father to bring the carefully itemized bill.

When I was first staying here alone in winter, Al came in for coffee every few days and quizzed me on my political and environmental views, making me defend every stand I took. We both enjoyed our mock arguments. His son, Alan, and Alan's wife, Shirley, live in a home they built a few hundred yards from Al's house, and his daughter, Margaret, and her family live a half-mile down the road. They are our closest neighbors in several ways.

December 9   Low -25, high -10; the wind stopped in the night.

Our first job was to dig the truck out of the barn, followed by digging a trail to the stack of bales and digging through the gates to get the cattle, which finished the morning.

In the afternoon Father took the 420 tractor, we followed in the three-quarter-ton truck, and we managed to get to the Lindsay pasture and feed the fifteen dry cows and eight bulls we left there. We turned them into a small pasture with running water in the tank and cleared the tank of six inches of ice. On the way home the pickup slid sideways into a hard-packed drift and the muffler was torn off.

Tonight George and I are both lying in our chairs, moving the heating pads from one aching muscle to the next.

December 10   Low -20, high zero; foggy and cold, with almost three feet of snow on the level.

We spent the day struggling through drifts to feed cattle and barely made it to the pasture across the tracks. We ate a cold supper and sat in the living room wrapped in blankets, but it seemed to take forever to warm up.

Many western or Great Plains novelists have written about including the land as a distinct character in novels, but it seems to me one almost must consider the weather as a separate entity, almost as an intelligence. We're especially conscious of it in spring, when the weathermen mention "stockman's warnings" and urge ranchers to get young livestock into shelter. The observant rancher already knows it by the time it's on the radio. He's seen the smoke rise heavily from the chimney, slide across the roof, and drop to the ground, and noticed the low spongy clouds and the heavy silence in the air that means a wet snowstorm coming.

December 11   Low -25, high -12; no wind.

George hauled more cake from Buffalo Gap in the morning after the snowplow came, while I helped Father separate some of the steer calves and give them extra feed.

We spent the afternoon feeding the cows—two pounds of cake and about ten pounds of hay each. Just as we finished struggling out of our coveralls— at 4 PM and dark—Father called to say he thought they needed more cake from now on, so we went back down and fed another two hundred pounds. To 145 cows, we're feeding about four pounds of cake each, or six hundred pounds total, and 1,450 pounds of baled hay per day, about twenty bales. We load and feed all of this weight by hand, since we can't get the big tractor through the drifts to the loose haystacks yet.

December 12   Low -30, high -15; cloudy, a little wind.

I woke early from a dream in which I couldn't breathe through either my nose or mouth. I tried to get out of bed—in the dream—but fell and lay there trying to make enough noise to wake George. I knew I was smothering and that he'd find me dead beside the bed in the morning. When I actually woke, I was gasping and covered with sweat, my nose plugged—just a cold coming on, but the feeling of panic kept me awake a long time.

The cold temperatures make chopping the ice difficult for George, whose breathing has never been very good. He doesn't seem able to get enough air into his lungs, and we still don't know if it's asthma or something else. In the evening we took a pot of chili to Bill. He says Margaret may be home for Christmas, but Bonnie won't be.

December 14   Low -20, high -10.

After we fed today, we went to town and got a few more gifts for Mike, since he will be here at Christmas. It was a rush trip, to get home in time to help Father separate the steer calves again. He intends to sell them first, and each night he cuts them away from the cows and shuts them in the corral to feed them alfalfa cubes.

Father spoke today of two particular cows we'd sold at least five years ago, and I asked him how long it had taken him to recognize individual cows. I know some, especially the ones with distinctive markings. He knows them all, every cow, and can usually tell what she was out of, and perhaps who her grandmother was besides. He said he's always been able to do it, since he was a child, which slightly dashed my hopes that perhaps someday I'd learn.

December 15   Low -25, high -10; brisk wind from south rearranged snowdrifts.

The cedar waxwings that visit our cedar trees annually on their migration south are crowding the trees around the folks' house, tippling on the berries and screeching raucously. When they pass through again, headed north in March, I'll know much of winter is past. They must be hardy birds to travel after the snow.

We increased the hay to the cattle by a few bales today, as they look terribly thin and weak. Some of them are sorefooted from walking in this snow and ice for so long.

I went to Jo and Harold's this evening to help clean the basement of the old house for the new hired man and his family. In one of the boxes I found an old journal written by my grandfather, Charles Hasselstrom, and borrowed it to read. I never met him.

He used accounting ledgers, recording the money spent in each month on the left-hand page and the money made on the right-hand page.

Money paid out in January 1928			Produce sold in January 1928		
2	groceries	$1.59	2	15 doz. eggs	7.50
4	bread and castor oil	.80	21	27 doz. eggs	9.45
21	oysters	1.00	31	one can of cream 8 g.	14.49
26	bulls from Wm. Snable	250.00			

He didn't record his daily activities, his thoughts or frustrations, but it's a wonderful document because it is so specific. A page in the front lists the workhorses by name (Queen, Betts, Beauty, Min, Alkili, Martha, Katie, Bell, Ester, Mary, May, and Dolly) and tells when their colts were born. On another page is his inventory for the year 1919, the year the journal opens. He valued the chicken houses and barns at $1,000, the fence posts at $1,500, and the farm machinery at $1,800, and recorded the expenses for the year: $1,352. At the end of 1918, he had thirty-five head of cows, twelve heifers, thirty calves, two bulls, thirteen steers, twelve horses, two brood sows, seventeen other hogs, and two hundred chickens, with a total value of $5,850.

December 16   Low -30, high -15; radio says chill factor is -60 with a cold wind drifting the snow again.

We had to dig the truck out of the barn again, dig out the stacks of bales, then dig the truck out several times while we fed the cattle. My back and shoulders are getting more used to the shoveling. The snow is so hard we can cut out perfectly square chunks. If we needed to make an igloo, it would be easy.

By noon the wind had dropped, and while we were eating dinner and trying to get warm the cattle from the Lindsay pasture straggled into the yard. All of us rushed out half-dressed and struggled through the drifts until they were all in the corral. So now we have every cow and calf we own standing in the same corral, a situation that makes it hard to feed them properly. The bulls and strongest cows shove the others aside and get most of the feed unless we separate them into several small bunches.

After we collected ourselves, we sorted the cows with steer calves into the pasture around our house and tried to turn the others out into the big pasture. But the wind was up again and they didn't want to go. So we fed everything a little cake and staggered back to the house.

We offered to go to Lindsays to see if all the cattle have come up, but Father's sure they would all stay together. That's good, because I don't think we could get there. The three-quarter-ton truck will ride up on top of a drift for a ways and then drop through and be stuck as hard as if it were in concrete.

I brought Father a pedometer for Christmas; he's been wanting one so they could measure their daily walks. Today I fastened it to my belt before walking down to the corral to begin feeding, and by noon I'd walked three miles.

December 17   Low -10, high zero.

We cut the twenty-one two-year-old heifers and put them on the hillside so we can give them extra feed; they'll calve for the first time in March. Now we have three separate bunches to feed and are moving at least seven hundred pounds of cake and twenty-three bales of hay a day—something like 2,400 pounds by hand.

Because of the extreme cold the drifts are crusted over, and each time you take a step you break through the top crust with a jerk, then hit another crust, and then another before your foot reaches the last layer above the ground, so walking is a real effort. All of us are having sharp pains in our legs.

I was reading Charley Hasselstrom's ledger today. Properly interpreted, it could provide an entire history of the times. Someone, probably my Aunt Anne, recorded $92.50 for the hospital bill when her father was operated on, $9.75 for a dress for her mother, and $226.60 for the funeral parlor when they buried him. I went over parts of it with my father, but he said it was too hard to look at—"Get it away from me."

December 18   Low -26, high -10; light wind in morning increased to sixty miles an hour by noon, with heavy wet snow falling.

Despite a cold wind, we managed to get feed to everything. In midmorning when the winds hit sixty, it drove the snow into our clothes, so that when we got into the pickup and it melted, we were soaking wet immediately.

After we changed clothes and had lunch, Father called and asked us to feed more cake to the cows. They were humped up with the cold, bawling, and gathered around the truck like sharks. I read somewhere that for every degree below zero they should have another pound of feed, and we're not feeding even close to that much.

Father ordered a truck for tomorrow to haul the rest of the steer calves, the best of the heifer calves, and about fifteen dry cows to the sale. He'd hoped to keep more of them through the winter, but it's too risky with the small amount of feed we have and the price it will cost us to get more. Also, the way the drifts are building up, we soon may not be able to get a truck in here to deliver feed or to haul cattle to the sale ring.

December 19   Low -20, high -10.

We were up early this morning but Father beat us to the corral, and we spent a cold two hours separating the cows from their calves and then sorting off the best of the calves to sell. We picked out 113 to sell, leaving us about seventy to take care of this winter. We left them separate from the cows. Weaning them in weather this cold, we risk wholesale pneumonia, but we'll have to move the cows soon, and the calves need more feed than the thin milk they're getting from their mamas.

I usually enjoy the few minutes' calm after sorting calves, while Father looks them over and allows himself a little pride in how they look. This year they look bad. The cold weather the last few weeks has knocked the bloom off them. Some are sorefooted and all of them are bonier than usual. Father looked at them awhile, then said, "We'll be glad we don't have them about February," and walked away.

Of course the ones we're keeping look even worse, the real dregs of bovine society: sick calves, calves born later than the rest, and calves from two-year-old heifers, which are always a little stunted. We decided to keep the dry cows and hope we can sell them next week, as we have a big load with calves.

The snowplow had just finished opening the road when the cattle truck came at eleven, and with much shoving and swearing, we loaded the calves. We loaded cake onto the Ford pickup to give it more stability on the icy roads, and Father took it to the sale. We had a quick lunch before tackling the feeding. Of course the cows spent a lot of time bellowing and running back to the corral to look for their calves.

Sometime recently I wrote a note on the bedside pad about a title for this journal: "Windbreak: The Journal of a Ranch Woman." I noticed today George has added "Breakin' Wind: The Journal of a Hired Hand."

December 20   Low -30, high -10.

Father called at six o'clock to tell me gloomily how cold it got last night and that another storm is predicted, so they plan to leave for Texas today.

"Have you heard about the guy who said, 'Cheer up—things could be worse'?" he asked.

"No."

"So I cheered up, and sure enough they got worse."

Usually he remains pretty optimistic, but this storm is beginning to get him down.

After breakfast I helped them hastily pack the car. We took the three-quarter-ton truck and had to tow them most of the way out the driveway. Then, at Father's request, we followed them to Hot Springs. The road was icy and visibility about one-quarter mile all the way, so it was a hair-raising trip. We got back home at two o'clock and had to scramble to finish feeding before it got dark at four o'clock.

Checking to be sure the folks' house was secure, I found a pad on their dining room table headed "Jottings from an old man to his Children":

> Start calves on one lb. of creep feed and increase to two lbs. as they all get to eating. Maybe there is enough feed bunks to feed them all at the same time. If not, build more.
>
> To conserve energy, when a pickup is not moving ahead, shut the motor off. Starters and batteries are cheaper than gasoline these days.
>
> Don't keep a lot of horses in the corrals feeding them hay. If there is snow on the ground a horse can get by in a pasture without water. Hay is expensive.
>
> Get the calves fed and watered before noon. John Lindsay used to say if he didn't get work done in the morning, he might as well go fishing for the rest of the day.
>
> When you feed cattle cake, know how much you are feeding them; don't guess at it. Remember, a hundred pounds costs $6.85 these days.
>
> Don't take chances and get caught in a storm. Remember a cow can stand more weather than you can.
>
> Don't forget I've never kept livestock in a house in which I live. Please observe and respect my way of life. Thank you.

This combination of practical advice and sarcasm (by livestock in the house he means our cat and dog) is typical of him; he always seems to assume we are wasteful and not very bright. On the other hand, he's put seventy years of work in on this ranch, and it must make him a little nervous to go away, leaving it in our hands. Destroying it all in one winter would be hard, but others have done it.

December 21   Low -10, high zero, with heavy, wet snow falling, high winds, lots of drifting—so it's a good thing the folks got out.

George and I used every bit of our energy to get feed to everything. The hose at the main tank was frozen. Father's been taking it into the house every night, as the flow of water isn't enough to keep it from freezing, but I forgot. I ran their bathtub full of hot water and put the hose in it until the ice drained out.

We're feeding the calves four thirty-pound buckets of alfalfa cubes in the morning with a hundred pounds of creep feed, and four more buckets of cubes in the afternoon—340 pounds of feed for seventy calves, or almost five pounds each. My arms are practically pulled out of their sockets when I stagger through the drifts with thirty pounds at the end of each arm. That makes lugging the fifty-pound bag of creep feed seem easy. I bent instead of squatting to pick up the buckets this morning and strained my back.

While we're pouring the feed into the bunks, the calves dash in, butting and kicking each other, and it's tricky not to get kicked. My knees and thighs are a mass of bruises where I've been kicked, nudged, and bludgeoned, but so far I haven't been knocked down.

In the afternoon George worked at reinforcing the stockyards, as the cattle had broken in during the night, led by the jumping cow we call Ugly. I spent the afternoon putting up plastic and insulation on the folks' porch and moving Mother's plants into the warmer part of the house. Tried to keep a fire in their woodstove in the basement, but the wood burned fast and my fingers remained stiff.

This evening Margaret called from home; she's in a back brace and probably will have to have a lot of surgery—even possibly have her spine fused—but she's cheerful anyway. Bonnie's thighs are set, but the doctor says one leg will probably be shorter than the other. She won't be home for Christmas. I took the truck and went up for a minute to leave Margaret a fruitcake and a pot of chili. Her table was stacked with things people had brought her in the hospital: cards, toys, books. She was amazed at how kind people have been, perhaps forgetting that she's always the first to help others.

She'd decorated their tree. It's covered with things Bonnie made in school and even some things Margaret made when she was in grade school. What a beautiful symbol of togetherness, of family life. When I got home I put a few decorations on the Norfolk Island pine in the living room. I am always pleased not to have to destroy a tree in order to observe Christmas. It looks bare and scraggly with its few ornaments; our history as a family is still so short.

December 22   Low -25, high -10.

We've been worried about the cows and bulls on the hillside south of the house. They're in the worst shape, thin and footsore. Each night they've been struggling up over the hill to get shelter from the cold north winds, and each day it takes them longer to stagger back down to feed. We've been afraid they'll get trapped on the other side where we can't get to them, so today we turned them into the alfalfa fields. Father cut and raked some hail-damaged hay that he didn't have time to stack, and they can clean that up. Unfortunately, a lot if it has drifted under, so we have to shovel to find the windrows, since cattle won't dig with their hoofs like horses.

Instead of bawling and rushing to the gates as they usually do, the cattle stand waiting for us to feed, hipbones sticking up like masts on a ship.

In the afternoon we managed to get out through the pasture—getting stuck twice—to get groceries. When we came back, the pasture route seemed to be drifted even worse than the road, so we tried the road—and got stuck three times. This may be our last trip out for a while unless we get the snow-plow, and he'll be busy with all the new drifting. Glad I've been laying in extra groceries for the last few weeks.

When we drove into the yard, a golden eagle was perched in a cottonwood tree beside the folks' house. I choose to interpret this as a good omen.

We're weaning the leftover calves—the ones not sold—and they stood in the corral bellowing frantically all morning until we fed them ten bales of hay and some cake. They're chewing on the corral planks, a steady gnawing like a million locusts. We got some blocks of mineral but it hasn't stopped them. I told Father about it when he called from Alliance, Nebraska, last night, and he said, "At the price of feed, it would be cheaper to feed them planks."

By the time George chopped the ice out of the water tank, it was almost empty. The chunks of ice were more than two feet thick. We're keeping the pump running full-time; if we shut it down to keep the tanks from running over, the pipes and hoses freeze. But when we let it run over, the ice freezes around the tanks and makes the footing hazardous for the cattle, so every day I take a bucket of ashes down and sprinkle it around the tanks. The gravel that usually helps the cows' footing is a couple of feet under the ice.

December 23   Low -30, high -7; windy.

The feed store wanted to deliver the twelve tons of alfalfa cubes we'd bought today, so we called the county grader. He got stuck and spent an hour waiting for a tow. We couldn't help, so George got the army-surplus tank heaters working, while I checked the folks' house, fed the barn cats, and hooked up the hoses on the tanks. We'd just finished feeding the calves when the semi came, but in spite of the work the grader had done, the driver was unwilling to drive into the yard; he was sure he'd get stuck. We had to dump the feed on plastic tarps in the yard beside the road.

We increased the cows' rations, since they're looking so thin and weak, to five pounds of cubes a day, a pound of cake, and ten pounds of hay each. We had to dig again to get to the bale stack, and then shovel more snow off the hay for the cattle we turned in to the alfalfa fields.

George said today, "You know, every other winter, I've had to listen to the old-timers talk about how much worse the winter of '27 was, or the Winter of '49. This year they just shut their mouths and keep shoveling."

December 24 Low -35, high -15.

I called Jim and Mavis and advised them not to come for Christmas. The entrance road is completely closed by huge drifts and the pasture route risky. But their pipes are frozen and they're sick of working with them, so they're coming anyway.

When we got to the corral this morning, we found a cow down. We tried to get her on her feet, but she was too far gone. She was lying with her head down-hill, so I suppose her lungs filled with fluid. She looked so thin I checked her teeth, and I found the bottom front ones worn nearly away. All the feed in the world wouldn't have helped her. We can't get through the drifts to the bone-yard, so tonight she's lying in the driveway, looking very small and pitiful.

We are continuing to feed cake, hay, and alfalfa cubes to all the cattle, but they still seem weak and lacking in energy, as well as terribly footsore. The yearling calves look gaunt even though they're getting all the creep feed and alfalfa cubes they can eat. Too much will make them bloat.

Jim tried to come in the main road, got stuck and dug out without our seeing him, and then parked the truck halfway to the house in the pasture and walked the rest of the way. I heard Mavis yell and opened the door in time to see her teetering through the drifts in high-heeled boots, shrieking, "Damn Christmas! To hell with living in the country."

WE HAD A GOOD visit around a supper of chili and cornbread, enhanced with scotch for the men, brandy for me, and pink squirrels for Mavis, and we played cards until late.

December 25, Christmas Low -25, high 10 above; feels like spring.

I'm keeping Father's journal too, now. He always leaves it for me so he'll know later what the temperatures were during the winter. Naturally I read back through what he's written. Mostly he sticks to the facts: the work done, which cows are with the bulls, how much rain we get. But it will be a wonderful record to have in the years ahead; already he uses it to settle arguments with Harold about exactly how much rainfall we got in a certain year, or how much snow. Mother also keeps one, though I've never seen it. I'm pleased to know we're all recording life in our own ways, though I wish I had children to pass all these journals to.

We all went together to feed and got Jim's truck in as far as the house at noon before stuffing ourselves on ham and turkey.

Mavis reminded me of the last time we were together on Christmas, a couple of years ago. It was the first nice day for a while, so we moved the cows home from over east. At the very last pasture gate I was shouting at George and Jim, who were riding in the pickup in front of the cattle while Mavis walked and I rode behind. My horse slipped on the ice and fell, with my right leg under her. My head hit the frozen ground and I was knocked cold.

When I came to, Jim, who had EMT training, was checking to see if my legs were broken, and Mavis, a nurse, was looking at my pupils and saying I had a concussion. George loaded me in the pickup and we headed for the house. After a minute I asked why Jim and Mavis were here.

George: "Because it's Christmas."

Linda: "Then why are we moving cattle?"

He laughed, and said later it was the first sensible thing I'd said all day. I was dizzy the rest of the day, my second concussion from having a horse fall with me. Mother always said my real father's family was famous for having hard heads. Grandmother Bovard fell on her head in a bathtub once and knocked a chunk out of the tub.

December 26   Low -30, high -5, with fifty-mile-an-hour winds most of the day.

Jim and Mavis went back to their frozen pipes. The folks called from Texas; they made it safely and are settling into their apartment, but someone had broken in and stolen their TV.

Started reading Loren Eiseley's *Star Thrower*. Ray Bradbury wrote at Eiseley's death that he had "stepped down to lace his bones with ancient dogs and prairie shadows." May we all.

Auden said Eiseley was "a man unusually well trained in the habit of prayer, by which I mean the habit of listening. The petitionary aspect of prayer is its most trivial because it is involuntary."

I like that thought. I've long since given up asking the being we call God for anything, but I often think of Him in appreciation—when enjoying the songs of the blackbirds, for example. I think he must be much more sensible than the Christians insist and makes allowances for people like me.

I remember my father, one Christmas Eve when I was a child, asking my mother and me if we really believed that a child had been born in a manger to take the world's sins on himself. At the time, I believed it passionately, but I was uneasy about my father in relation to religion. Even then he never went to church, but I knew I couldn't respect a God who would condemn him to hell.

December 27   Low -20, high 15.

We're low on propane in both houses but no truck could get up the road, so I called the county crew again and a grader made a few quick passes through the yard while we fed. He was stuck on the hillside leading to our house for a few minutes, and he left a narrow track with walls of snow six feet high on each side.

We haven't been able to get to our garbage dump since early in November, so I've got full garbage bags stacked in the basement waiting for the thaw. My compost pit is buried under five feet of snow, so I throw the scraps out on a drift and hope the rabbits and grouse will eat some of them. I save meat scraps for the barn cats.

In the afternoon George made two more trips to the Gap for cake, finishing off their supply. Most ranchers have now used more cake than we usually use for the entire winter, and the feed stores are frantically trying to get shipments in, but the highways are bad in the entire state. Harold says he's heard cattle are dying on trucks and in the sale ring as ranchers sell cows they can't afford to feed, cows already weak from inadequate feed for the past two months.

A story in the paper describes ranchers in Wyoming who have cattle literally freezing to death. They say the cattle are losing patches of hair, and under it are masses of pus. I've never seen anything like that, but I imagine we will.

December 28   Low -30, high -15, with sixty-mile-an-hour winds all day.

The cows hunched up behind any shelter they could find, and we dumped the hay out in big chunks so it wouldn't blow away. The corrals are piled with frozen manure on top of at least two feet of snow and ice. Cows hate to eat on filthy ground but they're so hungry they pick up every straw. The wind beats at them, and at us, incessantly. It's like a frozen nightmare with no end in sight.

The calves are either weaned or they're too depressed to bawl anymore. They just stand around the corral waiting for feed, or huddle in the shed, or gnaw on the corrals. They have no bare ground to lie on except under the shed. Every night they crowd in there, and the heat of their bodies warms up the mud so they emerge covered with filth—which promptly freezes. The poor things spend the time they're not eating just standing, shaggy with winter hair, covered in frozen mud, eyes glazed, looking half-dead.

Since George's son, Mike, was flying in tonight, we thought of getting the road grader, but the road would have blown shut before we could finish. Instead, my cousin John met him at the airport, brought him to our turnoff, and George walked to the highway to meet him. When I went out, the moon was shining, casting their shadows huge over the drifts. Mike dropped his suitcase and ran to hug me. He chattered enthusiastically about his Christmas presents and was eager for morning to come so he could help us feed. Lucky boy—what has been a nightmare for us is just a diversion for him.

Since I'm so tired at nights I'm not writing much but doing a lot of reading. I seem to spend long periods poised, thinking about a particular poem or story, as if I'm waiting for some impetus to actually begin writing it. During these times I read, or sew, or even feed cattle, and sometimes I take notes. My mind is working but it doesn't show. If I go to the computer during this phase, I may write a phrase or two and then sit, thinking, distracted by its blinking light, which seems to say, "Let's get on with it—time is money." Then suddenly something will force me to the typewriter or computer and I'll stay there working for hours, oblivious to meals, cramp, thirst, or even George. When this happens, he obligingly fixes something to eat. Sometimes he simply comes up behind me, hugs me, and goes away again.

December 29   Low -35, high -25.

Since the wind dropped last night, I called for the snowplow so we could go to town for George's appointment with the doctor and for groceries; the road was opened by 9 AM.

The two of us get gloomy about this time of year, plodding through our work without much conversation. Mike tells jokes, rolls in the snow with the dog, chases the cats, asks the names of all the cows, is openmouthed with wonder at seeing a great horned owl in a tree by the house, and generally gets us out of our rut. He's also a big help shoveling the alfalfa cubes into buckets to feed.

After feeding, we went to Rapid for groceries and bought two more army-surplus heaters to use in the stock tanks. George had an appointment at the

Air Force base hospital for a checkup. The doctor has finally concluded that George may not have asthma at all but an obstruction in his throat, possibly caused by radiation. He's making an appointment for us in Denver for further tests by the specialists there.

Even though it made us late with the evening feeding, we stopped for a pizza on the way home—Mike's choice. When we got home we couldn't get the truck up the hill because of new drifts. We had expected to have trouble; the snowshoes were in the back of the pickup. Mike thought it was great fun making three trips up the hill carrying the groceries and trying not to trip over his snowshoes. It's amazing how high our hill is with a load of groceries and how hard it is to walk on snowshoes when you can't see your feet. Mike and George fed the calves with flashlights while I put groceries away and built a fire.

December 30   Low -10, high 25; no wind. Felt like summer.

George and Mike hauled more cake from Buffalo Gap before feeding, afraid the store would run out again. Everyone's making trips to town while the good weather lasts.

I took a vacation from feeding, and spent the morning making a huge roast with potatoes and gravy, and a cherry pie. Whenever I passed Mike's room, I peered in and enjoyed the chaos. Usually it's so tidy. What a delight to see it strewn—overnight—with socks, underwear, and tee shirts with pictures of faces I don't recognize—teen idols, no doubt. He'd rummaged through the bookshelves and piled a dozen science fiction and western books on his bedside table for reading after he's supposed to be asleep. George and I pretend not to notice his nocturnal reading, since we both did it as children.

December 31   Low -30, high -15; with a high wind all day.

We kept the tank heaters burning all night, but the ice was still six inches thick on the tanks. Another cow was dead in the corral this morning. Her bottom teeth were broken and stubby—another one we should have sold but couldn't because the cold weather set in too quickly.

We noticed another cow limping painfully and put her into the corral, where she promptly lay down in a muddy hole beside the tank. We couldn't get her up, so we put hay and water beside her. Mike stood by her, urging her to eat, and wanted us to call the vet. I told him we just couldn't afford to do that for old cows, and it probably wouldn't help anyway. Once they lie down, it's usually the end. Cows can stand a terrific amount of cold weather and hardship, but when they decide it's over they seldom get up again.

Mike insisted we all make snow angels when we came in this noon, so now there is a hefty snow angel, a skinny tall one, and a short one that rolled all over the hill. Then I spoiled the mood by pointing out that all of us had done the same work all morning and wondering why they were reading while I fixed dinner.

Alan's wife, Shirley, brought us some cream from their cow, and we made ice cream with the hand-cranked freezer in the evening—a treat for Mike, and a strangely appropriate way to bring in the new year.

Bone
—for Georgia O'Keeffe

I am a saguaro, ribs thrust gray
against blue hot sky.
                              I am
a polished jawbone, teeth white
against the grass.
I have become all that I see:
an elegant bone gnawed clean,
leaving only bone the end,
bone the beginning,
bone the skyline mountain.

Christmas Letter, 1997

BRIAN BEDARD

WE'RE THANKING El Niño for the smooth, benign winter of 1997, glancing only occasionally over our shoulders at the hint of a howl in the wind, at the subtle stab of icicles in the breath of the Great White Wolf who is visiting lobo cousins in New Mexico or is chasing the moon in Canada. We know he's elsewhere, so we venture into the streets in shirtsleeves and light jackets, open-toed shoes and sunglasses, doing double takes on the bank thermometer and smiling like Cheshire cats.

Behind the smiles, our faces still hide the deep bruises of Winter '96 and, though to a visitor it might seem we are free-spirited as a beach full of California surfers, we're still remembering those ice storms in mid November and the downhill slide of a stillborn sky, the menace of sagging clouds. Each day a wavering dip towards the South Pole until we crunched into January, month of the flesh-chilling toilet seat and the end of all private warmth, month of -60° windchills and tales of dying and drifts.

We dance now but we drifted then, our brainwaves turned white as the fingers of snow on the roads. We tried to remember summer '96—lavender light on Badlands buttes, fields of flaming sunflowers east of Platte. Tried to focus on that season of travel and trust, the cycles of rain and sunny afternoons when the rain eased up and the dust grew thick on Climatis bursting purple up the wall of a white farmhouse.

We didn't speak of these visions, these small dependencies on the prairie's fleeting face. We spoke instead of other visits from the Wolf, other years now etched in memory and record book—'36, '49, '68, '82—seasons of dark dreams and death, trotted over town and plateau, over pine-black forest and frozen lake, over cornstubble and ice-covered cows, across the mouths of burrows, the stiff circles of nests, ruffling the feathers of pheasants pinned in ice, whispering in the bird-pecked ears of fallen deer.

Those seasons swirled in our speech, in the soft-spoken talk of farmers in small town bars and cafés, in the buzz of church kitchens, on phone lines that stretched over pasture and knoll. Spoken on the latest technology—the cellular phone—from pickup and van, from aging Buicks and Oldsmobiles; weather talk and weather threat, weather past and to come, cast in newspaper stats and in farmers' almanacs, in the telltale signs the locals can read. Newspapers noted those signs, quoted Czech farmers, Sioux medicine men, grandmothers and gnarled Norwegians—the future in caterpillar fuzz, the omen of coyotes' close prowl.

You can see why we're finding ourselves in Fat City this year, why we're praising the snow-melting warmth of the wind. We feel entitled, you see, to this odd-willed departure, this blessing of open roads. We earned this calm pocket of air, and we're breathing it in with the relish of kids freed from school. We're basking in 55° temps, storing them snug in the memory bank. We know we'll need them as keepsakes the next time the pasture turns polar. We'll need to see flakes masquerading as moths in a field of sky-splitting vines.

We hope you are well and warm, and, like us, are dead certain that spring is just a few sunstreaks away.

The Christmas Offering

O. E. RØLVAAG

Translation by Solveig Zempel

IT WAS CHRISTMAS EVE AND the moon shone brightly. The sharp, biting north wind burned the face. That same wind had worked itself into a fury far, far north of all human habitation. It had stormed down over the whole northwest of Canada, taken in all of North Dakota in one fell swoop, hadn't even given itself time to catch its breath and look around, before it raged far to the south in Minnesota. Here it took it easier, whining around the eaves, whistling down every lane, stirring up every little heap of snow it could find, but still burning just as cold as it had when it left the area up under the North Star. "What a cold north wind!" everyone remarked as soon as they came inside and could speak. "If we don't get more snow, and that right soon, everything will freeze solid!"

In a low, one-story house on a back street in Greenfield, an old couple sat by the Christmas Eve table. They were eating in the kitchen, and that was good enough for them, for here everything was clean and shiny and freshly polished for the holidays. All the nickel on the stove shone like a mirror, there were freshly ironed curtains at the windows, a new white paper fringe on the clock shelf, and the floor had been scoured and scrubbed so that one scarcely dared to step on it. The door to the little living room stood open. There the fire crackled so merrily in the stove that the north wind was put to shame as it blew along the walls. Another door led from the kitchen into the bedroom. That room had to get along on the warmth it received from the other two.

There was plenty of food on the kitchen table: lutefisk, lefse, rice cream, and coffee with extra tender Christmas cookies to go with it, everything that was necessary according to good old Norwegian tradition. The lutefisk was so delicate that it shook like aspen leaves in the wind when one barely touched the plate.

The two who sat here were both from Nordland in northern Norway. They were Simeon Stormo and his wife Anna Katrina. He was small, scrawny, and dried up, with thinning hair, but confident and gloating in manner. She was unusually tall and gaunt, all wrinkled skin on sinew and bone, and taciturn when Simeon didn't irritate her too much with his confident air of superiority. Last fall they had rented out their farm and moved to town to enjoy life in their old age. They might well have done so, too, for with their scrimping habits, they had saved more money than they could ever use up. And besides, they still owned a two hundred acre farm, well cared for and with good buildings. However, a few small problems interfered with their enjoyment of life in town. Simeon was used to pinching every penny before he let go of it, and his wife was certainly no wastrel either. But here in town, it seemed that money went out every time a person took a breath. They had never seen anything so terrible! On top of that, Anna Katrina decided that she didn't like living in town. And no wonder, for out on the farm she had had a whole world of living creatures to rule over and mother, while here she had only Simeon to struggle with! When they lived out in the country, she saw him only at meal times and scarcely even then during the busiest season. But now he hung around the kitchen and tried to correct her the livelong day, and for the first time she began to really get to know him!

Christmas comes but once a year, and Anna Katrina had spared nothing this evening. Now all the work was done, and there was no reason to hurry, so they took their time over the meal. But finally Simeon was satisfied, wiped the grease off his chin, shoved his plate in on the table so there was room for his elbows, looked at his wife, and thought she was going a bit far tonight. She had already helped herself three times to the fish, and lo and behold, if she wasn't going to have one more little bite. "It wasn't necessary to *stuff yourself* even if it was Christmas Eve!" thought Simeon. But then something happened which completely broke the holiday peace.

When Anna Katrina had finally stuffed enough into herself, and gone over to the stove one more time for a drop of coffee to wash it all down, Simeon picked up the devotional book which lay in the window every Sunday. He looked up the meditation for Christmas Eve, cleared his throat and read in a thick, mealy voice, with long pauses between sentences as well as within them. Simeon had never been any great reader. Now he couldn't see so well either, and this evening he felt so heavy with all the good food that he could scarcely breathe. He had the feeling that Anna Katrina didn't like all those pauses in the reading. She had even complained about it once, and said that it disturbed her concentration. Since then, the pauses had grown both in length and in number. This evening it was positively painful to try to follow along. After awhile Anna Katrina began to breathe heavily and regularly. Her head had dipped long before he got to the end. Just as he said amen and put the book down, he looked at her and couldn't resist saying—and not without a touch of malice:

"Tell me—do you mean to say that you can sit there sleeping while we are reading God's word?"

She gave a start as soon as he spoke, sat up, and looked at him with veiled eyes. She got up without a word and began to clear the table. Simeon moved his chair over to the stove, cleaned his pipe carefully, filled and lit it.

Just as she wiped off the table and put the book back in its place in the window, she remarked, "You're sure you have enough change for the special offering in church tomorrow?"

Simeon smacked his lips a couple of times before he answered. "Oh, I suppose I'll find something." His tone of voice was irritatingly indifferent.

She just wondered if he had anything for her too? The question was innocent enough, and she didn't mean anything wrong by it. But Simeon sat straight up in his chair. He took the pipe out of his mouth, blew out the smoke and stared at her. What sort of nonsense was this?

"For you too?" he repeated sharply.

Yes, that was what she'd said! She didn't plan to sit and watch the whole congregation march around the altar, as if she were the only one who didn't feel like giving the minister a shilling. They lived in town now, he'd better remember that!

"One shouldn't give an offering to be seen by others!"

"But one shouldn't give offense either!" She trod heavily across the floor with the cups and saucers.

Simeon didn't like this very much. He was well acquainted with her moods, and understood that now he would do well not to row out so far that he couldn't get ashore again should a storm really blow up. But he didn't understand what had come over her. Ever since they had moved to town, it had become positively dangerous even to talk to her. If he didn't tiptoe around and agree with everything she said, she was on him like a hawk! His tone was almost mild as he began to lecture her. "We should guard ourselves so we don't begin to imitate the world, I tell you! On Judgement Day we won't be asked which of us carried the offering to the altar, but *if* we gave."

She set the cups down and looked at him. Her voice became fuller and heavier, almost heated. "If that is the case, then I will go forward with the offering tomorrow, and you can sit there and look like a fool in front of the whole congregation!"

Simeon took a few angry drags at his pipe. "That's not what Paul says!"

"Oh, Paul, what does he know about how we should do things here in southern Minnesota!"

"Now watch your tongue, Anna Katrina! Paul, he was inspired—you know that much yourself!"

"He certainly wasn't so inspired that he would want an old woman to make a fool of herself!"

Simeon took his pipe out of his mouth and hit the stem against the palm of his hand in order to give the words of scripture more weight. "Women are to be silent in the house of the Lord!—That's what the Scripture says in so many words, and there's nothing I can do to change it!"

She came a step closer, her strong, sinewy face was flushed. "Well, it can say whatever it will, but tomorrow I will not sit in my place and watch every-one else go up! If you don't have any change, you can run right down to the restaurant and get some. And that's final!"

Simeon hunched his back, looked away and was silent. Now she had got-ten into one of her crazy moods again! He forgot to smoke, just sat there with his pipe against his teeth.

But when she got no answer, she came nearer, and there was a mighty power in the figure which bent over him. "Now I want to know. Do you have the money or don't you?"

"Haven't you gotten whatever you needed before?"

"I certainly have!" Anna Katrina began to laugh. Her laughter was hard and gusted as cold as the north wind which whistled around the eaves. "Well, don't say I didn't warn you!" she added ominously and began to wash the dishes.

Nothing more was said between them that evening, either on that subject or any other. Simeon filled his pipe one more time, although it was against his better judgement to smoke two pipes after supper. Anna Katrina washed the dishes and put them away, wiped up around the stove and was finished. And after awhile when they went to bed they were both as unwavering in their decision as before. She, that tomorrow she would march around the altar like the others, no matter what Simeon and Paul had to say about it. He, that such newfangled nonsense would never take hold in their house no matter how long they lived in town. For over thirty-five years he had offered whatever should be offered—and that's the way it would be in the future as well!

II

The pair of them slept heavily and uneasily that night. They had helped themselves generously to the lutefisk, now it seemed to press down on them, making them feel weak, but at the same time giving them no rest. Unpleasant dreams came and went, shining strangely in the darkness.

Simeon twisted and turned for a long time. And each time he became firmer in his decision, his heart became even harder. There would be no newfangled notions here. *No, sir,* he was still the master in his own house, thank goodness! He thought of many possible solutions, found one which might do, his eyelids became heavy, and he fell asleep before he knew it.

It took longer for her, she dozed off, but it didn't last long, and as soon as her eyes opened, her anger flared up again. She knew how contrary Simeon could be when he was in the mood, and what if he didn't have any change? It would be just like him, and then she would be in a pretty fix! Her hands clenched under the bedspread. Could she run over to Mrs. Carlsen tomorrow before church and borrow a few cents? But Mrs. Carlsen was a big fool, and gossiped about everything to anyone who would listen. Then it would soon be all over town that she had to run around to the neighbors on Christmas morning to borrow money for the offering!

Still, there were others besides Mrs. Carlsen? Yes, there were others. Anna Katrina turned over and slept for awhile, woke up again and didn't even realize that she had dozed off, for her thoughts continued on in the same restless way. Maybe she should get up and search among his doodads. She had used that method before.—Then Simeon turned over, yawned heavily, and pulled the quilt over his shoulders.—Well! He was actually lying awake keeping an eye on her during the night! Anger cleared her thoughts. She raised herself up on her elbow, and flattened the pillow with the palm of her hand, not even attempting to move cautiously. When she lay back down again, she fell asleep immediately.

Both lay quiet for a long time. But then Anna Katrina became fully awake when she suddenly realized that the solution was staring her right in the face. She saw in her mind's eye a fantastic, unbelievable picture. On the clock shelf, right next to the wall was hidden a cup, a rather pretty cup actually, with roses and an inscription "To Father" on it. A bridge for the moustache went over the top with a hole just the right size to drink through. She had given that cup to Simeon many years ago as a Christmas present. That had been in the days when they didn't have very much money, and while they were still in the habit of giving each other gifts. Now the cup stood on the clock shelf and hid something enticing within it. She had taken it down yesterday when she was dusting and putting new paper on the shelf, and had been astonished that Simeon had hidden so much money there. There were five ten-dollar bills in the cup. He had happened to collect this money the other day when he was down town, from Tobias Karstad, who had owed them for over three years. Tobias was coming out of the saloon just as Simeon strolled by. He was in such high spirits, that Simeon had spoken right up to him about the money. Tobias laughed heartily, slapped Simeon on the back, and said, "sure, of course!" He had been thinking of repaying those pennies this very day. He just had to go in and get some change. And Simeon had gone in with him, had been obliged to down a couple of drinks, but he got the money. Both she and Simeon were happy that day, for they had been anxious about this debt and had talked about it often.

Now she could clearly see that cup with everything in it staring her in the face. She tried to push the picture away. Should she do it? It would be possible. What kind of temptation had been placed before her? In the first place there would never be peace in the house if she laid a hand on Simeon's possessions. In the second place, she was not so foolish that she would throw away ten dollars on the minister, a stranger, so to speak. But the idea held on so stubbornly that she drew her hand out from under the quilt and shoved it out in the air as if to sweep temptation away.

But it didn't help. Another picture simply took its place, and that one wasn't the least bit easier to fight. She saw herself in that fine, town church, full of people in their Sunday best. Everyone marched up to the altar with their offering, even the smallest child who had to be lifted up in order to reach. She had seen that before on Thanksgiving Day, when she had been the only one to remain seated! Anna Katrina broke out in a cold sweat as she lay there and imagined herself sitting in the pew while all the others went up and placed their offerings on the altar. Here in town it was so much more disgraceful to remain seated. Well-dressed gentlemen even stood in the aisle and waited while the congregation moved forward. She had been the only one who remained seated!—No siree, she would not do that! Without even being aware of it, her hand came out and swatted at the quilt. Simeon grunted.—Yes, there he lay, the old fool. She felt now as she had felt so often before when a battle had arisen between them. She flared up in an impotent, helpless rage against the cruel fate which had laid such a cross as Simeon on her. She didn't think there could be a poorer specimen of manhood on God's green earth. And so scheming and nasty! When she finally dozed off, she slept heavily until daylight, well past her usual time to get up. Simeon was already rustling around in the kitchen. He had lit the fire in both stoves and put on the coffee pot.

III

A dull gray light lay over the desolate landscape. Outside the wind sang its heavy, unpleasant whoo-oo-oo through the endless, bitter cold.

Anna Katrina came out into the kitchen, but she couldn't bring herself to wish him a Merry Christmas. She was too honest for that. And he was so stubborn, that when she who had come in didn't say it, then it could go unsaid. She was scarcely to be trifled with today, the old hag! He went over to the window and rubbed the frost off to see how things looked outside.

She immediately began to set the table, glancing several times over at the clock shelf while she waited for the coffee to settle. Silently they sat at the table and ate their Christmas breakfast, both of them wrapped in thought. Afterwards he piously read the Christmas meditation from the devotion book. When he put the book away, they had still not exchanged a single word.

Then he put on his overalls, went out and took care of the cows and fed the chickens, came in again, and suddenly became very chatty. This was the worst cold he had ever seen in his life, it was downright dangerous to put your face outside the door! And then he wondered if it would be warm enough in church today, would it be bearable to sit there? There was nothing so dangerous as sitting in a chilly stone building. They ought to cancel services on days like this!

He had expected that she would make some reply to this, so that he would know what corner he had her in. However, she jolly well wouldn't do it. She stood over by the stove and cleaned a rooster for dinner and pretended that she didn't hear him. But uneasy glints sprang into her eyes, her lids blinked rapidly, and her cheeks burned warm and red. When she tore a thigh from the rooster, it seemed as though it had never been attached.

Then Simeon thought of something clever. He took the slop bucket and filled it with warm water from the container on the back of the stove, explaining all the while that their cow was likely to freeze to death. Something had to be done for the poor beast! He had tied a horse blanket over her yesterday evening and filled up the stall with straw; even so she stood there shivering and freezing, completely blue in the face. It was perhaps best if he stayed at home today and tried to thaw out the poor creature. After all, they had to save that cow!—Simeon chattered and puttered and drew his jacket on, Anna Katrina did her own work without paying the slightest attention. He went out with the bucket, came in and filled it again, and then stayed out for a long time.

When he came in at last she had put on her Sunday clothes and was ready for church. She had placed a freshly ironed handkerchief in her belt. The tip stuck coquettishly up in front of her left hip. When Simeon saw that, he knew which way the wind was blowing. He went out in the bedroom and changed, taking his time about everything. When she was so stubborn that she wouldn't take good advice, she could just sit there and stew!—Simeon stuck a match in his teeth and chewed, his eyes narrowed and took on a hard gleam.

When he came out again, she sat by the table in her hat and coat, paging through the hymnal. She stood up immediately and said, "Give me the money now!"

Simeon went to the corner where his overcoat hung, put it on and buttoned it up, pulled on one mitten and remarked shortly, "Are you going to give the offering here?"

Then she came towards him, powerful and threatening. "I won't ask you again."

"That's just fine then!" he wheezed, tore open the door and hurried out. He simply walked away from her, so she had to be the one to stop and lock the door and take the key. She stuck the key in her pocket, turned and watched him hurry up the street, and something painful bit into her. She started off, walked fast, then faster, and suddenly felt remarkably light on her feet. Simeon never looked back, never stopped, but hurried on as if his life depended on it. They were not going to wrangle over this any more!—A little ways up the street he caught up to a couple of other church goers, and was saved.—Just let her come now!

The weather was so bitterly cold that people hurried in as soon as they arrived. Walking down the aisle, Simeon was still in the lead, Anna Katrina a few steps behind. They were a strange sight to behold, he small and wizened, she tall and bony and large. They took their places in the middle of the church on the right-hand side.

It was nice and warm today, and pretty with all the lights turned on. There were flowers on the pulpit and altar, and a small Christmas tree on each side of the chancel. Shortly after they sat down, the organ came to life, soft music flowed out into the room and blended with the glowing lights and the flowers, creating a feeling of sacred peace. Today the choir sang both before and after the sermon. Anna Katrina, who was very fond of music, thought that everything was incredibly beautiful. But Simeon sat there and was out of sorts because they had turned the heat up so high that he had to take his overcoat off. They certainly ought to be a little more careful with the coal, with the big expenses the congregation had these days!

At last it was time for the offering. Two well-dressed young men directed the whole proceedings. Those who sat in the front pew on the right, went first, then those in the next pew as soon as the first was empty, and so on, pew after pew down the aisle. Seat after seat emptied. People streamed up the aisle, into the chancel, swung around behind the altar and came out on the other side. Every single miserable creature who was here today went up to give an offering.

Simeon took out his wallet and held it in his hand in such a way that she could see into it if she looked. He took out the half dollar which he had taken along for this purpose. Besides that there were only four pennies in his wallet. He shoved it over towards her, and he couldn't help smiling.

Anna Katrina didn't pay the slightest attention to him, she looked straight ahead. Suddenly she became restless. Her left hand came up, pulled the handkerchief out of her belt, and began to fumble nervously with it. And when one of the young men came and stood by the pew they were sitting in, and everyone there stood up, Anna Katrina stood up too, just as though she intended to go forward herself. Simeon became agitated. Had she gone so completely out of her head that she didn't know what she was doing? He fumbled with his wallet and tried to stick it into her hand, but she just made a sweeping motion behind her, as if she were brushing off her coat.

And so they walked up the aisle, she tall and majestic in front, he tripping along behind her. He wanted to talk to her, to reason a little with her. She surely wasn't intending to create a scandal in church on Christmas Day! But now he could only follow her silently. When they had gotten so far that the altar hid them, she stopped and fumbled with her handkerchief again, then took several steps forward until they were in full view of the whole congregation. But Simeon was hardly aware of that, for now he saw something really dreadful. Anna Katrina stretched out her hand and placed a whole ten dollar bill on the altar! Simeon could see the number in the corner as clearly as he could see the minister. This must be some terrible mistake, it was completely crazy! Surely he ought to pick up the bill! But there stood the minister nodding and smiling at him so beautifully that he slapped his fifty cent piece down on top of her ten dollar bill and stumbled along behind his wife. He felt as though he had been struck. He was so dizzy and weak in the knees, that he barely made it back to his place.

IV

On the way home it was she who walked ahead, and he who followed. But now she had acquired a youthful spring to her step. She seemed taller, and it wasn't easy to keep up with her. Simeon didn't even try. He needed to think things over before the moment of reckoning took place! He would really like to know where she could have gone to get all that money.—Hmm, hm, where could she have gotten it? There were some ominous aspects to this matter, that was for sure! When he got home, he didn't go into the house, but into the barn instead. Over in a corner lay a board. He lifted it up and took out three dollars and twenty-five cents in small change. Silently he took care of the cow and fed the chickens, taking his time about it.—It was best he thought about all this for awhile yet.—There was law and justice in this land, thank God, even against one's own wife!—His body scrunched together even more as he stood there and pondered his problem, his face became harder and grayer. Yes, sir—even against one's own wife it is possible to obtain justice!

Inside the kitchen Anna Katrina went about her duties as though nothing had happened. She didn't appear to have the slightest pang of conscience. When Simeon came in, he didn't even take time to remove his outdoor clothes, but went straight to the clock shelf, lifted down the fancy cup and counted the money out on the table. Just to be certain, he laid the bills side by side. Four there were, and four there remained.—He looked at his wife and cleared his throat, started to speak, and couldn't make his voice work. Simeon was a just man who had never knowingly done anything other than what was right and proper. And here was his own wife sneaking around and stealing from him even on this holy Christmas Day!

No, he was unable to say a word. Was there no justice in this world? Could our Lord let her go about here without the rod of punishment descending upon her as happened to those Israelites who returned from battle? Truly she went dancing about here right before his very eyes. She even looked happy! And now damned if she didn't begin to sing!—A strange urge to laugh came over him, but he couldn't quite get that out either, he just made a few gurgling noises in his throat. He felt so weak and helpless that it frightened him. He stuck the money in the inner pocket of his vest, hung up his overcoat, kicked his overshoes into the corner, and went straight to bed.

Out in the kitchen, Anna Katrina continued with her work. It wasn't true that she sang, she just hummed a Christmas melody which kept running through her head. Today she took her time with everything. The rooster she was cooking was old and tough, and Simeon always fussed when the meat wasn't good and tender. It was peaceful and quiet in the house. She hadn't taken the time to look at the last two issues of *Skandinaven* before all the Christmas rush. Now she pulled her rocking chair over to the stove and sat down to read. There were lots of amusing things in the paper, patterns and funny riddles and advice to housewives. They must have some really smart people to put it all together so well. After awhile she got up and began to fix dinner. She worked for a long time and even put on a white tablecloth as though they expected important company.

Finally everything was ready. The rooster was so tender that the meat fell from the bones when she touched it. Anna Katrina went out into the bedroom and announced that dinner was on the table.

But Simeon merely lay there and didn't move, didn't answer, didn't even bother to look up. Could he really be sleeping so soundly? She went over to the edge of the bed and shook him. Then something happened, something as unexpected as a bolt of lightning. Simeon stretched out his fist and poked at her so hard that she tumbled backwards, while he lay there and looked at her like a wounded animal. Then he turned to the wall and lay down again.

When Anna Katrina had regained her balance, she stood and stared at the bed in bewilderment, as if she were faced with something she didn't really understand. For thirty-five years they had fought, but never before had he dared to lay a hand on her. Her eyes widened, became round, and began to burn with a great light. Her nostrils flared. She drew in great gulps of air, as though she were short of breath. It cannot be denied that she even laughed. Once many years ago at a wedding she had downed a couple of whiskeys— life with Simeon had seemed so hopeless even then—and she had never forgotten what it felt like. Her body had seemed frisky and light. She had felt remarkably happy, and had been tempted to do something really silly. She felt exactly the same way now. And there was something so tempting about that furious, crumpled up figure in the bed, that she could not resist. She realized that she wasn't angry any more. No, how could she be angry, for she knew exactly what she was going to do and how she was going to go about it. Never in her life had she had a clearer head.

She went over to the bed and grabbed him by the neck. She had a large sinewy hand with unusually long fingers which could get a good grip. And now they really gripped! The other hand swept the quilt off him and grabbed hold further down on his body. She stepped back, straightened up, sighed, and there she had Simeon out on the floor. The hand on his neck did not let go. A feeling of revulsion came over her that she was forced to live with such a bag of straw. Thus they proceeded out of the bedroom, he ahead and she after him with her hand on his neck. When they came to the table she dumped him down in the chair which she had placed there. Then she heard herself say a few words which she had to wonder over, for they were well said, and she didn't know where she could have gotten them from.

"So!"—There was a little pause, for she had to take a deep breath. "Hereafter there will be but one flock and one shepherd in this house!—And now you will eat the food I have prepared for you!"—She still had hold on his neck. Tall and powerful she stood over him and waited to see if he would make any objections, but when she heard none, she let go and took her usual place at the other side of the table.

Outside it had begun to snow. The wind had died down completely. The snow came sailing down in large flakes, really fine, light Christmas snow. Now it was not so cold any more.

Making Bows

TED KOOSER

IN THE WEEKS JUST BEFORE Christmas, my father's store was busiest, its narrow aisles crowded with shoppers, its carefully arranged displays rumpled and disarrayed, and its floors slippery with melting snow. On Saturdays and when school let out in the afternoons, my sister and I helped out. She worked on the sales floor, and I made bows for the women in the gift-wrap booth.

The bow machine was set up in the furnace room. A single lightbulb hung over the card table upon which it sat. Behind my chair, the great gray furnace sighed and ticked, and piles of bald and disassembled manikins watched my back with wide unblinking eyes. In the shadows, bugs rustled across the floor, and above me the footfalls of customers knocked up and down the wooden floor. There I wound green and red satin ribbon into shiny bows that I dropped into a big cardboard box beside me. It was a job like those in fairy tales, in which a child is imprisoned in a castle and made to spin golden thread from flax straw.

Occasionally, my dungeon-keep would be visited by Otto Uhley, the store's janitor. He was a friendly humpbacked man whose nose was runny from first frost until after Easter, and who frequently dabbed at his upper lip with the tip of his tongue. Because the bow machine was in his basement, he looked upon the bow making as his responsibility and included me in his rounds of mop closets, toilets, and shipping room.

As if to inspect my work, he would dip his great knobby hands into the bow box and swirl them about. The satin splashed and sparkled around his thick hairy wrists. Although it was my responsibility to deliver the finished bows to the gift-wrap booth, Otto liked to do it for me. Up the narrow back stairs he'd go, the big box in his arms, his round face buried deep in the shiny satin.

Sometimes, his visits to the furnace room would be cut short by the appearance of my father, who occasionally fled from the crush of customers above to stand for a moment or two in the quiet warmth of the basement. Whenever he came down the stairs, Otto would hurriedly scuffle off to the other end of the darkness under the store.

My father was then in his early fifties. As much as he enjoyed storekeeping, there were times when he was gray with fatigue. He often worked ten or twelve hours a day. As much as he liked visiting with customers, there were moments when he would fall silent and stare off into space. There were evenings when he would drive the family in our old Plymouth out to the edge of town, only to get away for a few moments. There, a farmer kept a pen of sheep, and my father would pull the car off the road and stop. "See, children," he'd say, "how much the sheep look like the people who come to the store. Why, look! There's Dr. Mason's wife, and Mrs. Fitch, and, oh, there's Gladys Fitzpatrick, bless her soul . . ."

It was at such times, when the press of the store had become more than my father could bear, that he would stop in the furnace room, his shoulders sunken, his arms hanging down as if to let his responsibilities drip from the tips of his fingers. Though he would have preferred to stand there in silence, taking a few breaths, he would ask me how the bow making was going and would answer questions about how things were going on the sales floor above. Then, as quickly as he had appeared, he would be gone.

Except for these two visitors, I was alone. As the box filled with bows, my head filled with dreams. Behind me, the furnace breathed like an enormous and motherly old woman, pleased to have a boy among the dark folds of her skirts. Above me, the footsteps resounded with the spirit of giving. I could imagine women in rich furs, smiling and chatting, their shoulders sprinkled with new-fallen snow, their arms piled high with gifts, and upon each gift, one of my beautiful bows. I could imagine the presents spread about under the Christmas trees in their houses, each package lit by the winking lights. I could hear the rattle of the colorful paper as each package was torn open, my reverie enhanced by the rustle of the insects behind the furnace.

As the days drew closer to Christmas, the store became busier, and my box of bows was whisked away up the stairs before I'd had a chance to fill it. Sometimes, one of the women from the gift-wrap booth would come running down for it, thus spoiling Otto's opportunity to bury his wet nose in the gay colors. Sometimes, my father would come for the box, having passed by the booth in his endless rounds and seen that the women were nearly out of bows. The footsteps above me flowed together into a steady rumble along the wooden aisles.

In the evening, after the store had closed, my sister, my father, and I would pass through the aisles, finding the countertops in shambles and the floors a wet black swirl of grime. At the front door, waiting to let us out and lock up behind us, stood Otto, his nose dripping, his mop bucket at the ready.

And then, suddenly, it was Christmas Eve!

Late in the afternoon, I was told by my father that I could stop making bows. My work was finished. I shut off the light, put on my warm jacket, and walked snowy Main Street down to its end and back, enjoying the rush of last-minute shoppers, the Christmas carols being piped out under the awnings of the stores. I stopped to look at the animated display in the jewelry store window, tiny elves endlessly making toys in Santa's workshop. The cold air sang in my lungs. I hummed along with the carols as I walked back to the store. Christmas at last!

By the time the store closed that day, my father's face was gray and his hands trembled. He walked through the aisles, absentmindedly touching the counters, straightening the loose piles of unsold clothing. Our family was the last in the store. Even Otto had gone home before then, his arms full of packages, the floor left dirty behind him.

On the "Hold" shelf behind the counter in the gift-wrap booth would be several packages, left by mistake, forgotten, big boxes and small, all mysterious in their gift wrappings. Thinking that someone might come for them, my sister and father and I would wait an extra half hour, standing at the front of the store and peering out into the darkening street, the diminishing traffic. But no one came back. Finally, we loaded the mystery gifts into the Plymouth to take them home, leaving a note taped to the door: "If you have forgotten your package in our gift-wrap department, you may pick it up at the home of our manager." This was followed by our address.

By that hour we were the only people in the streets, the headlights of the Plymouth searching the ruts in the snow. In every window, a Christmas tree glittered. My sister and I sat among the packages as our father drove home.

My mother met us at the door, and the smell of cookies baking poured out into the cold air. It seemed that every light in the house was turned on. The Christmas tree stood in the corner of the living room with packages spilling out from beneath it. We unloaded the strangers' orphaned gifts and put them in the entryway, leaving the porch light on to guide their owners, should they come.

Soon, my father's older brother, Tubby, would come to spend the evening. We would hear him coming across the snowy yard, ringing a belt of harness bells that had been in our family for many years. When he came in, the cold night air slid from his topcoat. His gifts for the family, left all day in the trunk of his car at his office, were like blocks of ice. We set them under the tree with the others and sat down together for supper.

All through the evening, as we opened our packages, strangers came to the door to claim their gifts. Uncomfortable, shy, apologetic, they thanked my father for taking the gifts home. As they stood in the doorway, snow melted from their boots onto the carpet and the cold air flowed in around them. What would they have done, they asked, how would they have explained to their children? Each of them glowed with good luck and gratitude.

Finally, all the mysterious packages were gone and all of the family's had been unwrapped. Our family gathered in the living room, which was lit only by the tree, my uncle Tubby dozing in an armchair, my father and mother together on the couch, and my sister and I stretched out on the floor below the tree, looking through the glittering branches. It was quiet. Beyond the window, it was snowing. In a box in a corner of the room, the used Christmas wrappings rustled as they slowly unfolded. Near me, the shining bows sat in a little pile under the tree.

Family

CONSTANCE VOGEL

MAE TENDERLY REMOVED the Christmas ornaments from their tissue-paper nests: first, the tin peacocks that had perched on trees of her childhood. What fun she and her sister had had running around the house shaking the bristly tails at each other. Next, three green felt trolls with googly eyes her daughter, Gwen, had made in kindergarten. A tiny red sled like the one little Roger once had, lodged in a corner of the box. She remembered him sitting at the top of the sled hill lifting his mittened hands and shouting, "Push me, Mommy, push me."

This year tree trimming seemed like a chore. Each time she clipped a peacock on a branch, it fell forward. Something had eaten a hole in the felt of one of the trolls. And most important, for the first time Gwen and little Roger weren't coming home.

"We're going to Jack's parents for Christmas," Gwen had explained. "Next year it'll be your turn to have us." Next year I could be dead, Mae thought.

Little Roger's new girlfriend, Nikki, hadn't even held out hope for next year. She didn't celebrate holidays, and little Roger was so enamored of the girl he would never come alone. Will this be the pattern of the rest of her life, Mae wondered. From now on would she have only a small artificial tree pre-trimmed with plastic ornaments, as her neighbor had? Cover it with a pillow-case and store it in the attic for the rest of the year? Though he left the trimming up to her, Roger wouldn't like that. And Mae could not imagine setting up something that smelled of plastic, not pine.

Every time the phone rang, she hoped to hear little Roger's voice, "Nikki changed her mind. We'll be there on Christmas Eve." Or Gwen saying, "We're coming after all. We'll spend New Year's with Jack's parents." She'd hurry to the phone, only to hear an unfamiliar twang: "This is a courtesy call"— discourtesy calls, Roger called them—or someone for Chuck's Auto Shop, whose number was one digit from hers.

On Christmas Eve the children's carefully wrapped gifts still remained under the tree like forgotten toys in the rain, until Roger said matter-of-factly, "Looks like it's just you and I this year, Mae." He opened the bottle of champagne, put a Three Tenors CD on the player, and Mae rinsed the dust off the crystal stemmed glasses.

Settled in front of the fire, he lifted his glass and said, "Here's to a Merry Christmas . . . whatever that is." Lifting her glass mutely, she wondered when Roger had become so sardonic. Just this year? Or had she simply overlooked it when the children were at home? They pulled their gifts out from under the tree. Mae opened hers first, a sweater she'd found in a catalog. Pavarotti's "O Holy Night" filled the room.

"You remembered!" she said. But holding the sweater up, she saw that he'd chosen the shorter of two styles, suitable for a ninety-pound teenager with a slim midriff. "Long lay the world in sin and error pining," Pavarotti mourned. She peeked at the bottom of the box for the return slip.

Mae gave Roger a windbreaker jacket he was sure to like because he'd tried it on in the store. "Just what I wanted," he said, feigning surprise. "O night divine" swelled from the CD.

Mae folded the discarded wrapping paper and rolled up the ribbon to use again. Roger sat quietly in front of the fire. She didn't mind his not talking quite as much as she once did, now that they had a new puppy. They'd picked up the German shepherd mix at the Humane Society two days earlier. The dog, yet unnamed, immediately chose Mae to protect, lying at her feet, following her around the house.

Hoping the champagne had loosened Roger's tongue, Mae asked, "What do you think of our Roger's new girlfriend?"

"What about her?"

"She's an *atheist*, Roger. In the picture he sent she seems to have a pierced nose. He says she plays bass in a band."

Roger shrugged. "So?"

Mae sighed. "And what do *you* think, puppy?" she asked, stroking the dog who had fallen asleep.

After dinner, Roger threw another log on the fire and refilled the glasses. They began to watch *A Christmas Carol* on television. Mae was glad to see the black-and-white version. She'd had enough of colorful scenes where children fixed milk and cookies for Santa and families cuddled together in jingling Budweiser sleighs.

Specters led Scrooge down familiar paths. When the Ghost of Christmas Yet to Come pointed to Scrooge's gravestone, Mae was reminded of an inside joke between Roger and her. She turned to him, said, "You'll miss me when I'm gone."

Roger usually responded, "More than you know, Mae," or "Couldn't get along without you." But this time he paused. "You'll miss *me* more than I'll miss you," he said.

Mae felt dizzy. Cold, as if she, like Scrooge, were walking on her grave. Roger couldn't have said that; he would never be so cruel. But there was nothing wrong with her hearing, and he had a voice that could reach to the back of an auditorium, if he chose to speak. While Scrooge's reformation played out, she waited, expecting Roger to say, "I was only joking, Mae," or "I'm sorry. That came out wrong."

But when Tiny Tim said, "God bless us, everyone," and the credits began to roll, Roger went to the kitchen to fix himself a drink.

Mae followed. "Just what did you mean when you said, 'I'll miss *you* more than you'll miss *me*, Roger?" she asked.

Dropping ice cubes into his glass—one, two, three, four, five—he poured bourbon generously and took a slow sip, as if playing for time. Seconds hung like icicles over Mae's head.

"What I meant was, you'd miss my cooking, mowing the lawn, taking care of the insurance."

"Nice finesse. You're good at weaseling out of things," Mae said to his plaid-shirted back, as they returned to the living room. "You cook because you *like* to, and you know it. It's your choice."

"I-cook-because-I-like-to," Roger repeated mechanically as he picked up the *New York Times*.

Mae opened her library book, *Family: Writers Remember Their Own*, read a paragraph twice, then forgot it a second time.

Slamming the book shut, she asked, "Is there *anything* you'd miss about me?"

"I like having someone to go out for dinner with. I don't like to travel alone."

"You may have to," Mae muttered. "I'll buy you a one-way ticket to the North Pole. The climate will suit you."

Roger turned back to the *Times* as if Mae had never spoken. The fire had burned down. Mae grabbed the poker, jabbed at the embers, whirled around, and raised her arm as if to strike him. But, sighing, she turned back to the smoldering logs and stabbed until sparks flew. Grabbing her book, she went to her room to read in bed with the dog, as she did most nights. Later, she heard Roger close the fireplace doors and plod up the stairs to his room, where he often worked late into the night reading college entrance essays.

ON CHRISTMAS MORNING, Mae awoke to a blizzard of angry snowflakes swirling against the window. A leaden sky. There would be no walking the dog, no churchgoing, just a memory-long day in the house. The city had not plowed the sidewalks, not even the street. Coming downstairs to the kitchen, she saw Roger at the table, drinking a cup of coffee, staring out the window. She jerked the pot out from under the coffeemaker and filled her cup with a splash. What is he thinking? she wondered as she sat down. "Penny for your thoughts?" would be useless to ask. He would make up something: the stock market, the weather. She wanted an apology for last night's terrible remark. He'd probably forgotten. Just like a man.

"Morning," he said. "I wonder how much has fallen?"

"Morning," Mae mumbled through clenched teeth.

The house was still so gloomy after breakfast she plugged in the tree lights. One string had burned out, leaving a large black gap at the top. No way would she ask him for help, Mae decided. Teetering on the top rung of a step stool, she began to unwind the string, but she couldn't reach around the tree to catch the other end. She tugged, jerking so hard the tree fell toward her, ornaments clinking. She fought to keep it upright. "Help!" she yelled. The dog ran from the room, tail between its legs.

"Need some help, Mae?" Roger called, running down the stairs.

"I could have used some earlier," she snapped, head to one side to keep from being stabbed by the needles.

Roger grabbed the tree trunk. "Why didn't you call me?"

"I wanted to prove there was *something* you'd miss about me," Mae said sarcastically. "So that when I'm gone, you'd tell people, 'The thing I miss most about Mae is her excellent arrangement of the Christmas tree lights. I've never been able to do as well.'"

Roger rolled his eyes, removed the light string, and rearranged others to fill the gap.

"So efficient," Mae said, sneering, as Roger went back upstairs.

LOOKING OUT THE WINDOW before dinner, Roger said, "Snow's really coming down. The Weather Channel predicts ten inches. Might as well open that second bottle of champagne."

Preoccupied, Mae didn't answer. Last night's remark had been coming back like an old greeting card to the top of a drawer. The dog, at her side, put its soft muzzle in her hand.

"Roger," she said, "we've got to find a name for the dog. What about Schatzie?"

"That's for a small dog," he answered.

"Goldie? Because she's worth her weight in gold."

"Too much like that movie actress," Roger said.

"Nefertiti? Bathsheba? Hilda? Beverly?" She ticked the names off on her fingers, but she lost Roger to *Newsweek*.

Later, setting the table with the lace cloth and ivy-patterned china her mother had left her, she called to Roger, in the kitchen, "We've got to name the dog *something.*"

Coming to the door, he waved the turkey baster at her. "Let's call her Rover and be done with it."

"Too masculine for my pretty girl," Mae whispered in the dog's ear. The shepherd slurped Mae's face.

Mae finished setting the table, walked into the kitchen, and collided with Roger. Startled, the dog jumped up and jostled her glass. Champagne fell on its head.

"Look what you've made me do!" she screamed at Roger.

He laughed. "You've just baptized your dog."

She glared at him, ripped a paper towel from the holder to wipe the dog's head. She wanted to throw her glass at Roger. How dare he be so jovial after last night!

SITTING AT THE OPPOSITE end of the otherwise-empty table, Roger seemed very far away. Mae formed a telescope with her hands, pretending to focus on him.

"Why are you doing that, Mae?" he asked, frowning as he made a gravy well in his mashed potatoes.

Hopeless. He's hopeless, Mae thought. No sense of humor at all. If only there were talking, laughing, as when the table was full of children and grandparents. Snow kept falling, heavy and silent as the air in the house. Mae remembered another happier Christmas when Gwen and another dog had climbed up a drift so high they reached the garage roof. She had that picture someplace. After dinner she would dig it out—something to look forward to.

During the meal, Roger kept refilling their glasses. Mae knew she was drinking more than she ever did, but what the hell, there was a blizzard outside and she was trapped with a man who wouldn't communicate. She decided she wouldn't talk until he did.

But soon, unable to bear the quiet, she said, "I wish Gwen had invited us sometime to Cleveland, or little Roger had brought his girlfriend home."

"She doesn't celebrate Christmas, Mae. Remember?"

"Fine. I wouldn't have said the word. Not once. I would've ordered out Chinese."

Roger helped himself to more stuffing.

She tried again. "Now that we've baptized the dog, we have to name her. Isn't that the way it goes?"

"Cranberries?" he said, pointing to the cut-glass dish.

"Very original, Roger. We'll have the only dog in the country named Cranberries. Sit, Cranberries. Paw, Cranberries," she said to the dog waiting under the table for falling food. "When she dies her headstone will say, 'Here lies Cranberries.'"

"Hmmph," Roger responded. Was that a laugh? she wondered. She could hear his jaw crack as he chewed. She slammed her fork down on the plate. "Damn it, Roger, stop stuffing your face and *say* something!"

He sighed, wiped his mouth, laid his napkin down slowly as if this were his last meal. Tipping the chair back, he steepled his fingers. "I've got the perfect name," he said. "We'll call her 'Family.' That way, if we ever *do* get an invitation from the kids, we can give them a dose of their own medicine: 'Sorry, Gwen, little Roger, we can't make it for Christmas. We're spending the day with Family.'"

Mae began to laugh, so hard tears fell. She choked, and Roger had to slap her on the back.

"Here, Family," she called, snapping her fingers. "Up, girl, up." The dog scrambled from under the table and jumped into the chair Mae was patting. She tied a red napkin around the dog's neck, heaped a plate with turkey, stuffing, potatoes, green beans, a roll, and cranberries, and set it in front of Family.

The dog looked from Mae to Roger as if to ask, "Is this for real?" She licked the plate until it shined, then slavered for more.

As they ate Yule-log cakes, they watched Family tear into a silver-wrapped rawhide bone. "I know what we can say to people who ask what we did today," Mae said. "We opened presents around the tree. Our Family loved the gifts."

"That's good, Mae," Roger said. "Or, how about, 'Roger cooked a delicious dinner for Family?'"

Glad to have his attention, Mae went on, "How about this, Roger? We'll say, 'We stayed home. Christmas should be spent with Family.'"

Roger smiled back, pushed back his chair. "I'm stuffed," he said, leaving the table.

Mae poured coffee and brought two cups into the living room. Roger was already dozing in his chair, his stomach rising, falling, as he snored. She curled up at her favorite end of the sofa and warmed her hands on her cup.

An Iowa Christmas

PAUL ENGLE

EVERY CHRISTMAS SHOULD begin with the sound of bells, and when I was a child mine always did. But they were sleigh bells, not church bells, for we lived in a part of Cedar Rapids, Iowa, where there were no churches. My bells were on my father's team of horses as he drove up to our horse-headed hitching post with the bobsled that would take us to celebrate Christmas on the family farm ten miles out in the country. My father would bring the team down Fifth Avenue at a smart trot, flicking his whip over the horses' rumps and making the bells double their light, thin jangling over the snow, whose radiance threw back a brilliance like the sound of bells.

There are no such departures any more: the whole family piling into the bobsled with a foot of golden oat straw to lie in and heavy buffalo robes to lie under, the horses stamping the soft snow, and at every motion of their hoofs the bells jingling, jingling. My father sat there with the reins firmly held, wearing a long coat made from the hide of a favorite family horse, the deep chestnut color still glowing, his mittens also from the same hide. It always troubled me as a boy of eight that the horses had so indifferent a view of their late friend appearing as a warm overcoat on the back of the man who put the iron bit in their mouths.

There are no streets like those any more: the snow sensibly left on the road for the sake of sleighs and easy travel. We could hop off and ride the heavy runners as they made their hissing, tearing sound over the packed snow. And along the streets we met other horses, so that we moved from one set of bells to another, from the tiny tinkle of the individual bells on the shafts to the silvery, leaping sound of the long strands hung over the harness. There would be an occasional brass-mounted automobile laboring on its narrow tires and as often as not pulled up the slippery hills by a horse, and we would pass it with a triumphant shout for an awkward nuisance which was obviously not here to stay.

The country road ran through a landscape of little hills and shallow valleys and heavy groves of timber, including one of great towering black walnut trees which were all cut down a year later to be made into gunstocks for the First World War. The great moment was when we left the road and turned up the long lane on the farm. It ran through fields where watermelons were always planted in the summer because of the fine sandy soil, and I could go out and break one open to see its Christmas colors of green skin and red inside. My grandfather had been given some of that farm as bounty land for service as a cavalryman in the Civil War.

Near the low house on the hill, with oaks on one side and apple trees on the other, my father would stand up, flourish his whip, and bring the bobsled right up to the door of the house with a burst of speed.

There are no such arrivals any more: the harness bells ringing and clashing, the horses whinnying at the horses in the barn and receiving a great, trumpeting whinny in reply, the dogs leaping into the bobsled and burrowing under the buffalo robes, a squawking from the hen house, a yelling of "Whoa, whoa," at the excited horses, boy and girl cousins howling around the bobsled, and the descent into the snow with the Christmas basket carried by my mother.

While my mother and sisters went into the house, the team was unhitched and taken to the barn, to be covered with blankets and given a little grain. That winter odor of a barn is a wonderfully complex one, rich and warm and utterly unlike the smell of the same barn in summer: the body heat of many animals weighing a thousand pounds and more; pigs in one corner making their dark, brown-sounding grunts; milk cattle still nuzzling the manger for wisps of hay; horses eying the newcomers and rolling their deep, oval eyes white; oats, hay, and straw tangy still with the live August sunlight; the manure steaming; the sharp odor of leather harness rubbed with neat's-foot oil to keep it supple; the molasses-sweet odor of ensilage in the silo where the fodder was almost fermenting. It is a smell from strong and living things, and my father always said it was the secret of health, that it scoured out a man's lungs; and he would stand there, breathing deeply, one hand on a horse's rump, watching the steam come out from under the blankets as the team cooled down from their rapid trot up the lane. It gave him a better appetite, he argued, than plain fresh air, which was thin and had no body to it.

A barn with cattle and horses is the place to begin Christmas; after all, that's where the original event happened, and that same smell was the first air that the Christ Child breathed.

By the time we reached the house my mother and sisters were wearing aprons and busying in the kitchen, as red-faced as the women who had been there all morning. The kitchen was the biggest room in the house and all family life save sleeping went on there. My uncle even had a couch along one wall where he napped and where the children lay when they were ill. The kitchen range was a tremendous black and gleaming one called a Smoke Eater, with pans bubbling over the holes above the firebox and a reservoir of hot water at the side, lined with dull copper, from which my uncle would dip a basin of water and shave above the sink, turning his lathered face now and then to drop a remark into the women's talk, waving his straight-edged razor as if it were a threat to make them believe him. My job was to go to the wood-pile out back and keep the fire burning, splitting the chunks of oak and hick-ory, watching how cleanly the ax went through the tough wood.

It was a handmade Christmas. The tree came from down in the grove, and on it were many paper ornaments made by my cousins, as well as beautiful ones brought from the Black Forest, where the family had originally lived. There were popcorn balls, from corn planted on the sunny slope next the watermelons, paper horns with homemade candy, and apples from the or-chard. The gifts tended to be hand-knit socks, or wool ties, or fancy cro-cheted "yokes" for nightgowns, tatted collars for blouses, doilies with fancy flower patterns for tables, tidies for chairs, and once I received a brilliantly polished cow horn with a cavalryman crudely but bravely carved on it. And there would usually be a cornhusk doll, perhaps with a prune or walnut for a face, and a gay dress of an old corset-cover scrap with its ribbons still bright. And there were real candles burning with real flames, every guest sniffing the air for the smell of scorching pine needles. No electrically lit tree has the warm and primitive presence of a tree with a crown of living fires over it, sug-gesting whatever true flame Joseph may have kindled on that original cold night.

There are no dinners like that any more: every item from the farm itself, with no deep-freezer, no car for driving into town for packaged food. The pies had been baked the day before, pumpkin, apple, and mince; as we ate them, we could look out the window and see the cornfield where the pumpkins grew, the trees from which the apples were picked. There was cottage cheese, with the dripping bags of curds still hanging from the cold cellar ceiling. The bread had been baked that morning, heating up the oven for the meat, and as my aunt hurried by I could smell in her apron the freshest of all odors with which the human nose is honored—bread straight from the oven. There would be a huge brown crock of beans with smoked pork from the hog butchered every November. We would see, beyond the crock, the broad black iron kettle in a corner of the barnyard, turned upside down, the innocent hogs stopping to scratch on it.

There would be every form of preserve: wild grape from the vines in the grove, crabapple jelly, wild blackberry and tame raspberry, strawberry from the bed in the garden, sweet and sour pickles with dill from the edge of the lane where it grew wild, pickles from the rind of the same watermelon we had cooled in the tank at the milkhouse and eaten on a hot September afternoon.

Cut into the slope of the hill behind the house, with a little door of its own, was the vegetable cellar, from which came carrots, turnips, cabbages, potatoes, squash. Sometimes my scared cousins were sent there for punishment, to sit in darkness and meditate on their sins; but never on Christmas Day. For days after such an ordeal they could not endure biting into a carrot.

And of course there was the traditional sauerkraut, with flecks of caraway seed. I remember one Christmas Day, when a ten-gallon crock of it in the basement, with a stone weighting down the lid, had blown up, driving the stone against the floor of the parlor, and my uncle had exclaimed, "Good God, the piano's fallen through the floor."

All the meat was from the home place, too. Most useful of all, the goose— the very one which had chased me the summer before, hissing and darting out its bill at the end of its curving neck like a feathered snake. Here was the universal bird of an older Christmas: its down was plucked, washed, and hung in bags in the barn to be put into pillows; its awkward body was roasted until the skin was crisp as a fine paper; and the grease from its carcass was melted down, a little camphor added, and rubbed on the chests of coughing children. We ate, slept on, and wore that goose.

I was blessed as a child with a remote uncle from the nearest railroad town, Uncle Ben, who was admiringly referred to as a "railroad man," working the run into Omaha. Ben had been to Chicago; just often enough, as his wife Minnie said with a sniff in her voice, "to ruin the fool, not often enough to teach him anything useful." Ben refused to eat fowl in any form, and as a Christmas token a little pork roast would be put in the oven just for him, always referred to by the hurrying ladies in the kitchen as "Ben's chunk." Ben would make frequent trips to the milkhouse, returning each time a little redder in the face, usually with one of the men toward whom he had jerked his head. It was not many years before I came to associate Ben's remarkably fruity breath not only with the mince pie, but with the jug I found sunk in the bottom of the cooling tank with a stone tied to its neck. He was a romantic person in my life for his constant travels and for that dignifying term "railroad man," so much more impressive than farmer or lawyer. Yet now I see that he was a short man with a fine natural shyness, giving us knives and guns because he had no children of his own.

And of course the trimmings were from the farm too: the hickory nut cake made with nuts gathered in the grove after the first frost and hulled out by my cousins with yellowed hands; the black walnut cookies, sweeter than any taste; the fudge with butternuts crowding it. In the mornings we would be given a hammer, a flatiron, and a bowl of nuts to crack and pick out for the homemade ice cream.

And there was the orchard beyond the kitchen window, the Wealthy, the Russet, the Wolf with its giant-sized fruit, and an apple romantically called the Northern Spy as if it were a suspicious character out of the Civil War.

All families had their special Christmas food. Ours was called Dutch Bread, made from a dough halfway between bread and cake, stuffed with citron and every sort of nut from the farm—hazel, black walnut, hickory, butternut. A little round one was always baked for me in a Clabber Girl baking soda can, and my last act on Christmas Eve was to put it by the tree so that Santa Claus would find it and have a snack—after all, he'd come a long, cold way to our house. And every Christmas morning he would have eaten it. My aunt made the same Dutch Bread and we smeared over it the same butter she had been churning from their own Jersey (highest butterfat content) milk that same morning.

To eat in the same room where food is cooked—that is the way to thank the Lord for His abundance. The long table, with its different levels where additions had been made for the small fry, ran the length of the kitchen. The air was heavy with odors not only of food on plates but of the act of cooking itself, along with the metallic smell of heated iron from the hard-working Smoke Eater, and the whole stove offered us its yet uneaten prospects of more goose and untouched pies. To see the giblet gravy made and poured into a gravy boat, which had painted on its sides winter scenes of boys sliding and deer bounding over snow, is the surest way to overeat its swimming richness.

The warning for Christmas dinner was always an order to go to the milk-house for cream, where we skimmed from the cooling pans of fresh milk the cream which had the same golden color as the flanks of the Jersey cows which had given it. The last deed before eating was grinding the coffee beans in the little mill, adding that exotic odor to the more native ones of goose and spiced pumpkin pie. Then all would sit at the table and my uncle would ask the grace, sometimes in German, but later, for the benefit of us ignorant children, in English:

Come, Lord Jesus, be our guest,
Share this food that you have blessed.

There are no blessings like that any more: every scrap of food for which my uncle had asked the blessing was the result of his own hard work. What he took to the Lord for Him to make holy was the plain substance that an Iowa farm could produce in an average year with decent rainfall and proper plowing and manure.

The first act of dedication on such a Christmas was to the occasion which had begun it, thanks to the Child of a pastoral couple who no doubt knew a good deal about rainfall and grass and the fattening of animals. The second act of dedication was to the ceremony of eating. My aunt kept a turmoil of food circulating, and to refuse any of it was somehow to violate the elevated nature of the day. We were there not only to celebrate a fortunate event for mankind but also to recognize that suffering is a natural lot of men—and to consume the length and breadth of that meal was to suffer! But we all faced the ordeal with courage. Uncle Ben would let out his belt—a fancy western belt with steer heads and silver buckle—with a snap and a sigh. The women managed better by always getting up from the table and trotting to the kitchen sink or the Smoke Eater or outdoors for some item left in the cold. The men sat there grimly enduring the glory of their appetites.

After dinner, late in the afternoon, the women would make despairing gestures toward the dirty dishes and scoop up hot water from the reservoir at the side of the range. The men would go to the barn and look after the livestock. My older cousin would take his new .22 rifle and stalk out across the pasture with the remark, "I saw that fox just now looking for his Christmas goose." Or sleds would be dragged out and we would slide in a long snake, feet hooked into the sled behind, down the hill and across the westward sloping fields into the sunset. Bones would be thrown to dogs, suet tied in the oak trees for the juncos and winter-defying chickadees, a saucer of skimmed milk set out for the cats, daintily and disgustedly picking their padded feet through the snow, and crumbs scattered on a bird feeder where already crimson cardinals would be dropping out of the sky like blood. Then back to the house for a final warming up before leaving.

There was usually a song around the tree before we were all bundled up, many thanks all around for gifts, the basket as loaded as when it came, more so, for leftover food had been piled in it. My father and uncle would have brought up the team from the barn and hooked them into the double shafts of the bobsled, and we would all go out into the freezing air of early evening.

On the way to the door I would walk under a photograph of my grandfather, his cavalry saber hung over it (I had once sneaked it down from the wall and in a burst of gallantry had killed a mouse with it behind the corncrib). With his long white beard he looked like one of the prophets in Hurlbut's illustrated *Story of the Bible,* and it was years before I discovered that as a young man he had not been off fighting the Philistines but the painted Sioux. It was hard to think of that gentle man, whose family had left Germany in protest over military service, swinging that deadly blade and yelling in a cavalry charge. But he had done just that, in some hard realization that sometimes the way to have peace and a quiet life on a modest farm was to go off and fight for them.

And now those bells again as the horses, impatient from their long standing in the barn, stamped and shook their harness, my father holding them back with a soft clucking in his throat and a hard pull on the reins. The smell of wood smoke flavoring the air in our noses, the cousins shivering with cold, "Good-bye, good-bye," called out from everyone, and the bobsled would move off, creaking over the frost-brittle snow. All of us, my mother included, would dig down in the straw and pull the buffalo robes up to our chins. As the horses settled into a steady trot, the bells gently chiming in their rhythmical beat, we would fall half asleep, the hiss of the runners comforting. As we looked up at the night sky through half-closed eyelids, the constant bounce and swerve of the runners would seem to shake the little stars as if they would fall into our laps. But that one great star in the East never wavered. Nothing could shake it from the sky as we drifted home on Christmas.

The Shop

JOSEPH M. DITTA

CHRISTMAS IS A SLUSHY season, but for most people the holidays make up for the outward cold and damp by adding gaiety and warmth to the heart. The season's lights and garlands transform Main Street at night into a glittering promenade. Children love the atmosphere, though they lack the nostalgia that moves their parents, many of whom were born here, like their own parents, and can remember the glittering town in former days.

What had kept the town from disappearing was its core of residents whose families could trace their histories back to the territorial days. These were numerous enough to make a difference, for they seldom left. Such families took pride in their having stuck it out through the awful years of depression and drought, and they took pride in what was passed on to them and educated their children to be receivers of this heritage. But people have always come to the town in a slow trickle, for a whole world of reasons, and some stuck. Most didn't. But over time the town had grown. When it reached a respectable population of some fourteen thousand, it acquired the necessary critical mass to suddenly grow faster.

Fourteen thousand people with money in their pockets, especially at Christmas, may not be an economic magnet big enough to attract department stores like Dayton's or Younkers—megastores that ply the Midwest—but it is magnet enough to draw in the more modest second-tier stores like Kmart and Shopko. And so, these came and anchored the town—Shopko in the north, Kmart in the south—and like little economic fiefdoms, each lorded over its banner-crowded realm, having gathered to itself a host of smaller concerns —hamburger joints, used-car lots, gas stations, gift shops, antique stores, roadside Christmas-tree stands in winter and produce stands in late summer and fall (tomatoes, melons, corn, squash), motels, cafés, arcades—all the sorts of things that attract people to and keep them moving around the area.

It is a familiar story, this pattern of growth, with consequences that are also familiar—the old settled merchants on Main Street who knew their customers by name and knew their histories, who sold on credit based on trust, and who prospered in proportion as the people did and suffered declines in the same proportion—these began to see their ways of life uprooted and transformed and had to find new ways of doing business or die. Many closed up their shops, so that for quite a while Main Street was a dead zone, with empty buildings announcing sadly to passersby the fates of many a longtime resident. The Christmas season was often a time of pain, when the cold and slush were all the heart had to feed on.

There was one shop on Main Street, however, that remained unchanged. It was located at the extreme south end, in the most disreputable neighborhood of the town, sandwiched between two seedy bars, which were, perhaps, responsible for the atmosphere in that area of disreputability. This shop was unchanged, for it alone, in that town, specialized in trading with the destitute, exchanging money for lost hopes and dead dreams, selling to the same a woman's fallen world in the pathetic circle of a diamond ring, purchasing for airy nothing a young—or not so young—man's disillusioned attempt at independent living, exchanging, in the dimness of a clustered corner, for some glinting valuable a Smith & Wesson, a cloud of emotional fatigue hanging in the exchanger's face, only the eyes alive to whatever burned in the breast. In this shop, the holidays were more a time of heartache than of joy.

This shabby shop did not change, for the people from whom and to whom it bought and sold are always with us, and the economic development that swept over the larger world, and thus swept up in the process our little town, had no effect on these—the fallen, the cast-outs, the runaways, the down-and-outers, the dreamers with golden rings in need of fifty bucks.

And now, after the turn of the century, when new ways of commerce are making large incursions into the snowy gay fiefdoms of the north and south, this little shop, adding to its regular stores shelves packed with electronic goods, still plies, as always, its regular trade, its customers as furtive as they have always been. The family of its proprietor, the Wahls—out of the country around Stockholm—is one of the town's oldest, a family that has always been marginal, always tainted by a certain sordidness in the makeup of its men, and always uninvited. The present Wahl—named, euphoniously, Warren —is a widower, over fifty, whose only daughter left the family years ago. He is a tall, spare man with long blond hair turning gray, large, droopy eyes, and a full, graying beard.

If you came in out of the cold, you would see this man sitting on a stool behind a counter of glass cases, whose two sixty-watt bulbs, one at each end, illuminate the entire store as well as the watches and rings, necklaces, bracelets, leather wallets, gold pens and pencils, earrings, belt buckles, snakeskins, tie tacs, pocketknives, and other belongings dearly purchased in the sweat of the brow and traded for coin enough to buy a bus ticket or fill a car with gas, their owners never to return to redeem what they had parted with. As you entered, old Warren's droopy eyes would fasten upon you, and you would see in them the recognition of life's pathos, and the sympathy that always said, "We can do business."

On this occasion, the person who had poked her head in the door was the aforementioned daughter, herself a runaway, long ago having settled differences between herself and her parents by making out for the coast, where she found work and marriage and hardship and degradation and tragedy enough to fill many an hour recounting. She had been hardened by experiences her father could not imagine and was now coming home to start anew in the town of her birth. She came in the holiday season the better to reconcile with him, for he was the sole reason for her homecoming. She was, for her part, ready to make peace and hoped the many years of absence had worked their balm in him. She shut the door behind her but stood in the musty dimness of the entrance, awaiting a sign of recognition.

This came after a few moments during which father and daughter each took the measure of the other. He knew when she stepped in that she wasn't one of the people who typically seek his services. She was expensively dressed, wearing a dark full-length coat over tan woolen slacks, a gay colored silk scarf around her neck and throat, and her short, wavy blond hair speaking of salon styling. At first he stared, wondering who she was and why she might have come in, but the surprise gave way to recognition, and his face hardened. He said, finally, "Ahhh, you didn't come all this way after all this time just to visit me."

"Yes, I did," she affirmed, and walked in, stopping at the counter in front of him.

"Well," he said, uncertainly, suspiciously, "you look good."

"You look the same, a little gray now."

"Nooo, a lot gray now. A lot you care, anyway. Don't say you do or I'll get angry, and I won't be responsible for what I'll do."

"I don't want to make you angry."

"Why have you come?"

"To stay."

"To stay? You mean you're coming home? Moving in?"

"Not in on you, if that's what you mean. I've been wanting to come home."

"Home," he said sarcastically, "you can't come home. Your mother's dead, she's buried in the cemetery where her grandparents are—she's home. There's no place for you there. The house is gone. I live upstairs now, in the apartment. There's room only for me, none for you. The town has changed since you left. Changed a lot in the last few years. Nothing is the same. There's no more 'home.'"

"I'm not leaving."

"Suit yourself."

He sat down again on the stool, looking over the counter at her, his droopy eyes filled with sadness and anger. She couldn't tell by his attitude whether he was more angry or hurt, but she knew she would have to heal the wounds that gave rise to both those feelings before she could consider herself "home." He was, after all, the only thing that connected her to this place, the town where she was born, where her mother died, where he, himself, was born and lived and will die.

"I've been in town a couple of days, Dad. I've already found a place. It's one of those new apartments in that complex by the highway. I'm looking for work now."

"Fine, fine!" he ejaculated, as though he didn't want to hear.

"This is the address," she said, writing it on a page in a little notebook she took from her purse, tearing it off and leaving it on the counter. "It'll be Christmas soon. We should be together. We have to start somehow. You'll come? Tonight? Tomorrow? Come tonight. Please, Dad. When you shut up here, come. I'll have dinner ready."

He said nothing, looking past her toward the door. He did reach for the page and held it between thumb and index finger, like he had a butterfly by the wings.

"Why?" he asked, his eyes turning up at her face. "What's the point? Dinner? Like . . . like . . ." He didn't or couldn't make himself finish the thought or utter it aloud.

"I'm sorry," she said tearfully, turning and walking to the door. She looked back at him, his droopy eyes following her and looking sadder than she could bear. He was mumbling something she couldn't make out. "Six," she said in a raised voice, "come at six."

When she stepped back into the cold, the brightness of the day blinded her. She stood a moment to adjust. An unshaven man in blue jeans and a green down coat and seed cap walked past her and entered the Longhorn Bar. When its door opened she caught a whiff of beer and heard the sounds of video poker being played and the loud cursing of someone within, a certain prelude to violence, she thought. That night her father didn't come.

She thought about him all through the evening—her father, the pawnbroker, the dealer in cash. She thought about the seediness of the shop and the people who came and went from it, the suspicion, always there, that he fenced stolen goods, the dimness and furtiveness, the meager living he derived from it, the contempt people felt for him in town, especially the merchants. She thought about him because he was what she had run from all those years ago, because she was ashamed of him and of herself through him. Ashamed of his droopy eyes, of the stories he would tell of the desperate people he bought from or traded with or loaned money to, of the squalid look of the shop, which always filled her with the feeling that her father was a scavenger, a jackal who fed off the misfortunes of those life dealt most harshly with; ashamed of what she knew, through him, she was herself. But it all was different now. She had to make him know that.

Two days after her first visit, she returned to the shop. It was late in the afternoon. He was sitting, as before, on the stool behind the glass cases. He didn't acknowledge her. He just stared, with those sad eyes that made people —strangers—who came in feel like here was one who understood all. She looked across the distance at him and he returned her look, silent, as he would be for anyone who walked in.

Finally, she walked to the counter and said, "You didn't come."

"I didn't," he returned, and said no more.

"Does that mean you won't come?"

"It means . . ." But he didn't finish what he started to say.

Taking that as a good sign, she pleaded: "Will you come tonight? At six? I want to talk. We can talk, can't we? And have dinner, too?"

"Why?"

"I don't understand what you mean, 'Why?' Why, what? Why can't we talk?"

He was silent. He looked away from her as though it pained him to see her. She could feel it.

"You have so much sympathy for the down-and-outers who come in and trade their wedding rings for cash but none for your daughter?" She didn't want to say that, but it came, and the comparison struck her. He looked at her, unsympathetically.

"I haven't thought of you for ten years," he said, evidently having gnawed on his resentment during the last two days. "For ten years I have had no daughter. Why? Why was that? Because for ten years my daughter has had no father. She has not called, she has not written, she has not visited, she has not thought about me or her mother. I buried your mother and went home to an empty house. I had no daughter then. I have no daughter now. I have no daughter. No daughter. No daughter. None!" He had risen from the stool, shouting into her face, and then turned and went into the little back room which was divided from the shop by a black curtain that hung from a cord stretched from wall to wall behind him.

She was speechless; the blood drained from her face. She stood, staring at the black curtain, dry-eyed but overwhelmed with guilt for the way her father felt so betrayed. She knew she deserved it, and she knew, also, that the only way to get around this impasse was to tell him everything that happened to her during those ten years. But she had to get him to agree to listen, to come to her. She couldn't tell him here. The shop affected her now exactly as it had when she was eighteen. And he knew it. She could tell he did by the way he looked at her. His resentment was stirred by it, made much worse than it might have been. She took the notebook from her purse and wrote a short note, saying only that she was sorry and that she wanted to make up for the ten years and wouldn't he let her try? She tore the page out and put it on the counter and left.

The town had grown dramatically since she left. There was work wherever she went to look for it. In New York she had worked at many jobs, but the one she had taken to the best was as manager of a women's boutique. She knew the business well: the fabrics, colors, and styles that would sell and those that wouldn't; who to buy from and who not to, and how to make terms. She found work readily. In a week's time she had a routine that she knew she could live with and which would provide her a decent income. During the week, however, she had not been back to visit her father.

She thought about him every day. Christmas was drawing near, and she thought she should go to the apartment above the store one night, knock, and when he opened the door, just step in and force herself on him and refuse to leave. Wouldn't the season make him charitable? she thought. He would have no choice then but to listen. But she was afraid to do it, afraid her father would do something irrational out of the intensity of his feelings, in spite of the season. As she mulled over what to do, she had an idea. She sent him a present, a box of chocolates wrapped in Christmas paper with a red bow. She added a note, which read: "Dear Dad, I have not told you I love you since I was a child. I'm saying it now. I love you. Enjoy the chocolate."

She hoped that by asking nothing of him, she would arouse no resentment, and, in the spirit of Christmas, he would accept the gift. Then, after a decent time allowed to pass, she would send another. Then another. He would, by degrees, come to feel a little something of the old warmth, enjoy the gifts, and perhaps soften a little toward her, maybe, even, more than a little. This seemed like a good plan. She went to work cheerfully the next few mornings. But one evening, when she got home, she found the package on the floor in front of her door.

It had been opened and the note torn to pieces and then the whole thing rewrapped. At first, she was devastated. But when she thought about it, she realized her father was curious enough to open the package and read the note —the return address was on the outside and he had to know it was from her! He could have just rejected it and had it returned. He didn't do that. She took it as a good sign, even though it wasn't the sign she wanted.

So, the next day, she sent another present—this time a tie—with another note. It was returned exactly like the first one. A day after that, she sent another, with the same result. But before she could send a fourth, she got a note in the mail from her father that begged her to leave him alone. He didn't want to be reminded of her, he wrote, and if she really cared for him, as she said she did, she should stop bothering him.

That note was like a knife in her chest. She felt wounded to the core. Why was he so determined to hate her? She acknowledged her fault and begged to be forgiven, but he was cold and unfeeling toward her. She stopped sending presents. She hoped that he would write again, perhaps to thank her for not annoying him. But he didn't. Apparently, he seemed content to live his life as he did before, as though she didn't exist.

Days passed. She desperately wanted to reconcile with her father, but the prospects of that happening had now grown dim. She would be alone for Christmas, again. It was at this time that the nightmare of her life in New York began to torment her. Alone, she could not bear it. She wanted to tell her father of the marriage, of the beatings and the divorce, of the prostitution and the drugs, of the loss of her children, of the long rehabilitation, of the loneliness during which she had worked herself back to health, and of what her future might hold and how important to it he was. But she despaired of all this now. He wouldn't and probably couldn't help her. She thought of those eyes and knew there was no sympathy in them for her and never would be. He lived his whole life in the squalor of that shop, where sympathy was gold, and destitution was entered in his books as profit and loss, and seediness was the very atmosphere of success. It was her very own soul. She despaired.

On December 23, she wrote a last note, "Dear Father, you cannot know how I have suffered and still suffer." She sealed the envelope and mailed it and went to work. She spent the day in a dreamlike trance. On her way home, she resolved to do as she had planned. She turned off all the lamps in the apartment and plugged in the Christmas tree she had put up in the corner of the living room. Then she filled the bath with hot water and placed a kitchen knife beside the tub. Then she put Christmas carols in the CD and turned the volume low, undressed, and sat in the water, letting her hands sink to the bottom.

After a long time, when she was overheated and sweating, she picked up the knife and put it to her wrist. The warm colored lights of the tree dimly illuminated the bathroom. Bing Crosby's voice crooned at the threshold of her hearing. And once again, the blackness of the void troubled her heart. She thought of her father, of his resentment, of the life he lived in that shop, and the turmoil of her heart was subdued. If she could break through to him, she thought, they could rescue each other. Had he not been waiting for her all these years? She put the knife down and let the water out of the tub. When she crawled out, she felt so drained she went to her bed and fell asleep.

When the letter came on the day after Christmas, Warren Wahl didn't open it. He placed it on the counter, and there it sat all afternoon. It was a busy day for him. People came and left: a teenager wanting to hock a shiny new pocketknife; a young man looking for a wedding ring he could buy with his few dollars; someone wanting to sell a digital camera; another a computer. A young woman came in last, pale and thin, and tremblingly tore her engagement ring from her finger with a tearful jerk. She held it out to him, and he gave her seventy-five dollars. She swore she would be back next week to redeem it, but he knew he would never see her again. The aftermath of Christmas was filled with creatures like her. When he locked the shop and had only to close the lights in the glass cases before going upstairs, he picked up the letter and tore it open. When he read the brief lines, he sighed aloud and said, "At last, my daughter is home."

My First Christmas Tree

HAMLIN GARLAND

I WILL BEGIN BY SAYING that we never had a Christmas tree in our house in the Wisconsin coulée; indeed, my father never saw one in a family circle till he saw that which I set up for my own children last year. But we celebrated Christmas in those days, always, and I cannot remember a time when we did not all hang up our stockings for "Sandy Claws" to fill. As I look back upon those days it seems as if the snows were always deep, the night skies crystal clear, and the stars especially lustrous with frosty sparkles of blue and yellow fire—and probably this was so, for we lived in a Northern land where winter was usually stern and always long.

I recall one Christmas when "Sandy" brought me a sled, and a horse that stood on rollers—a wonderful tin horse which I very shortly split in two in order to see what his insides were. Father traded a cord of wood for the sled, and the horse cost twenty cents—but they made the day wonderful.

Another notable Christmas Day, as I stood in our front yard, mid-leg deep in snow, a neighbor drove by closely muffled in furs, while behind his seat his son, a lad of twelve or fifteen, stood beside a barrel of apples, and as he passed he hurled a glorious big red one at me. It missed me, but bored a deep, round hole in the soft snow. I thrill yet with the remembered joy of burrowing for that delicious bomb. Nothing will ever smell quite as good as that Wine Sap or Northern Spy or whatever it was. It was a wayward impulse on the part of the boy in the sleigh, but it warms my heart after more than forty years.

We had no chimney in our home, but the stocking-hanging was a ceremony nevertheless. My parents, and especially my mother, entered into it with the best of humor. They always put up their own stockings or permitted us to do it for them—and they always laughed next morning when they found potatoes or ears of corn in them. I can see now that my mother's laugh had a tear in it, for she loved pretty things and seldom got any during the years that we lived in the coulée.

When I was ten years old we moved to Mitchell County, an Iowa prairie land, and there we prospered in such wise that our stockings always held toys of some sort, and even my mother's stocking occasionally sagged with a simple piece of jewelry or a new comb or brush. But the thought of a family tree remained the luxury of millionaire city dwellers; indeed it was not till my fifteenth or sixteenth year that our Sunday school rose to the extravagance of a tree, and it is of this wondrous festival that I write.

The land about us was only partly cultivated at this time, and our district schoolhouse, a bare little box, was set bleakly on the prairie; but the Burr Oak schoolhouse was not only larger but it stood beneath great oaks as well and possessed the charm of a forest background through which a stream ran silently. It was our chief social center. There of a Sunday a regular preacher held "Divine service" with Sunday school as a sequence. At night—usually on Friday nights—the young people let in "ly-ceums," as we called them, to debate great questions or to "speak pieces" and read essays; and here it was that I saw my first Christmas tree.

I walked to that tree across four miles of moonlit snow. Snow? No, it was a floor of diamonds, a magical world, so beautiful that my heart still aches with the wonder of it and with the regret that it has all gone—gone with the keen eyes and the bounding pulses of the boy.

Our home at this time was a small frame house on the prairie almost directly west of the Burr Oak grove, and as it was too cold to take the horses out my brother and I, with our tall boots, our visored caps and our long woolen mufflers, started forth afoot defiant of the cold. We left the gate on the trot, bound for a sight of the glittering unknown. The snow was deep and we moved side by side in the grooves made by the hoofs of the horses, setting our feet in the shine left by the broad shoes of the wood sleighs whose going had smoothed the way for us.

Our breaths rose like smoke in the still air. It must have been ten below zero, but that did not trouble us in those days, and at last we came in sight of the lights, in sound of the singing, the laughter, the bells of the feast.

It was a poor little building without tower or bell and its low walls had but three windows on a side, and yet it seemed very imposing to me that night as I crossed the threshold and faced the strange people who packed it to the door. I say "strange people," for though I had seen most of them many times they all seemed somehow alien to me that night. I was an irregular attendant at Sunday school and did not expect a present, therefore I stood against the wall and gazed with open-eyed marveling at the shining pine which stood where the pulpit was wont to be. I was made to feel the more embarrassed by reason of the remark of a boy who accused me of having forgotten to comb my hair.

This was not true, but the cap I wore always matted my hair down over my brow, and then, when I lifted it off invariably disarranged it completely. Nevertheless I felt guilty—and hot. I don't suppose my hair was artistically barbered that night—I rather guess Mother had used the shears—and I can believe that I looked the half-wild colt that I was; but there was no call for that youth to direct attention to my unavoidable shagginess.

I don't think the tree had many candles, and I don't remember that it glittered with golden apples. But it was loaded with presents, and the girls coming and going clothed in bright garments made me forget my own looks—I think they made me forget to remove my overcoat, which was a sodden thing of poor cut and worse quality. I think I must have stood agape for nearly two hours listening to the songs, noting every motion of Adoniram Burtch and Asa Walker as they directed the ceremonies and prepared the way for the great event—that is to say, for the coming of Santa Claus himself.

A furious jingling of bells, a loud voice outside, the lifting of a window, the nearer clash of bells, and the dear old Saint appeared (in the person of Stephen Bartle) clothed in a red robe, a belt of sleigh bells, and a long white beard. The children cried out, "Oh!" The girls tittered and shrieked with excitement, and the boys laughed and clapped their hands. Then "Sandy" made a little speech about being glad to see us all, but as he had many other places to visit, and as there were a great many presents to distribute, he guessed he'd have to ask some of the many pretty girls to help him. So he called upon Betty Burtch and Hattie Knapp—and I for one admired his taste, for they were the most popular maids of the school.

They came up blushing, and a little bewildered by the blaze of publicity thus blown upon them. But their native dignity asserted itself, and the distribution of the presents began. I have a notion now that the fruit upon the tree was mostly bags of popcorn and "corny copias" of candy, but as my brother and I stood there that night and saw everybody, even the rowdiest boy, getting something we felt aggrieved and rebellious. We forgot that we had come from afar—we only knew that we were being left out.

But suddenly, in the midst of our gloom, my brother's name was called, and a lovely girl with a gentle smile handed him a bag of popcorn. My heart glowed with gratitude. Somebody had thought of us; and when she came to me, saying sweetly, "Here's something for you," I had not words to thank her. This happened nearly forty years ago, but her smile, her outstretched hand, her sympathetic eyes are vividly before me as I write. She was sorry for the shock-headed boy who stood against the wall, and her pity made the little box of candy a casket of pearls. The fact that I swallowed the jewels on the road home does not take from the reality of my adoration.

At last I had to take my final glimpse of that wondrous tree, and I well remember the walk home. My brother and I traveled in wordless companionship. The moon was sinking toward the west, and the snow crust gleamed with a million fairy lamps. The sentinel watchdogs barked from lonely farmhouses, and the wolves answered from the ridges. Now and then sleighs passed us with lovers sitting two and two, and the bells on their horses had the remote music of romance to us whose boots drummed like clogs of wood upon the icy road.

Our house was dark as we approached and entered it, but how deliciously warm it seemed after the pitiless wind! I confess we made straight for the cupboard for a mince pie, a doughnut and a bowl of milk!

As I write this there stands in my library a thick-branched, beautifully tapering fir tree covered with gold and purple apples of Hesperides, together with crystal ice points, green and red and yellow candles, clusters of gilded grapes, wreaths of metallic frost, and glittering angels swinging in ecstasy; but I doubt if my children will ever know the keen pleasure (that is almost pain) which came to my brother and me in those Christmas days when an orange was not a breakfast fruit, but a casket of incense and of spice, a message from the sunlands of the South.

That was our compensation—we brought to our Christmastime a keen appetite and empty hands. And the lesson of it all is, if we are seeking a lesson, that it is better to give to those who want than to those for whom "we ought to do something because they did something for us last year."

What I Took from Minnesota Christmases

ROSANNE NORDSTROM

BEFORE I MARRIED ROGER, he often talked about the many times during his childhood when his family had gone to St. Paul, Minnesota, for Christmas. His stories sounded like the Christmas celebrations I'd always wished my family could have: lots of people who enjoyed each other in a beautiful house with good food. "Usually," he said, "we arrived on the evening of the twenty-second or twenty-third and had a lutefisk dinner at my grandmother's."

"You had what?"

"Lutefisk. It's cod cured in lye."

"You're kidding me. Wouldn't that be dangerous to eat?"

"Nah, Rose, it's delicious. My father, brother, and I have contests to see who can eat the most. That meal is the beginning of the Christmas feasts."

"What do you do on Christmas Eve?"

"We go to my uncle's house. That's where all my cousins live. My grandmother and at least one of her sisters come also. It's a good thing my uncle has a really long dining room table."

"And you eat?"

"Reindeer."

"No. I don't believe it."

"Well, we did have it once. We always have Swedish meatballs and potatoes, loganberries, a vegetable or two, sausage, and limpa. Sometimes we have fruit soup, and my aunt really did serve reindeer. She's Finnish. Maybe that was part of her family's Christmas. For dessert there is always rice pudding and homemade cookies."

"Well, except for the reindeer meat, which I wouldn't think of eating—that would be like eating Rudolph—the Christmas Eve meal sounds pretty tasty."

"On Christmas Day, we usually have ham or turkey for dinner."

As a child I ate ham or turkey with my family, too, but the feeling in the air wasn't one of celebration. One year my mother took a photo of my father on the living room couch. He looked like he was taking a nap, but I suspect he'd passed out from overindulgence in alcohol. My mother had arranged a plastic Christmas-tree centerpiece with flanking candles on the couch beside him before she took the shot. I wanted to believe that the picture was hugely funny and that my father would be surprised to see it. I had a suspicion, though, that he would be angry, not amused. I couldn't figure out why my mother would do something that would make him mad.

Often my mother said, "Things would be so much better if we lived with family." All my relatives from both sides lived in other states and they rarely visited us. We never went to see any of them. I wondered just how my life would improve if these strangers were present more often. Would they be happy to see me? Would they pay attention to me?

In 1976, after Roger and I had been married for six years, he and I went to St. Paul for Christmas at his grandmother's. During the five-hour ride between Madison, Wisconsin, and St. Paul, I found myself humming one of my favorite songs from first grade, the one about going over the river and through the woods to get to grandmother's house.

My maternal grandmother died before I was born. She spent the last decades of her life in a mental institution in western Iowa. I saw my paternal grandmother only once. She died in a South Dakota nursing home when I was in fourth grade. I'd only met Roger's grandmother a few times and didn't know her, but she looked perfect for the part. She was short and a bit plump. She wore her pure white hair in a bun. Her eyes were blue and her skin looked soft. She did what I thought were grandmotherly things. She was an avid gardener and baked delicious cookies.

Roger and I arrived at her house on the evening of December 23 just in time for lutefisk. Yuck! Given enough cream sauce I can eat it, as I did that night. However I remain firmly convinced that a person has to possess both

Scandinavian genes and a childhood history of eating lutefisk as part of winter festivities to actually enjoy the taste as Roger does, as many in his family do.

The next day Roger's parents and his sister and brother arrived while he and I were out touring and shopping. On the business streets of St. Paul, I saw a few Native Americans and a lot of people who looked like Roger: tall, thin, and blond. I started to have a twinge or two of concern about the family celebration that evening. Would I fit in? Would I feel uncomfortably different? I can pass for tall but not for thin or blond. I have not even the smallest drop of Scandinavian blood coursing through my veins, a fact that was mentioned with family concern before Roger and I married. All his ancestors are Swedish.

I'd forgotten these little worries by the time Roger and I arrived at his uncle's that night. I stepped out of the car into a gentle snow shower and saw a huge brick house on a hill. Inside I walked into a hall-like living room with a fireplace at one end and an enormous tree surrounded by presents at the other. I glanced to my right and saw the long table in the dining room, which was set with china and crystal. Immediately I smelled Swedish meatballs. My mouth watered in anticipation.

After the flurry of divesting ourselves of winter coats and a round of introductions for my benefit, I sat on one of the chairs by the fireplace and was soon joined by a young man who didn't look any more Scandinavian than I do. He had dark brown hair and eyes and was of medium height with a stocky build. He introduced himself as the boyfriend of Roger's oldest cousin. He and I went through the usual where-are-you-from, what-do-you-do questions and answers, and then he slipped into stories about a folk-dance group that he and Roger's cousin belonged to. Soon I was laughing. My laugh was once described to me as operatic. It is not quiet. I realized it was by far the loudest noise in the room, and I remembered that I'd been worried that morning about feeling different and not fitting in. Next I noticed that I was the only young woman in the room who wasn't wearing a long skirt. I had on a dress that came to just below my knees. From then on I became more of an observer than a participant. All evening I kept thinking that everything looked as wonderful as I'd imagined it when I heard Roger's stories: big, beautiful house, a roaring fire, a tree with a treasure trove of wrapped presents, beautiful linen and crystal for delicious food, and generations of a large family gathered to celebrate. But these weren't my people. I didn't look like them. When I felt comfortable, I laughed more and talked more than any three or four of them together. I was close to my daydream wishes for a happy family Christmas, but I wasn't quite there.

After a noon dinner on Christmas Day, all of the cousins and great-aunts and uncles, with some of their families, started coming to Roger's grand-mother's. A three- or four-year-old girl joined me on the living room couch. She wanted someone to color with her. While I drew, I looked around the large living room. Roger and several of his cousins were standing or sitting by a card table working a jigsaw puzzle. They were quiet. His father, uncle, and one cousin were reading newspapers, holding them in front of their bodies so that it looked like there were three newspapers with legs in the chairs next to the fireplace. Roger's brother and some other cousins were on the sunporch play-ing Scrabble, a game that only got noisy during arguments about the exis-tence of certain words. There were women sitting at the dining room table. Their voices were soft and unanimated. I colored until my eyelids had drifted to an almost closed position. I excused myself to go upstairs for a long win-ter's nap. As I flung a comforter across my shoulders, I thought these people could all use a shot and a beer. I fell asleep before I considered that it was shots and beers that had ruined so many of my childhood holidays.

The women at the dining room table may have been discussing Roger's grandmother. She was in her late eighties and lived with an unmarried sister in her early nineties. The house was the one Roger's grandfather had brought her to after their wedding. Some part of the family had decided these two were no longer able to handle life in a house on their own. To my eyes, both of the old ladies were in good mental and physical health. I thought it was cruel to even think about moving either of them to a retirement/nursing home.

I heard, "They can't take care of this big house. They're too old to wash windows and clean ceilings."

I thought to myself: Why don't you hire someone to come in and clean for them?

I heard, "The bathroom is on the second floor. Those stairs are too steep to climb up and down all day long."

I thought: Those stairs might be good exercise, might be keeping them healthy.

I heard, "It's so much work for them to take the bus to go grocery shopping."

I thought: Have one of the cousins drive their grandmother and great-aunt to the grocery store.

In my silence, I felt absolutely helpless. I could do nothing to stop the plans for a nursing home. I felt like I was among strangers whose ways were foreign. I did talk to Roger. "Do you think it's a good idea for your grandmother to leave her home?"

"No, probably not."

"Well, can't you talk to your mother about stopping this."

"No, I avoid conversation with her if I think it might involve emotional upset."

That evening I was back on the couch with my arms crossed as I watched each grandchild take an ornament from the Christmas tree until they were gone. Roger got a butterfly, an airplane, an elf on a swing, and a clear glass ball. Some of the cousins shed tears. There would never be another Christmas at grandmother's house. Well you have your own selves to thank for that, I thought.

A DECADE PASSED. Roger and I moved from Madison to Chicago. He and I were nearing our forties. His grandmother had died. His father had retired. Both his sister and brother had graduated from college. His brother went on to Lutheran seminary and married. After ordination, he and his wife and year-old son moved to Clarissa, Minnesota, a small town (population 663) in the northwest corner of the state. There they had another child, a girl.

ROGER AND I MADE plans in 1987 to drive to Clarissa for Christmas with his brother's family. We drove through Racine, Wisconsin, to pick up Roger's parents. From there it is about seven hours to the Twin Cities, and then another two and a half to Clarissa. I didn't know any songs to hum to myself. The words would have gone like this. Do you really want to do this? Are you sure? Are you sure?

I had concerns. To begin with, Roger and I had already been to Clarissa a couple of years earlier, a summertime visit. I grew up listening to my mother's stories about growing up during the Depression in the poorest family in a small town in western Iowa. At least once in every story, she made the point that small towns were purely awful places to live. The smallest place I've lived in had a population of eighty thousand, so I couldn't judge if my small-town opinions matched my mother's. I never did expect much from tiny, out-of-the-way places. I always hoped they'd at least be cute.

Clarissa wasn't even that. The main street had a grocery store, meat market, bakery, hardware store, drugstore, café, and post office. Not one of those buildings was quaint or even attractive. The park was a rectangle of grass stuck between the café and post office. It didn't have a white bandstand or a landscaping of native grasses and summer flowers. There was a swing set and other children's equipment and a memorial to the town's war dead. This town of almost seven hundred people had seven churches. My first thought was, I bet a lot of the farmers around here drink way too much; they probably beat their wives and children. Then I wondered where people got books. I didn't see a library, not even a video store. I tried to imagine living in such a bleak place. How many books would I need to get through a week? A month? As far as I could tell, the nearest bookstore was at least thirty miles away.

I was concerned about spending Christmas in the house of a Lutheran minister. It's true that he was also Roger's brother, but he was nine years younger. He and Roger weren't exactly close. I found his wife easy to talk to, but she and I didn't have a lot in common. She liked being a mom. I'd never wanted children and had always thought of motherhood as a state to be avoided at all costs. She had grown up in a small town in North Dakota and seemed sweet and wholesome. While I didn't think of myself as dissolute, I had an edge that didn't bring the word *sweet* to mind. She was religious and I definitely wasn't. Oh, well.

My biggest concern was about spending several days in the company of Roger's parents. Whenever Roger and I were around them, I felt like everything I said and did was judged harshly. It also seemed like Roger disappeared. I could see his body, could watch him move and make polite conversation, but any connection I felt between us ceased to exist. Years later my sister-in-law told me about a weekend with her in-laws that left her feeling bereft. She told Roger's brother, "I don't know what goes on inside you when we are with your parents, but you don't act like the man I know and love. I can't reach you. I hate it." Me, too. I always hated that feeling, plus I always worried that it happened because I was loud, opinionated, and emotional.

As Roger and I drove his parents north, I wondered if any of us would have a merry Christmas. When Clarissa was still two and a half hours away, the sky went from twilight to dark. Little gusts of snow blew across empty fields and the highway. Had that been my first trip to Clarissa, I'd have been upset about missing scenery, but I knew from my previous trip that what I couldn't see was open land with few trees and fewer buildings.

Nighttime hid the plain little main street. The parsonage was a large house with multipaned windows. Light poured out of each one. We entered from a side door into a warm kitchen. Every inch of counter space and most of the table was covered with cookies and other seasonal delights. "Are you having a party tonight?" I asked my sister-in-law.

"Nah," she shrugged, "it's just that everybody brings the minister treats."

The next morning, December 24, we woke to a light snow. All during the day, church members stopped by bearing gifts. That evening we had a traditional Scandinavian Christmas dinner sans lutefisk but with lefse (this Norwegian flat bread looks like a tortilla but is made from potatoes and is especially tasty spread with butter). My sister-in-law's ancestors were from Norway. Shortly after coffee and cookies, Roger's niece and nephew started the great present unwrapping. Each of them got giddy with excitement as the four adults opened gifts at a more sedate pace.

Although I hadn't been to church in almost two decades, I decided to accompany Roger to the midnight service at his brother's church. As a child, I loved going to midnight Mass on Christmas Eve. Every year I looked forward to the transformation of the altar area: a nativity with almost life-sized figures in a wooden stable surrounded by undecorated pine trees. Poinsettias and candles hid most of the altar. The priests wore white vestments trimmed in gold, and the choir sang glorious music. Today I don't remember the Clarissa church at all, though I'm told it was small and had exceptional stained-glass windows. I don't remember how it was decorated. I don't remember what Roger's brother as minister wore. What I do remember is the part of the service when the church went pitch black except for the light of the Advent candles. That light was passed from minister to ushers to the first person in each pew, who passed the light to his or her neighbor until everyone in the church held a lighted candle. In that small church, in a tiny town far from others in the northwest corner of Minnesota, I sang by candlelight and felt it was a silent and holy night. Probably the beauty, ritual, and music of that service reminded me of how I felt as a child going to midnight Mass.

Christmas Day was replete with more people visiting, another huge meal, playing with the two children, talking, and napping. Around suppertime, the air outside was filled with song. Inside, we crowded around the open front door to listen to a group of college-age carolers. Light snow fell, and I was sure I'd fallen asleep somewhere and dreamed myself into a made-for-TV movie. It felt good.

A DECADE AND A HALF PASSED. Roger's father died. His mother lives alone in the house she and her husband finished building when Roger was a junior in high school. Roger's brother and his wife had another child, and then they moved to Iowa. Today Roger's brother is pastor of a church just outside of Cedar Falls. Since he moved to Iowa, he has endured two brutal battles with cancer. The last one ended with a bone marrow transplant. Roger was the donor. He and I are now in our mid fifties. We never did have children, but one found us about a decade ago. That child, Paco, is now almost twenty and has lived with us on and off since we met, even though no legal relationship has ever existed.

THIS YEAR ROGER'S BROTHER and his wife and their thirteen-year-old daughter left Cedar Falls on the morning of December 25 and headed for Chicago to see us. Their other two children are now in college and creating lives of their own. They stopped in Racine for Roger's mother. While they were driving south, Roger and I were next door. For the past three years those neighbors have invited others from five or six houses to join them for the holiday. We have brunch followed by an exchange of gifts. These are the Christmases I dreamed about as a child. We neighbors are good friends. We have social gatherings throughout the year. We take care of each other's houses and animals when needed. We gather for neighborhood political action if that's needed. We never lack for conversation, and my laugh doesn't stand out in either volume or frequency.

Around four in the afternoon, I began to put together our Christmas dinner. Before going next door, I'd set the table. As I do every year, I admire the Christmas Spode. I started with the rice pudding from Roger's mother's recipe. One cooks the rice in milk with two sticks of cinnamon, which ensures that the house soon smells of that spice. Then I got the meatballs, already made, into the oven and the potato sausage simmering on top of the stove. By the time everyone arrived around six, I was mostly finished. Both Roger's mother and brother walked in and said, "It smells just like grandma's house."

They placed the gifts they brought under the decorated tree. Four of the ornaments are the ones from Roger's grandmother's tree. This year his mother brought another butterfly, a close relative to the one already on the tree. Both were from Minnesota from sometime in the 1930s.

By the time we were ready for dinner, Paco had joined us. With him was his nineteen-month-old daughter. Her mother is Belizean, and she, too, was born in Belize. Paco's daughter liked the Swedish meatballs, which she insisted on sharing with her dad. He has enjoyed many holiday celebrations with us, so for him the meatballs weren't a new taste treat.

Roger and I sat at opposite ends of our dining room table. From time to time I looked at him and realized that, in the three decades we'd been married, his family hadn't been to our house on Christmas Eve or Christmas Day. I knew that it had probably taken me that long time to create the life and family I needed so that I could feel comfortable with what I've kept of his family's traditions and what I've changed. I liked the way my table looked loaded with Scandinavian food and lit by candles. Both Paco and his daughter have dark skin, which reflected that light beautifully. They are also both charming and outgoing, and Roger's mother, who sat across from them, responded with smiles. I find it difficult to imagine what Roger's brother, his wife, and children have gone through because of his cancer, but they were in good spirits that evening. Yes, I thought to myself, this is a family Christmas.

After eating our fill, we took coffee, rice pudding, and Spritz cookies made from Roger's great-great grandmother's recipe into the living room and unwrapped presents. All of us had fun, but the center of attention was Paco's daughter. At first she sat on her dad's lap and let him tear off papers and bows. Then she began to help him. Soon she was over by the tree, where she had room to maneuver her favorite present, a choo-choo train that she could sit on. When she pushed a button, the entire living room was filled with the sound of a train riding over tracks, clickety-clack. I was delighted to discover that particular noise drove Paco crazy. His daughter was giving him a taste of the feelings I'd had while enduring his noise over the years.

Earlier in the evening, my sister-in-law had mentioned that she found the sound of the el going along its tracks soothing. The el crosses over the street at the end of our block. She said it reminded her of the sound of winter wind blowing across the North Dakota prairie, one of her childhood memories. She decided to help Paco's daughter fill the house with the sound of trains. Soon the two of them were on the floor, coloring and playing with the cats' new toys.

During my first Minnesota Christmas, I sat in a living room crowded with presents and people among whom I had not one blood relative and I felt out of place. Even so, I was attracted to many of the ways Roger's people, whose ancestors hailed from Scandinavian countries, celebrated Christmas. Theirs looked and tasted so much better than the Christmases I grew up with. It took me a long time to bring what I wanted to the celebrations: smiles and laughter, joyful noise, people I was happy to see who I knew were just as happy to see me. This year I had it all.

Stringing Lights

KENNETH ROBBINS

ON A COLD BLUSTERY December 13, Daryl Sweardon climbs the nine-foot
A-frame ladder up the side of his 1929 vintage four-gabled house with red
painted bricks halfway up and aluminum siding covering the rest. It is his
home of thirty-five years, his respite from the car lot where he makes his living. It is his hobby. Only he hates the roof and he doesn't know why. These
are his thoughts as his hands achieve the top rung and he is contemplating
stepping onto the slanted roof.

> *Jesus. Got better things to—*
> *Told her, call the fellow, easier that way.*
> *Every year, hate this damn Christmas and Christmas lights.*
> *You'd think she'd have bought new ones this year but oh no, not her.*
> *Tradition, she says.*
> *Tradition.*
> *Tevya and his traditions, you think Tevya ever had to hang Christmas lights—*
> *Too cold for this—*
> *No sir, not him, lucky Jew bastard, they don't do Christmas—*
> *Damn string lights—*
> *The fellow says on his signs all over town, here to hang your Christmas—*
> *Good old days one light went bad the whole string went bad—*
> *None of this "Time to hang the Christmas lights, Daryl, it's that time, Dear."*
> *Need to reroof this whole damn house.*

Lookit, bird shit froze stiff.

Wonder how much the guy costs. A rip-off most likely, he and his Hang Your Christmas Lights, Dear.

Can't afford—

Slant's steeper this year maybe.

Watch the ice—

Watch the bird shit—

Too damn cold for this—

Work all week so I can come home to—

Tradition.

THE NAILS ARE already fixed. He finished that job twelve years ago when Kirsten bought the streamer lights especially designed for houses with eaves. Daryl is clever with a hammer; My Man with a Tack Hammer, according to Kirsten, each time he takes on a home repair task. Only this is not a home repair. It is, instead, a chore. A chore that has tradition tacked all over it.

Wonder what she'd do if I suddenly keeled over?

What kind of man would want to make money off old people who need Christmas lights strung?

I ain't old. Just crusty . . . like snow.

Keel over one day and then she'll say My Man Missed a Tack Hammer.

Can't believe that guy bought the Ford Escort full price—

Christmas does that to people, makes them do stupid—

Santa Claus tries to fit down this chimney, he'll be stuck until first thaw.

Damn lights're tangled—

Would you look—can see from here to nowhere clear as Elmer's Glue—

Cold—cole—co—

Folks that claim global warming haven't been on this roof.

Wouldn't have thought there'd be ice—

Knots, knots, knotsknotsknots—

Bet that fellow charges extra to untangle your lights—

I'll untangle his—

Wonder what she has for me this year?

Last year, what was it, can't remember—

Who in their right mind would buy a Ford Escort as a Christmas gift?

People turn stupid this time of year—
Okay, okay now, where is it—

"Hey, Kirsten—you got the extras down there?"

"Extra what?"

"You know, colored thing-a-ma-jigs for the sockets? I got a couple burned out bulbs here."

"How do you know? You've not plugged in the lights yet, have you?"

"Just answer me straight, Kirsten—You got any extra bulbs down there?"

"I don't know. I'll check in the house."

"Well, will you hurry? It's cold up here."

"If you had hung the lights when I told you—"

"What?"

"If you had only hung the lights at Thanksgiving. It was fifty degrees Thanksgiving Day, Daryl."

"Will you check in the house for the extra bulbs?"

The wind is cutting, especially after he is forced by his task to remove his work gloves. It hasn't snowed for over a week, and still there are residual drifts around the edges of the chimney and behind the pipe that vents the bathtub and other indoor plumbing. He contemplates the snow.

Should be in Florida—
Warm sultry days—
Santa comes calling in a red bikini—love to see that.
Who made that up, anyway, Santa down chimneys, couldn't keep a suit red long that way—
Sun's got no warmth today.
Shit shit shit.

THE COLD MAKES HIS knuckles stiff, and he slices the inside of his left forefinger on the hook. He sucks on his finger. It bleeds red. His finger drains his attention from the task at hand, and his foot, his right foot snug inside his L. L. Bean winter boots, so thick he can't feel the rough shingles underfoot, finds the edge of the ice that masquerades as snow and loses its grip. Daryl Sweardon is suddenly aware of the fall that is happening in spite of his fabled mountain-goat agility, the fall that fills his brain with—

Where's the—
Okay, okay, okay—
Grab the gutter—gutter, the damn gutter—
How much would that man cost.
Help the damn aged—
Not old!—crusty, like—
The damn roof, the damn roof, where's the —

FOR A MOMENT, a split second, his hands, both red with his blood and white from the cold, grasp the vent pipe from the bath, only it is old, as old as the house, and it cracks free at the base, leaving Daryl holding a cold chunk of metal, so cold it clings to the palm of his hand, as he slides dangerously close to the brink of the eave.

His thought, as he reaches the edge and begins his descent to the hard lawn below, is of Little Lizzy, his sister, twelve years his junior, who had—

Stuck her tongue—
Who in her right mind would stick her tongue—
Where's the gutter?
Stick her tongue to a frosty doorknob in the mud room!
Little Lizzy, I need you—

OVER THE EDGE, Christmas tree lights falling around him, the venting pipe glued to his palm, his L. L. Bean boots flailing, it seems a year and a day before he finds the earth, enough time for—

God forgive me.
Don't deserve this, break my back—
Sorry, Santa, next year I'll do better—
If we lived in Florida, there wouldn't be ice—
Or frozen bird doo—
Break my back, oh, Jesus, too old for this!
Wonder what she got me this year?

HE FEELS THE THUD and hears the cracks as the Christmas lights, now aglow, shower around him like falling stars: red and white and green and purple. His head whams the frozen turf, the yard he mowed religiously every week in the summer and raked each fall half a dozen times, the grass that is now a foot beneath the crusty snow.

Don't move.
Can I move?
Move? Where to, Florida?
No ice in Florida except in mixed drinks—
Kirsten will weep if she has to go to my funeral.
Too young to die. Too old to hang Christmas—

KIRSTEN IS THERE, hovering over him, his coffin already open and her husband's body stowed there, a smile on his ugly, unshaven face. A smile, an idiotic smile that's growing to a grin. "What's so funny, Daryl, you could be dead."

"I landed in a snow bank," he says.

If we lived in Florida I'd be dead right now, no snow to catch me there.
Love damn winter—
Wouldn't live any place else—
I can do this, I can—
She's got such a beautiful face!

"Did you break anything? Daryl, talk to me."

"Don't think so."

Jesus, I can move my legs.
Heard a crack—
Something must have broken, something—

HE STANDS AND SWATS at his coveralls, sending a spray of snow here and yon.

She holds her hand in front of his face. "How many fingers, Daryl?"

"It's Christmas, honey, not a time for riddles."

"You fell from the roof! You could have broken your back. You could have died, Daryl, and you're making fun?"

"No, not making fun. It's just these Christmas lights." He sees the broken bulbs lying in the imprint his body left in the snow. There, the broken slivers of glass, decorating the snow, send off their streamers of light reflected from the low southern sun.

"We're throwing them away, Daryl, right now."

"No, we're not. It's tradition, isn't it?"

"You're not going back on that roof, are you?"

"Not this year I'm not. Got to get my hand off this pipe thing first."

"Oh, Daryl, what in the world—"

"I'll never make fun of Little Lizzy and her tongue again." He wraps a long arm around his wife's shoulders, pleased that it still works, pleased that his legs can carry him without pain into the house he calls his respite. "It's just I'm a bit too old for this, don't you think?"

"Oh, now, don't you start."

"And I was wondering. You got the phone number of this fellow?"

The door closes gently on the frozen world, the Christmas lights lying like gems on the white, white snow.

First Profession

JAMES CALVIN SCHAAP

THAT I WHOLEHEARTEDLY agree with Missy Simpson's lecture about our oversentimentalizing Christmas, that I laud her efforts on behalf of our country church's nativity pageant, and that I know no one more determined to put us on the map out here—none of that alters my opinion about Missy Simpson: she's just not my favorite human being.

So I understand why my daughter was owly when I picked her up from church a few nights ago. Angela had to listen to Missy's lecture, a lecture I heard in part after letting the car run outside in the cold and stepping into the church, rehearsal having gone about ten minutes late. What else is new?

Missy Simpson is just like her mother. I can't tell you how often I've noticed those associations since we've moved back. You see some kid with a peculiar walk coming out of Casey's, you swear it's his father, then you remind yourself that you've simply lost an entire generation. That realization ages you even more. Like nothing else, I wanted to leave Chicago and come back here, but it's not always been good for the ego.

But I was saying about Missy that, like her mother, she gets her way by a force of character she claims she doesn't have. "Oh, what do I know?" she'll mutter, every other paragraph. But what's between the browbeating is a big John Deere with dual wheels. She's accustomed to acting on things at the drop of a hat, of simply plowing forward. She's great to have on your team; give her a half hour and she can change the world. Oppose her, you lose.

"There's an awful lot of silliness connected to Christmas celebrations already," she crabbed at the kids at the end of practice that night, "and we don't want to add to them." She had all of them—shepherds, wise men, Mary and Joseph, the whole works—in the first two pews for her address. "Did Jesus cry?—well, of course he did. He was human. Humans cry. Case closed. So this foolish little line, 'No crying he made,' is just ridiculous. Animals singing and all of that? It only sentimentalizes the real story—that Jesus came for us, for sinners."

I knew how our Angela would take that. For most of her life, she's thought *The Lion King* was the greatest story ever told.

"And let's remember that Jesus was born in a barn because, quite literally, there was no room in town." Missy pointed in the air. "Have any of you ever *not* found a motel? It's awful. Jeff and I were in Athens, Ohio, once, years ago, and we could find nothing—but that's another story."

Thank goodness, I thought.

"And Christmas carols in the mall? That's probably the biggest sacrilege of all—'The Hallelujah Chorus' as Muzak."

My daughter has no idea what Muzak is.

"That's why we have to be authentic—as authentic as possible—because we don't want to sentimentalize."

Angela is thirteen, and she understands the word *sentimentalize* no better than she does the phrase "the unpardonable sin." In fact, sentimentality has been her way of seeing things. I'm sure she rather likes hearing "O Holy Night" in Wal-Mart.

"And that's why we have to make the truth stick," Missy told them.

I thought her choice of words somewhat inappropriate because I knew what was coming. She'd given this speech before, I know, because she started a controversy the last time she suggested what she was about to push on the kids.

"Angela," she said, pointing at my daughter, "you live on a farm."

Angela, trust me, has never wanted to be thought of as a "farm girl."

"You bring us the straw—and some manure."

Angela would rather burn her Disney videos than be the kid responsible for bringing the smelly stuff from the barn.

"Shepherds were tough hombres," Missy told them, ranging back and forth in front of them like something caged. "Shepherds were lowlifes, and God sent his angels to them for a reason: because they were." Her face lit up. "That's the point of Christmas," she said, as if she'd just stumbled on the gospel. "He came to save ordinary people—not just kings and princes, but the lowlifes."

Missy Simpson didn't see me in the back of the church with the other parents. All of the focus was on Angela. Missy wanted a bit of manure in church. It was a big deal two years ago, when we first moved here, a big stink, you might say. But generally Missy Simpson wins major battles—even most of the minors. You volunteer a lot in a little church like ours, and you swing some clout; righteousness pays.

"We need manure on the manger. We need you guys looking like it's on you—the shepherds, the lowlifes. We need straw around the church." I swear she could have played Moses if Charlton Heston stumbled. "On Christmas Eve this isn't going to be a church, it's going to be a barn."

Angela, our daughter, was appointed by presidential fiat to be the manure pipeline, and I knew she didn't like it. She's not always been happy with our being here, so far from her childhood Chicago friends.

But there's more. Angela really wanted to be Mary, but Roberta Dekker got the job. On a scale of ten, Roberta Dekker is, I'm sad to admit, a nine to my Ang's six. Roberta reads with expression, carries herself in a fashion Bert Parks would admire, and has eyes to kill for. She gets, well, most everything, my daughter would say. So there was that, too. Honestly, Ang didn't want to be a manure-caked, cross-gendered shepherd when rodeo queen Roberta got Mary's song.

So that afternoon, when the two of us left the church, she didn't say a word, not a word, all the way home. Only when I pulled into the garage did her mouth open at all. "Whose idea was it anyway to move to the sticks?" she said before slamming the door.

She's growing up. Most of the time, my daughter has the sentimentality of a child, but time is pushing her farther along toward a world she can see is more complex than she sometimes wishes it were. Occasionally, she wants to hide. Don't we all.

We bought her a horse for Christmas, but there's no place to hide a horse really, so she's had it since Thanksgiving. I honestly thought there was a verse in the Bible that says "your young women will love horses." Angela is on speaking terms with Macintosh (she named it after a computer?), but all this schmaltzy *Black Beauty* stuff?—no way. Actually, I think she likes him, even if publicly she acts otherwise. I've been in the barn with the chickens several times and heard her talking to him. It's our moving out here in the middle of nowhere that irritates her.

Then again, maybe it's just the time in her life when everything irritates her. She hovers on a precipice of childhood, like the coyote in *Road Runner* cartoons, and a fall is inevitable. I remember the first time I took her to the dentist, and Dr. Lowell, a kindhearted guy, stood there in front of her and told her she was going to have to watch the sweets—take it easy on candy. She was six maybe, and she couldn't have put on a heavier face. But back then she had no sense of coulds and couldn'ts, no experience with the real meaning of the word *no*. Today, she does. She's beginning to understand a world in which some are rodeo queens and many others are not.

She's an inhabitant of two worlds really, and it's the mix that confuses her, like it does all of us. She could get along swimmingly in a world of light, and she could, like all of us, learn to negotiate if darkness were forever the shape of things. But it's the mixture that's tough. She would prefer that she not be the conduit for manure, especially when she was nothing but smudgy shepherd herself. She still would prefer her Christmases in Norman Rockwell style, even though she's beginning to know better.

We opened our presents in the afternoon of Christmas Eve this year. Mark is home from college, and Randy brought Lexie, his girl—but that's another story.

At Christmas my wife, whom I love dearly, loses all sense of perspective. She claims there are ten times more great presents for a boy like Barry, who's ten, than a girl like Ang. She may be right.

Besides, Barry's her baby. So this year, when Angie's biggest present was a real live horse given to her already three weeks before and far too big, of course, to lug into the family room and adorn with a bow, when her little brother looked over a range of Christmas booty that threatened to take over the family room, and when Randy and his sweetheart were forever embarrassingly stuck to each other, our Angela looked down at some tatted hankies from her grandma, a new Bible from her parents, and an Iowa Hawkeye sweater, and felt indecently shortchanged. She waited until the crumpled paper was picked up, then left the house in silence.

Now a word in defense of my daughter. It wasn't the lack of presents that got to her. She knew very well that Macintosh was hers, and hers alone. I'm thinking that what bummed her out was a lack of climax. A day after Halloween the march toward Christmas begins. Everywhere you hear music. Dozens of gizmos appear on TV ads only in the months of November and December. Christmas specials air nightly after Thanksgiving.

Angela, the child, lived in anticipation of "Christmas." And "Christmas" to her annually reaches its climax around the tree. That Christmas Eve afternoon, her thirteenth, the ritual of presents simply didn't deliver the goods. I really believe she wasn't as angry with us as she was let down by the climax of a drumroll that had risen to this very day and then simply fallen away in a whimper. That's what bugged her, I think.

We moved back to the open reaches of my childhood hometown for many reasons, but one of them, I know, is critters. I wasn't born on a farm, but we live in a place where there are far more animals than human beings, and sometimes even today I think I ought to quit my job at the bank and go to vet school—that's how much I love animals. Always have.

Missy Simpson wasn't wrong. On the acreage we bought out here beneath the broad prairie skies, we've got manure in all shapes and sizes. That was my excuse for leaving the house late that afternoon. If the nativity scene was going to grip us with authenticity, I'd have to collect the dung. Ang wouldn't. No way. So I followed her out to the barn.

When I got out there, I suppose I shouldn't have been surprised that she wasn't with the horse. I thought she would be, but she wasn't. I found her instead with the chickens, sitting cross-legged on the floor in her old fleece jacket and jeans, actually sitting on the straw, her elbows on her knees, chin in hands. My daughter is becoming a woman who is, in a way, no longer my daughter. Her shoulders have broadened, and even in that slumped-over position I could begin to discern an hourglass. If she heard me come up behind her, she didn't say a word.

We had been losing chickens, five of them in eight days—a couple of leghorns, a Rhode Island red, and then the one that really ticked me off—a Buff Oppington, a fluffy and fat brown honey of a hen, if chickens can be likable. Just exactly who was the murderer had remained a mystery, since the victims were hardly touched, just a plump hump of feathers, necks split. Coons we've had before, but a raccoon doesn't simply drink blood. I didn't have a clue about the murderer when I put out the box trap.

The first time it had happened, Ang had been furious, not because she likes chickens. Sometimes I have to push her out to get eggs. She had told me that if whoever or whatever was doing the killing would eat them, she could take it. "But just to do that," she said, unable to even describe the murders.

I was mad, too. When I saw that Buff down, I would have taken on a skunk with a straw broom.

Christmas Eve, early, as we were opening presents, the murderer had arrived and walked into my trap, and there he was in front of her, very much alive.

"What is it?" she asked me when I came up from behind her.

The animal was long, and blessed—graced—with glossy fur. It looked up at her nervously and paced back and forth, back and forth, like the king of beasts.

I couldn't believe it. "It's a mink," I said. "Good night, it's a mink."

"Are they rare?" she asked.

"Not rare, but wily. I never thought I'd catch a mink in a box trap. This one must be retarded."

"He doesn't look retarded," she said. "He's gorgeous."

And he was. His tiny eyes were translucent in a face that looked classic, Greek or Roman. Nimble and agile, his body flowed in that cage. Like a cat, he showed no expression, and his stoicism seemed noble. But how can I do justice to the beauty of his fur? He was brown, no chestnut, no reddish—he was mahogany, with a sheen of darkness over the ends of each follicle of warm, beautiful fur that, even in the soft yellow light of the coop, shone like a red planet. He was beautiful. He was, as Ang said, gorgeous. "You can see why people want coats," I said.

She was transfixed, as if that mink were a kaleidoscope. "Can we keep him?" she asked.

"It's no sheep, Ang," I told her. "You're lucky enough to see him. They're nocturnal, totally. I don't know what brought him in so early—must have figured the place was a piece of cake."

"You think *he* did it?" she asked.

"I *know* he did," I told her, pointing at the dead leghorn across the room.

"I can't believe he's a murderer," she said. "I won't. Why should he? He's too perfect, Dad. He's just beautiful. Look at him."

"He sucked the blood out of five of our hens," I told her.

Back and forth, back and forth, the mink ranged through the trap.

And then she said what was really on her mind. "I've been thinking, Dad—you know, the story—about what happened?" For the first time she looked up at me. "About what happened in the stable in Bethlehem?" She shrugged her shoulders, annoyed with her own words. "Seems as if you can't even say anything without it sounding like a commercial."

"What happened?" I said.

"That old story—I know it's silly and it's dumb and it's not in the Bible. You know that old story about how all the animals in the barn suddenly spoke at Jesus's birth?"

"Of course," I said.

And then she looked back at the murderer, the beautiful mink. "You think it was all of them who spoke?" she asked.

I didn't know right away what she meant.

"I mean, like cows and sheep," she said. "You know, they don't do nothing really but give milk and grow wool."

"What are you saying, Ang?" I asked.

"I'm wondering, you know, if all the animals talked that night," she said. "All of them?" She never took her eyes off that mink.

We were in a barn she didn't always like. It was Christmas Eve, and in front of her eyes a beautiful killer pranced like a prince.

"Who talked?—that's what you're asking? That's what you want to know?" She didn't say a thing. "I'll tell you what I think, Ang—even the killers got a word in that night." That's what I told her.

She nodded like someone who was no more a child, as she watched the beautiful mink move back and forth, back and forth. "It's really a big deal, isn't it?" she asked.

"Christmas?" I said.

She nodded again.

"Everything sings," I told her.

She brought her hands right up to the cage, without touching it. "'The lion lies down with the lamb'—isn't that right?—something like that?"

"It's Christmas," I said. And then, for some reason, I couldn't help myself. "You get it, Ang?"

Once more, her back to me, she nodded her head gloriously.

And that was my daughter's first profession, and it couldn't have come at a sweeter time—for her, or for Missy Simpson, who was trying to teach Angie exactly what she learned.

I put the trap in the trunk of the car, and later that night, after the stinky program, Ang watched as I let it out along a bare country road, six, maybe seven miles from home. I had this sickening feeling that sooner rather than later that prince would be back in our barn.

But later that night, when things had settled down in the house and I went out to check on things, I told myself that a couple of chickens was a small price to pay for Christmas joy.

It was cold and crystal clear and perfectly quiet out there in the middle of nowhere. Over the long hills west of our place the stars glittered against a midnight sky. It would have been a great night for the angels, I thought.

And who's to say, I'm thinking, they weren't out there somewhere singing? The snow between the barn and the house made a cushion that added heft to the silence and brightened everything for miles.

Inside the house it was Christmas Eve. But outside it was too. I swear, I heard music.

Julebukking

BETH DVERGSTEN STEVENS

THE DOORBELL RANG. My parents and I looked at each other and wondered who would be on our doorstep at this hour of the night. Christmas was over and New Year's hadn't yet arrived. It was cold and snowy outside and we weren't expecting company.

I jumped up and reached the door first. As I flung it open, a jolly band of Christmas revelers greeted me with "Merry Christmas, Beth!" I stared at them openmouthed. I didn't recognize a single person. Of course, with masks and nylon stockings covering their faces, that was the plan.

"Mom! Dad!" I shouted. "Come here!"

Slowly I backed up into the entryway and continued to stare at them. The strange-looking group huddled on our back porch didn't really frighten me. After all, they knew my name. But they didn't speak. They just stood there and looked at me through the open door. I couldn't tell if they were smiling or scowling. One of them bowed toward me. Several shorter ones waved at me. Then they shuddered in unison as a gust of cold Minnesota air blew snowflakes down their backs.

"Come in, come in!" my parents called as they hurried toward me. They motioned the group inside. I couldn't believe Mom and Dad were inviting these strange people into our house.

The group nodded silently, stomped the snow from their feet, and stepped into the warmth of our kitchen. One, two, three, four . . . soon there were nine people crowded into the small room. They stood quietly, but a few shaking shoulders told me they were people who wanted to laugh. At what? It was all strange to me.

Mom scurried to pile Christmas cookies onto a plate. Dad grabbed a tall bottle of something caramel brown from the "grown-ups only" cupboard and set it on the counter. Dad filled a saucepan with water, added sugar, and placed it on the stove. The costumed crowd waited patiently. Everyone seemed to know what was going on, except me.

Finally my father turned to the crowd and said, "Welcome, Julebukkers!" He winked at me, then peered closely at the group. "Who have we got here tonight?" He and my mother circled slowly around them, examining each person from head to toe, looking for clues. Only a few muffled sounds escaped from the strange people.

So this was it—some sort of game! Maybe I could figure out who they were too. I looked more closely at our guests. The shoes on one of the characters looked familiar; I'd seen those buckles before. But where? And who wore them?

And the red scarf. I'd seen that before too.

The person with the tattered fur coat—was that a man or a woman? The legs wore nylon stockings, but I thought they looked larger than most women's legs—and a little too hairy.

Mom and Dad were laughing as they discussed their observations. Dad patted one large round stomach with his fingertips. A deep grunt resulted. "It's the real thing," Dad announced to everyone gleefully. There were barely muffled snorts and hoots as all attention was turned to the large-bellied man.

Dad rubbed his chin. "I think I know a couple of these julebukkers. How about you, Jewell? And Beth? Any ideas who these tricksters could be?"

My mom laughed. "I'd recognize that feather hat anywhere. Is that you, Fran?" But the woman in the hat only shook her head no.

"Oh, I see," my mother responded slowly. "You've traded clothes for the evening. Hmmm . . . then it must be Laverne."

The woman in the hat reached out and pinched my mother's cheek gently. Then she pulled the nylon stocking and hat off her head in great relief. "Finally!" she exclaimed. "I thought you'd never get it."

"I think Mr. Clause here is actually my friend, Mr. Ellingson," my dad ventured. He slipped his arm around the man's shoulder. "Could I be right?"

The man nodded, then pulled the mask off his face and laughed out loud. My dad clapped Ernie on the back and handed him a steaming cup of hot sweet water and brown liquor. Ernie and Laverne munched on cookies and sipped their hot toddies as the game continued.

I was beginning to see a pattern. Fran and Laverne were both in my mom's Bridge Club. Ernie's wife was too. I wondered if she was standing there someplace in the group.

Then I turned my eye on the shortest person, somebody just a little taller than I. Scrunching my eyes and walking all around, I looked at him or her from top to bottom. I studied the hand-knitted stocking cap slung low over the eyebrows. I looked at the turtleneck sweater that covered the nose and stretched up to the bottom of the winged sunglasses. The cowboy boots. The black stretch pants with the knobby knees and padded fanny. I started to giggle as recognition streamed through me. LuAnn! We'd played dress-up in her brother's old boots and her sister's old sunglasses. We'd spent hours padding ourselves in places we hoped would someday be naturally padded.

"I know her!" I yelled and pointed. "It's LuAnn!"

Hoots of laughter filled the kitchen as LuAnn peeled away the stocking cap and blond hair fell free. Off came the sunglasses. Down came the turtleneck. She slid out of her heavy jacket and gave me a squeeze. "This is so much fun," she said. "You've got to come with us! Mom, Dad, and I were the ones who got it started tonight." When she realized what she'd said, her hand flew up to cover her mouth. "Oops! I can't say any more until you've guessed everybody," she whispered loudly.

So we knew Elizabeth was in the group too. It didn't take long to find her, dressed as a Norwegian elf (a *nisse*) in the buckled shoes that had looked so familiar.

Somebody coughed on purpose and someone else did a little dance in a circle. Another person gestured in a familiar way. It wasn't long before Mom and Dad started to recognize the unique characteristics of their dear friends. Ruth and Charlie were there, disguised as a bent and bespectacled old woman beside a large hairy woman draped in fur.

Goldie was dressed as a balding old man, Arlene as a princess, and her husband as a toothless old cowboy.

I looked for Fran. But she wasn't there at all. LuAnn explained that the group was heading to her house next. "We went to Charlie and Ruth's at six thirty. By the time they guessed who we were and then got dressed up themselves, it was past seven. We'll be out until midnight!"

"I've never done this before," I said. "What am I supposed to do?"

"It's easy. You just have to cover every part of your body or disguise it so no one will recognize you. You're not supposed to talk or move in any way that might allow people to figure out who you are. That's kind of hard," she confided. "But if you get really hot and you want people to guess, you can always give them some clues," she said with a giggle.

LuAnn pulled me aside as the grown-ups warmed up with their hot drinks and cookies. "We've got to find a really good disguise for you," she said conspiratorially. "Let's look through the dress-up clothes. Choose things that no one will recognize." We dug through all the old clothes until we found some potential pieces.

My parents joined us in the search, and before long, three more costumed julebukkers headed out the door for another round of "Christmas fooling" with their friends. It was indeed midnight before our merry group disbanded, and when we finally crawled into our own warm beds, there were smiles on our faces and warm memories in our hearts.

The Burglar's Christmas

WILLA CATHER

TWO VERY SHABBY LOOKING young men stood at the corner of Prairie Avenue and Eightieth Street, looking despondently at the carriages that whirled by. It was Christmas Eve, and the streets were full of vehicles; florists' wagons, grocers' carts and carriages. The streets were in that half-liquid, half-congealed condition peculiar to the streets of Chicago at that season of the year. The swift wheels that spun by sometimes threw the slush of mud and snow over the two young men who were talking on the corner.

"Well," remarked the elder of the two, "I guess we are at our rope's end, sure enough. How do you feel?"

"Pretty shaky. The wind's sharp tonight. If I had had anything to eat I mightn't mind it so much. There is simply no show. I'm sick of the whole business. Looks like there's nothing for it but the lake."

"O, nonsense, I thought you had more grit. Got anything left you can hock?"

"Nothing but my beard, and I am afraid they wouldn't find it worth a pawn ticket," said the younger man ruefully, rubbing the week's growth of stubble on his face.

"Got any folks anywhere? Now's your time to strike 'em if you have."

"Never mind if I have, they're out of the question."

"Well, you'll be out of it before many hours if you don't make a move of some sort. A man's got to eat. See here, I am going down to Longtin's saloon. I used to play banjo in there with a couple of coons, and I'll bone him for some of his free-lunch stuff. You'd better come along, perhaps they'll fill an order for two."

"How far down is it?"

"Well, it's clear downtown, of course, 'way down on Michigan Avenue."

"Thanks, I guess I'll loaf around here. I don't feel equal to the walk, and the cars—well, the cars are crowded." His features drew themselves into what might have been a smile under happier circumstances.

"No, you never did like street cars, you're too aristocratic. See here, Crawford, I don't like leaving you here. You ain't good company for yourself tonight."

"Crawford? O, yes, that's the last one. There have been so many I forget them."

"Have you got a real name, anyway?"

"O, yes, but it's one of the ones I've forgotten. Don't you worry about me. You go along and get your free lunch. I think I had a row in Longtin's place once. I'd better not show myself there again." As he spoke the young man nodded and turned slowly up the avenue.

He was miserable enough to want to be quite alone. Even the crowd that jostled by him annoyed him. He wanted to think about himself. He had avoided this final reckoning with himself for a year now. He had laughed it off and drunk it off. But now, when all those artificial devices which are employed to turn our thoughts into other channels and shield us from ourselves had failed him, it must come. Hunger is a powerful incentive to introspection.

It is a tragic hour, that hour when we are finally driven to reckon with ourselves, when every avenue of mental distraction has been cut off and our own life and all its ineffaceable failures closes about us like the walls of that old torture chamber of the Inquisition. Tonight, as this man stood stranded in the streets of the city, his hour came. It was not the first time he had been hungry and desperate and alone. But always before there had been some outlook, some chance ahead, some pleasure yet untasted that seemed worth the effort, some face that he fancied was, or would be, dear. But it was not so tonight. The unyielding conviction was upon him that he had failed in everything, had outlived everything. It had been near him for a long time, that Pale Spectre. He had caught its shadow at the bottom of his glass many a time, at the head of his bed when he was sleepless at night, in the twilight shadows when some great sunset broke upon him. It had made life hateful to him when he awoke in the morning before now. But now it settled slowly over him, like night, the endless Northern nights that bid the sun a long farewell. It rose up before him like granite. From this brilliant city with its glad bustle of Yuletide he was shut off as completely as though he were a creature of another species. His days seemed numbered and done, sealed over like the little coral cells at the bottom of the sea. Involuntarily he drew that cold air through his lungs slowly, as though he were tasting it for the last time.

Yet he was but four and twenty, this man—he looked even younger—and he had a father someplace down East who had been very proud of him once. Well, he had taken his life into his own hands, and this was what he had made of it. That was all there was to be said. He could remember the hopeful things they used to say about him at college in the old days, before he had cut away and begun to live by his wits, and he found courage to smile at them now. They had read him wrongly. He knew now that he never had the essentials of success, only the superficial agility that is often mistaken for it. He was tow without the tinder, and he had burnt himself out at other people's fires. He had helped other people to make it win, but he himself—he had never touched an enterprise that had not failed eventually. Or, if it survived his connection with it, it left him behind.

His last venture had been with some ten-cent specialty company, a little lower than all the others, that had gone to pieces in Buffalo, and he had worked his way to Chicago by boat. When the boat made up its crew for the outward voyage, he was dispensed with as usual. He was used to that. The reason for it? O, there are so many reasons for failure! His was a very common one.

As he stood there in the wet under the street light he drew up his reckoning with the world and decided that it had treated him as well as he deserved. He had overdrawn his account once too often. There had been a day when he thought otherwise; when he had said he was unjustly handled, that his failure was merely the lack of proper adjustment between himself and other men, that some day he would be recognized and it would all come right. But he knew better than that now, and he was still man enough to bear no grudge against anyone—man or woman.

Tonight was his birthday, too. There seemed something particularly amusing in that. He turned up a limp little coat collar to try to keep a little of the wet chill from his throat, and instinctively began to remember all the birthday parties he used to have. He was so cold and empty that his mind seemed unable to grapple with any serious question. He kept thinking about ginger-bread and frosted cakes like a child. He could remember the splendid birth-day parties his mother used to give him, when all the other little boys in the block came in their Sunday clothes and creaking shoes, with their ears still red from their mother's towel, and the pink and white birthday cake, and the stuffed olives and all the dishes of which he had been particularly fond, and how he would eat and eat and then go to bed and dream of Santa Claus. And in the morning he would awaken and eat again, until by night the family doc-tor arrived with his castor oil, and poor William used to dolefully say that it was altogether too much to have your birthday and Christmas all at once. He could remember, too, the royal birthday suppers he had given at college, and the stag dinners, and the toasts, and the music, and the good fellows who had wished him happiness and really meant what they had said.

And since then there were other birthday suppers that he could not re-member so clearly; the memory of them was heavy and flat, like cigarette smoke that has been shut in a room all night, like champagne that has been a day opened, a song that has been too often sung, and acute sensation that has been overstrained. They seemed tawdry and garish, discordant to him now. He rather wished he could forget them altogether.

Whichever way his mind now turned there was one thought that it could not escape, and that was the idea of food. He caught the scent of a cigar sud-denly, and felt a sharp pain in the pit of his abdomen and a sudden moisture in his mouth. His cold hands clenched angrily, and for a moment he felt that bitter hatred of wealth, of ease, of everything that is well fed and well housed that is common to starving men. At any rate he had a right to eat! He had de-manded great things from the world once: fame and wealth and admiration. Now it was simply bread—and he would have it! He looked about him quickly and felt the blood begin to stir in his veins. In all his straits he had never stolen anything, his tastes were above it. But tonight there would be no to-morrow. He was amused at the way in which the idea excited him. Was it pos-sible there was yet one more experience that would distract him, one thing that had power to excite his jaded interest? Good! He had failed at everything else, now he would see what his chances would be as a common thief. It would be amusing to watch the beautiful consistency of his destiny work itself out even in that role. It would be interesting to add another study to his gallery of futile attempts, and then label them all: "the failure as a journalist," "the fail-ure as a lecturer," "the failure as a business man," "the failure as a thief," and so on, like the titles under the pictures of the Dance of Death. It was time that Childe Roland came to the dark tower.

A girl hastened by him with her arms full of packages. She walked quickly and nervously, keeping well within the shadow, as if she were not accustomed to carrying bundles and did not care to meet any of her friends. As she crossed the muddy street, she made an effort to lift her skirt a little, and as she did so one of the packages slipped unnoticed from beneath her arm. He caught it up and overtook her. "Excuse me, but I think you dropped something."

She started, "O, yes, thank you, I would rather have lost anything than that."

The young man turned angrily upon himself. The package must have contained something of value. Why had he not kept it? Was this the sort of thief he would make? He ground his teeth together. There is nothing more maddening than to have morally consented to crime and then lack the nerve force to carry it out.

A carriage drove up to the house before which he stood. Several richly dressed women alighted and went in. It was a new house, and must have been built since he was in Chicago last. The front door was open and he could see down the hallway and up the staircase. The servant had left the door and gone with the guests. The first floor was brilliantly lighted, but the windows upstairs were dark. It looked very easy, just to slip upstairs to the darkened chambers where the jewels and trinkets of the fashionable occupants were kept.

Still burning with impatience against himself he entered quickly. Instinctively he removed his mud-stained hat as he passed quickly and quietly up the staircase. It struck him as being a rather superfluous courtesy in a burglar, but he had done it before he had thought. His way was clear enough, he met no one on the stairway or in the upper hall. The gas was lit in the upper hall. He passed the first chamber door through sheer cowardice. The second he entered quickly, thinking of something else lest his courage should fail him, and closed the door behind him. The light from the hall shone into the room through the transom. The apartment was finished richly enough to justify his expectations. He went at once to the dressing case. A number of rings and small trinkets lay in a silver tray. These he put hastily in his pocket. He opened the upper drawer and found, as he expected, several leather cases. In the first he opened was a lady's watch, in the second a pair of old-fashioned bracelets; he seemed to dimly remember having seen bracelets like them before, somewhere. The third case was heavier, the spring was much worn, and it opened easily. It held a cup of some kind. He held it up to the light and then his strained nerves gave way and he uttered a sharp exclamation. It was the silver mug he used to drink from when he was a little boy.

The door opened, and a woman stood in the doorway facing him. She was a tall woman, with white hair, in evening dress. The light from the hall streamed in upon him, but she was not afraid. She stood looking at him a moment, then she threw out her hand and went quickly toward him.

"Willie, Willie! Is it you?"

He struggled to loose her arms from him, to keep her lips from his cheek. "Mother—you must not! You do not understand! O, my God, this is worst of all!" Hunger, weakness, cold, shame, all came back to him, and shook his self-control completely. Physically he was too weak to stand a shock like this. Why could it not have been an ordinary discovery, arrest, the station house and all the rest of it. Anything but this! A hard dry sob broke from him. Again he strove to disengage himself.

"Who is it says I shall not kiss my son? O, my boy, we have waited so long for this! You have been so long in coming, even I almost gave you up."

Her lips upon his cheek burnt him like fire. He put his hand to his throat, and spoke thickly and incoherently: "You do not understand. I did not know you were here. I came here to rob—it is the first time—I swear it—but I am a common thief. My pockets are full of your jewels now. Can't you hear me? I am a common thief!"

"Hush, my boy, those are ugly words. How could you rob your own house? How could you take what is your own? They are all yours, my son, as wholly yours as my great love—and you can't doubt that, Will, do you?"

That soft voice, the warmth and fragrance of her person stole through his chill, empty veins like a gentle stimulant. He felt as though all his strength were leaving him and even consciousness. He held fast to her and bowed his head on her strong shoulder, and groaned aloud.

"O, mother, life is hard, hard!"

She said nothing, but held him closer. And O, the strength of those white arms that held him! O, the assurance of safety in that warm bosom that rose and fell under his cheek! For a moment they stood so, silently. Then they heard a heavy step upon the stair. She led him to a chair and went out and closed the door. At the top of the staircase she met a tall, broad-shouldered man, with iron gray hair, and a face alert and stern. Her eyes were shining and her cheeks on fire, her whole face was one expression of intense determination.

"James, it is William in there, come home. You must keep him at any cost.

If he goes this time, I go with him. O, James, be easy with him, he has suffered so." She broke from a command to an entreaty, and laid her hand on his shoulder. He looked questioningly at her a moment, then went in the room and quietly shut the door.

She stood leaning against the wall, clasping her temples with her hands and listening to the low indistinct sound of the voices within. Her own lips moved silently. She waited a long time, scarcely breathing. At last the door opened, and her husband came out. He stopped to say in a shaken voice,

"You go to him now, he will stay. I will go to my room. I will see him again in the morning."

She put her arm about his neck. "O, James, I thank you, I thank you! This is the night he came so long ago, you remember? I gave him to you then, and now you give him back to me."

"Don't, Helen," he muttered. "He is my son, I have never forgotten that. I failed with him. I don't like to fail, it cuts my pride. Take him and make a man of him." He passed on down the hall.

She flew into the room where the young man sat with his head bowed upon his knee. She dropped to her knees beside him. Ah, it was so good to him to feel those arms again!

"He is so glad, Willie, so glad! He may not show it, but he is as happy as I. He never was demonstrative with either of us, you know."

"O, my God, he was good enough," groaned the man. "I told him everything, and he was good enough. I don't see how either of you can look at me, speak to me, touch me." He shivered under her clasp again as when she had first touched him, and tried weakly to throw her off.

But she whispered softly,

"This is my right, my son."

Presently, when he was calmer, she rose. "Now, come with me into the library, and I will have your dinner brought there."

As they went downstairs she remarked apologetically, "I will not call Ellen tonight; she has a number of guests to attend to. She is a big girl now, you know, and came out last winter. Besides, I want you all to myself tonight."

When the dinner came, and it came very soon, he fell upon it savagely. As he ate she told him all that had transpired during the years of his absence, and how his father's business had brought them there. "I was glad when we came. I thought you would drift West. I seemed a good deal nearer to you here."

There was a gentle unobtrusive sadness in her tone that was too soft for a reproach.

"Have you everything you want? It is a comfort to see you eat."

He smiled grimly. "It is certainly a comfort to me. I have not indulged in this frivolous habit for some thirty-five hours."

She caught his hand and pressed it sharply, uttering a quick remonstrance.

"Don't say that! I know, but I can't hear you say it—it's too terrible! My boy, food has choked me many a time when I have thought of the possibility of that. Now take the old lounging chair by the fire, and if you are too tired to talk, we will just sit and rest together."

He sank into the depths of the big leather chair with the lions' heads on the arms, where he had sat so often in the days when his feet did not touch the floor and he was half afraid of the grim monsters cut in the polished wood. That chair seemed to speak to him of things long forgotten. It was like the touch of an old familiar friend. He felt a sudden yearning tenderness for the happy little boy who had sat there and dreamed of the big world so long ago. Alas, he had been dead many a summer, that little boy!

He sat looking up at the magnificent woman beside him. He had almost forgotten how handsome she was; how lustrous and sad were the eyes that set under that serene brow, how impetuous and wayward the mouth even now, how superb the white throat and shoulders! Ah, the wit and grace and fineness of this woman! He remembered how proud he had been of her as a boy when she came to see him at school. Then in the deep red coals of the grate he saw the faces of other women who had come since then into his vexed, disordered life. Laughing faces, with eyes artificially bright, eyes without depth or meaning, features without the stamp of high sensibilities. And he had left this face for such as those!

He sighed restlessly and laid his hand on hers. There seemed refuge and protection in the touch of her, as in the old days when he was afraid of the dark. He had been in the dark so long now, his confidence was so thoroughly shaken, and he was bitterly afraid of the night and of himself.

"Ah, mother, you make other things seem so false. You must feel that I owe you an explanation, but I can't make any, even to myself. Ah, but we make poor exchanges in life. I can't make out the riddle of it all. Yet there are things I ought to tell you before I accept your confidence like this."

"I'd rather you wouldn't, Will. Listen: Between you and me there can be no secrets. We are more alike than other people. Dear boy, I know all about it.

I am a woman, and circumstances were different with me, but we are of one blood. I have lived all your life before you. You have never had an impulse that I have not known, you have never touched a brink that my feet have not trod. This is your birthday night. Twenty-four years ago I foresaw all this. I was a young woman then and I had hot battles of my own, and I felt your likeness to me. You were not like other babies. From the hour you were born you were restless and discontented, as I had been before you. You used to brace your strong little limbs against mine and try to throw me off as you did tonight. Tonight you have come back to me, just as you always did after you ran away to swim in the river that was forbidden you, the river you loved because it was forbidden. You are tired and sleepy, just as you used to be then, only a little older and a little paler and a little more foolish. I never asked you where you had been then, nor will I now. You have come back to me, that's all in all to me. I know your every possibility and limitation, as a composer knows his instrument."

He found no answer that was worthy to give to talk like this. He had not found life easy since he had lived by his wits. He had come to know poverty at close quarters. He had known what it was to be gay with an empty pocket, to wear violets in his buttonhole when he had not breakfasted, and all the hateful shams of the poverty of idleness. He had been a reporter on a big metropolitan daily, where men grind out their brains on paper until they have not one idea left—and still grind on. He had worked in a real estate office, where ignorant men were swindled. He had sung in a comic opera chorus and played Harris in an *Uncle Tom's Cabin* company, and edited a socialist weekly. He had been dogged by debt and hunger and grinding poverty, until to sit here by a warm fire without concern as to how it would be paid for seemed unnatural.

He looked up at her questioningly. "I wonder if you know how much you pardon?"

"O, my poor boy, much or little, what does it matter? Have you wandered so far and paid such a bitter price for knowledge and not yet learned that love has nothing to do with pardon or forgiveness, that it only loves, and loves— and loves? They have not taught you well, the women of your world." She leaned over and kissed him, as no woman had kissed him since he left her.

He drew a long sigh of rich content. The old life, with all its bitterness and useless antagonism and flimsy sophistries, its brief delights that were always tinged with fear and distrust and unfaith, that whole miserable, futile, swindled world of Bohemia seemed immeasurably distant and far away, like a dream that is over and done. And as the chimes rang joyfully outside and sleep pressed heavily upon his eyelids, he wondered dimly if the Author of this sad little riddle of ours were not able to solve it after all, and if the Potter would not finally mete out his all comprehensive justice, such as none but he could have, to his Things of Clay, which are made in his own patterns, weak or strong, for his own ends; and if some day we will not awaken and find that all evil is a dream, a mental distortion that will pass when the dawn shall break.

CONTRIBUTORS

Bess Streeter Aldrich (1881–1954) was one of Nebraska's most popular writers, publishing more than one hundred articles and short stories, nine novels, one novella, and two collections of short stories. *Mother Mason*, her first novel, was published in 1924. Her critically acclaimed *A Lantern in Her Hand* (1928) chronicles the joys and the travails of a pioneer woman home-steading with her family in Nebraska.

Brian Bedard is professor of English and chair of the English Department at the University of South Dakota. He also directs the creative writing pro-gram and serves as editor of the *South Dakota Review*. His short stories have been published nationwide in such forums as the *Alaska Quarterly Review*, *Cimarron Review*, and *Quarterly West*. A trio of stories on a single theme was nominated for a Pushcart Award in 2000. More recent work appears in the *North Dakota Quarterly*, the *MacGuffin*, and *Blue Line*.

Ann Boaden lives and writes in Rock Island, Illinois, where she teaches English at Augustana College. Her fiction and nonfiction have appeared in such publications as *Big Muddy: A Journal of the Mississippi River Valley*, *British Heritage*, the *Heartlands Review*, the *Hyde Parker*, *Wascana Review*, *Knight Literary Journal*, and *Northwoods Journal*.

Willa Cather (1873–1947) is considered one of America's most distin-guished novelists. Her works, set often in desolate regions of Nebraska and the American Southwest, pay homage to those lands and their formidable in-habitants. She is noted for her depiction of strong, intelligent, self-sufficient female characters. *My Ántonia, O, Pioneers!*, and *Death Comes for the Archbishop* are established classics in American literature. Cather was awarded the Pulitzer Prize for Fiction in 1923 for *One of Ours*.

Joseph M. Ditta, professor of English at Dakota Wesleyan University in Mitchell, South Dakota, is a past recipient of an artist grant in literature from the South Dakota Arts Council. He has published more than two hundred poems in magazines and reviews, among them *Poetry*, the *Missouri Review*, the *Mississippi Valley Review*, *Southern Humanities Review*, and the *New York Arts Review*. His fiction has been published in the *South Dakota Review*, the *Connecticut Review*, and *Weber Studies*. "Raphael in Brooklyn" was nominated for a Pushcart Award in fiction.

Paul Engle (1908–1991) won the Yale Series of Younger Poets Prize for *Worn Earth* in 1932, became a Rhodes Scholar in 1933, began to teach in the Iowa Writers' Workshop in 1937, and directed the workshop from 1943 to 1966. Engle and Chinese poet Hualing Nieh Engle together founded the International Writing Program in 1967. The couple was nominated in 1976 for the Nobel Peace Prize for their humanitarian work with foreign writers. Engle was the author of more than a dozen books of poetry, a novel, numerous short stories and critical essays, a children's book, and a full-length libretto.

Hamlin Garland (1860–1940) achieved popular and critical success upon the publication of his collection of short stories, *Main-Travelled Roads* (1891). His memoir, *A Son of the Middle Border*, appeared in 1917. He received the Pulitzer Prize in 1922 for *A Daughter of the Middle Border*.

Linda M. Hasselstrom is a poet, essayist, and working ranch woman. She is the author of *Windbreak, Going over East, Road Kill*, and *Caught by One Wing*. Hasselstrom has received numerous awards for her writing, including a National Endowment for the Arts fellowship in poetry and a South Dakota Arts Council literature fellowship. In 1990 she became the first woman to win a Western American Writer award from Augustana College in Sioux Falls, South Dakota.

Jon Hassler's novels include *Staggerford, Simon's Night, The Love Hunter, A Green Journey, North of Hope, Dear James, Rookery Blues*, and *The Dean's List*. Works for young readers include *Four Miles to Pinecone* and *Jemmy*.

Born in Minneapolis in 1933, Hassler received his degree from St. John's University in Minnesota, where he later served as an English teacher and writer-in-residence. In 2000 he received the Distinguished Minnesotan Award for his contributions to literature and education.

Ted Kooser is one of Nebraska's most prolific poets, authoring nine collections of poetry, including *Sure Signs, One World at a Time, Weather Central,* and *Winter Morning Walks: One Hundred Postcards to Jim Harrison,* winner of the 2001 Nebraska Book Award for poetry. His work has appeared in the *New Yorker, Poetry,* the *American Poetry Review,* the *Hudson Review, Kansas Quarterly,* the *Kenyon Review, Antioch Review, Poetry Northwest, Prairie Schooner, Shenandoah, Tailwind,* and elsewhere. He also writes fiction and literary criticism. He has received two National Endowment for the Arts fellowships in poetry, the Pushcart Prize, the Stanley Kunitz Prize, the James Boatwright Prize, and a Merit Award from the Nebraska Arts Council. He is editor and publisher of Windflower Press, a small press specializing in contemporary poetry. He teaches as a visiting professor in the English Department of the University of Nebraska-Lincoln.

Rosanne Nordstrom resides in Chicago, Illinois. Her grandparents and parents were born in and lived in Iowa. Portions of her memoir, *My Life with Paco,* from which "What I Took from Minnesota Christmases" is taken, are being published by Indiana University Press in a forthcoming anthology.

Dorothy Dodge Robbins received her Ph.D. from the University of Nebraska–Lincoln and taught Great Plains literature at Dakota Wesleyan University. Currently she teaches English at Louisiana Tech University. She is coeditor of *Christmas Stories from Louisiana.* Her critical writings have appeared in *Critique,* the *Midwest Quarterly,* the *Southern Quarterly, Centennial Review,* and the *Texas Review.*

Kenneth Robbins is the author of four published novels, nineteen published plays, and numerous works of short fiction, essays, memoirs, and reviews. He is the recipient of the Toni Morrison Prize for Fiction, the Associated Writing Programs Novel Award, and the Charles Getchell New Play Award. He lived for four years in North Dakota and thirteen years in South Dakota before relocating to Louisiana.

Ron Robinson is the author of numerous published novels and plays, including *Thunder Dreamer; Diamond Trump; Cats Are from Saturn, Dogs Are from Pluto;* and *Kitchen Dance.* A native of Iowa, he now makes South Dakota his home.

O. E. Rølvaag (1876–1931) left Norway for the United States in 1896, eventually settling on the Great Plains. For twenty-five years he served as professor of Norwegian language and literature at St. Olaf College in Northfield, Minnesota. Originally penned in his native Norwegian language and later translated, *Giants in the Earth* (1927) and *Peder Victorious* (1929) met with critical and popular success. Both novels depict pioneer life on the Dakota prairies in the 1870s. In 1926 Rølvaag was knighted (Order of St. Olav) by King Haakon VII in Norway.

Mari Sandoz (1896–1966) was a noted Nebraska novelist, biographer, historian, teacher, and Plains Indians authority. Her Great Plains series spans the Stone Age to the twentieth century and is considered by critics to be her definitive work. Among her most popular literary works are her novel *Cheyenne Autumn* and her biography of her father, *Old Jules.* "The Christmas of the Phonograph Records" originally appeared in her memoir, *Sandhill Sundays and Other Recollections.*

James Calvin Schaap has resided in the far northwest corner of the state of Iowa for most of his life. He is the author of numerous essays, stories, novels, and collections of short stories. *Touches the Sky* is a historical novel concerning the Ghost Dance of late nineteenth-century South Dakota and the Wounded Knee Massacre. He is a professor of English at Dordt College in Sioux Center, Iowa.

Jane Smiley's novels include *The Age of Grief, The Greenlanders, Ordinary Love and Good Will, Moo, The All-True Travels and Adventures of Lidie Newton, Horse Heaven,* and *Good Faith.* From 1981 to 1996 she taught at Iowa State University in Ames, Iowa. She won the Pulitzer Prize for *A Thousand Acres* in 1992. Currently Smiley resides and writes in northern California.

Beth Dvergsten Stevens writes books, stories, and hands-on activities for children, families, and teachers. Her first book, *Celebrate Christmas Around the World,* is a teacher resource book. She is the author of a series of eight nonfiction books about historical toys published by Perfection Learning Corporation. Her stories, crafts, and activities have appeared in many national children's magazines. She also writes a weekly crafts column for the *Waterloo/Cedar Falls Courier* in Iowa.

Mary Swander is on the English faculty of Iowa State University and has published three volumes of poetry *(Heaven-and-Earth House, Driving the Body Back*, and *Succession*), a book of literary interviews (*Parsnips in the Snow*), and works of nonfiction (*The Desert Pilgrim, Land of the Fragile Giants, The Healing Circle: Authors on Recovery from Illness*, and *Bloom and Blossom*). She is the recipient of a Whiting Award, a National Endowment for the Arts grant for the Literary Arts, two Ingram Merrill Awards, the Carl Sandburg Literary Award, and the Nation-Discovery Award. Her poems, essays, and short stories have appeared in the *Nation*, the *New Yorker*, the *New York Times Magazine*, and the *New Republic*.

Constance Vogel, a Pushcart Prize nominee, has published in more than 150 journals, including *Spoon River Poetry Review, River Oak Review*, the *MacGuffin, Thema, Blue Mesa Review, Blue Unicorn, Willow Review*, and *After Hours*. She is the recipient of a poetry award from *Rambunctious Review* and was a finalist for the Frith Press, Bacchae Press, and Thorntree Press chapbook competitions. She served as a reader in the Poetry Center of Chicago Annual Juried Reading in 2001.

Larry Woiwode is the author of eight novels, including *What I'm Going To Do, I Think* (1969) and *Beyond the Bedroom Wall* (1975). His stories and poetry have appeared in the *New Yorker*, the *Atlantic, Esquire, Harper's* and the *Paris Review*. He has been a Guggenheim Fellow, a John Dos Passos Prize winner, a recipient of awards from the William Faulkner Foundation and the American Academy and Institute of Arts and Letters, and a nominee for both the National Book Critics Circle and National Book Awards. A North Dakota native, he returned in 1978 and now lives on a 160-acre farm near Mott where he continues to write.

OTHER BUR OAK BOOKS OF INTEREST

A Bountiful Harvest
The Midwestern Farm Photographs
of Pete Wettach, 1925–1965
By Leslie A. Loveless

Buxton
A Black Utopia in the Heartland
By Dorothy Schwieder, Joseph Hraba,
and Elmer Schwieder

Central Standard
A Time, a Place, a Family
By Patrick Irelan

Driving the Body Back
By Mary Swander

The Folks
By Ruth Suckow

Harker's Barns
Visions of an American Icon
Photographs by Michael P. Harker
Text by Jim Heynen

An Iowa Album
A Photographic History, 1860–1920
By Mary Bennett

Iowa Stereographs
Three-Dimensional Visions of the Past
By Mary Bennett and Paul C. Juhl

Letters of a German American Farmer
Jürnjakob Swehn Travels to America
By Johannes Gillhoff

Neighboring on the Air
Cooking with the KMA Radio Homemakers
By Evelyn Birkby

Nothing to Do but Stay
My Pioneer Mother
By Carrie Young

Picturing Utopia
Bertha Shambaugh and the
Amana Photographers
By Abigail Foerstner

Prairie Cooks
Glorified Rice, Three-Day Buns,
and Other Reminiscences
By Carrie Young with Felicia Young

Prairie Reunion
By Barbara J. Scot